EXTRAORDINARY TIME OF GOOD VS EVIL

Judith Coates

BOOKS BY THE AUTHOR

JUDITH COATES

Be Who You Be

Let Your Light Shine

my life, my story

(with Beyond The Heart Clubhouse)

J L COATES

Second Chances

Awakening

Two Women, Two Stories

Shattered

The Seeker, the Sentinel and the Orb

Total Equals the Sum of the Parts

A Change of Heart

Journey

Library and Archives Canada in Publication

Judith Coates

ISBN: 978-1-7751668-2-5

ISBN e-book: 978-1-7751668-3-2

Printed in USA by KDP

Cover photo used with permission from Peter Heck of Hectic Travels

For My Mom

who never stopped believing in me.

I miss you every day.

ACKNOWLEDGEMENTS

Thank you once again to my editor, Dianne Tchir who has taken my words and made them coherent. Keep fighting Dianne. We are not finished yet. There are still more books waiting for your magic touch.

Thank you to my readers Clarice Nelson and Father Froese for you valuable insight and input. These are more important to me than you realize. Thank you to Peter and Dalene Heck of Hectic Travels for the use of their photo for the cover.

You may be wondering how this story came to be. One Sunday morning I was sitting in church supposedly listening to the Priest's sermon when the words "what would happen if Jesus and Hitler lived at the same time" flashed through my mind. Jesus being the personification of all that was good, Hitler, the personification of all that was evil. Based upon this idea, the words flowed through my pen and, three years later you are holding the finished product in your hand.

I have always been fascinated with the plight of the Jewish people during World War ll. The biblical story of Jesus and incidents from the war became the back drop of my story. Any relationship to actual people or places is purely coincidental and the product of my vivid imagination. I have taken the liberty of writing about real events and changed them to serve my purpose.

When Fr. Froese handed my manuscript back to me he said, "This is a story of hope and the value of forgiveness." Even in this crazy mixed up world of today one statement boldly stands out "treat others as you wish to be treated."

When I was finished I realized this was not the end of the story. Instead of writing "the end" I found myself writing "to be continued."

Thank you for travelling with me through this journey. This story has been a labor of love and I am pleased to be able to share it with you.

To believe in God or a guiding force because someone tells you to is the height of stupidity. We are given senses to receive our information with. With our eyes we see and with our skin we feel. With our intelligence it is intended we understand. But each person must puzzle it out for him or herself."

Sophy Burnham quote

The Artists Way

Sin leads man to consider himself the god of creation,

to see himself as the absolute master and to use it

not for the purpose willed by the Creator, but for his own interests.

Pope Francis

PART ONE

The Early Years

CHAPTER ONE

In an earlier time, and in a different world, two sperm penetrated two eggs. From those fateful couplings, one in love, the other in hate, the world would be forever changed.

"That looks like a good spot," he pointed, "over there by that big tree."

Hand in hand, the young couple leaves the rocky path and climbed the grassy hill. The view below them is spectacular: a green lush valley surrounded by high rocky hills. They see tendrils of smoke rising from the chimneys of the houses nestled below. Neatly plowed fields appear laid out like a checker board, some black, some yellow. They could see the path they walked twisting and turning up from the valley below,

While Joe stood looking at the peaceful scene below, Maria opened the picnic basket he had placed on the ground. She took out a red checkered tablecloth and spread it out under the branches of the huge tree, and then continued to take out the bread, wine, cheese, and sliced tomatoes she had so lovingly packed, and arranged them neatly in the center of the cloth.

"Come and eat Joe. Lunch is ready."

He turned and sat on the grass across from her. "Someday Maria I am going to build a big beautiful house in the valley for us. Just you wait and see. It will be the biggest and grandest house in the village, even bigger than John Schmidt's."

"Joe, you are a carpenter and a very good one, but it will take you a lifetime to save enough money for that. Here, eat" she said, handing him a slice of fresh buttered bread.

"You are probably right Maria," he sighed, "but there is no harm in dreaming."

They ate in the silence of two people in love and comfortable with each other. A year from now they planned to have the banns posted in the church, and be married.

When Joe finished eating he lay back on the grass, chewed on a toothpick, and gazed at the cloudless blue sky above them. "This is the life. I wish we could stay here forever. It is so peaceful and quiet."

Mary smiled as she packed everything back into the picnic basket and then sat with her back propped against the huge trunk of the tree. She noticed Joe had fallen asleep and she was content to sit and watch him. The sun warmed her face, a gentle breeze ruffled the leaves on the tree and the man she loved is beside her.

I wish it could always be this way she thought. *One more year is not such a long time to wait. By then, I will be seventeen and Joe nineteen. Many girls are married at this age even though our parents think we are too young. "'Wait until you are sure," they keep telling me, but I know my love for Joe will never change.*

"Joe," she called reaching over, gently shaking his shoulder. "It's time to go. I promised mother I would be back in time to help her with supper. She isn't feeling well today."

He opened his eyes, smiled, reached for her, and pulled her down on top of him. Alone, under the tree, their usually chaste kisses took on a new sense of urgency. He rolled her onto her back and then climbed on top of her.

14

"Joe, stop. We mustn't do this. Get off of me, we have to go."

Even as she said these words, Maria felt an urgency rising in her, a passion she never felt before. She didn't want him to stop. She felt his hand reach under her skirt and lifted her hips as he slid her underwear down and off. At some point, he removed his shirt and lowered his pants to his knees. Keeping her eyes closed, she ran her hands up and down his back, pulling him closer to her. She opened her legs as she felt his hardness pressing against them.

"Joe, we must stop. We have to wait until we are married."

Then he shuddered, and she felt a warm liquid spill on top of her thigh, and run down the inside of her leg into her private parts. She held him tightly as he shuddered again and again.

"Maria, I love you," he whispered in her ear. "One year is too much to wait." Then he lay still on top of her. She moaned as her body released itself.

All at once, he rolled off her and turned his face away. He stood with his back to her, adjusting his pants and putting his shirt back on.

"I am sorry," he said, reaching into his pocket for a handkerchief. Clumsily he attempted to wipe all traces of him from her. "Please forgive me? I didn't mean to."

Maria lay there, with her eyes closed, until her breathing slowed. Taking the handkerchief from Joe's hand she finished what he started slipped on her underwear and readjusted her skirt.

He reached down, and pulled her by the hand, helping her to her feet. He looked ashamed and bewildered.

Cupping her hands around his face she whispered," Joe I love you. I wish we could be married now, today, instead of waiting." Kissing him on the cheek she added, "We must not allow this to happen again. One more year is not such a long time to wait."

After gathering up the picnic basket they walked back to the village, hand in hand, each lost in their private thoughts. *Why did I allow that to happen? I should have had more self-control. What if she hates me now? I vow, from this day forward, I will wait until we are married.*

Now I am a woman. Now I know what the others are talking about as they whisper among themselves. I know that the physical act was not completed, but now I'm not sure I can wait for one more year.

When they came close to the village he kissed her on the cheek. "I love you Maria. I'm sorry about today. I promise you that won't happen again."

Maria smiled at him, "I love you too."

Joe turned left toward his workshop; Maria walked straight ahead to return to her home.

* * * * *

At the same time in the village below, a man slapped a woman across the face and snarled. "You will do as I say. Do you understand me? I told you to go in there and spread your legs for me."

"Please, not again. It hurts. The doctor said that you are making me sick inside. He said you must stop and give me time to heal."

16

He slapped her across the face again, and twisting her arm up behind her back forced her to the floor. He ripped off her under clothing, pulled down his pants, and slammed into her. She screamed in pain as he brutally took what he thought he owned.

When he was finished he stood up. Buttoning the front of his pants he sneered "clean yourself up and make my lunch. I am hungry."

Wincing from the pain inside her, she lifted herself off the floor and limped to the bathroom. Blood and semen trickled down her legs; her insides felt as though they were ripped apart.

She poured cold water from the pitcher into the wash basin sitting on the small counter, and then used the dirty rag that lay beside it to wash as best she could. She checked to see if there was any blood on the back of her dress. Seeing none, she rinsed out the rag and dumped the bloody water into the slop pail beside the cupboard.

In the other room, using the same rag she wiped up the mess he left on the floor. She picked up her torn underwear from the floor, looked at it, gathered it into a ball and tossed it into the garbage. *They cannot be mended.*

Trembling from exhaustion and pain she dutifully went into the kitchen to prepare his lunch. All they have is a few potatoes and a piece of left over pork sausage from the night before.

I hate him; she mutters under her breath, *God how I hate him. I wish I were dead because that is the only way he will stop hurting me. The doctor tells me to say no, to make him stop, but he takes whatever he wants, whenever he wants. His animals get more respect than I do.*

She winces at the disgusting noises he makes as he gobbles his lunch. *I don't know how much more of this I can take. The Doctor says he is ripping me a part inside, but I don't know how to make him listen.*

When he finished eating he stood up, put on his filthy, gray, faded jacket and walked out the door, slamming it behind him. He never came back.

Nine months later, to the day, she went into labor. For two days she struggled and strained to free the child from her womb. Finally, as her body was torn apart, the child's head emerged between her legs.

"It is a great big boy," the midwife proclaimed, "he will be a big eater; you will need much milk to feed him."

"Name him after his father, Heinrich Mollen."

She did not look at her son, but turned her head away and breathed her last. Perhaps, if she had known the terror her son would one day unleash upon the world, she wouldn't have tried so hard, and let him die inside her.

CHAPTER TWO

Six weeks later Maria came to Joe's workshop in tears. Taking her by the arm, he led her inside, out of the glare of the blazing sun.

"Maria, why are you crying? Has something happened?"

Maria looked around. "Are you alone? Is there anybody here besides you? I have something I need to tell you."

"No, I am alone. Come and see, I have been working on Mrs. Schwartz's table; you can barely see where it was broken. She will be pleased at the good job I have done."

"Joe," she blurted out, "I've missed my monthly time twice and I am sick every morning. I have heard the women say this is what happens when you are with child."

Joe turned on her angrily. "How can that be? Who have you been with? You know that we have never been together that way." His hands curled into fists, ready to strike her.

"Joe, I have never even looked at another man, you know that. I have only been with you. I don't know how this could have happened."

"Does anyone know? Have you told anyone?"

"No, I wanted to tell you first. You know what will happen to me if the villagers find out. I will be cast out, and my parents will have to disown me."

"Get away from me." Joe was furious. It was all he could do not to strike her for deceiving him. "Go to whoever did this to you and tell him. I never want to see you again. Go, get out of here."

"Joe, please believe me."

He turned his back to her, his shoulders shaking with anger. "Go Maria, before I do something I will be sorry for."

She looked at him, then turned and began to walk away, tears streamed down her cheeks. She hadn't expected him to be so cruel, nor to accuse her of betraying him. The consequences looming in her future were unbearable.

Joe spent the next several days reliving his feelings of betrayal and anger at her. He couldn't sleep or eat. When he thought of her being with another man, he wanted to beat her and demand to know who he was.

Later, as he began to calm down, he remembered the day of the picnic and how he had been unable to control spilling himself on her. *Was it possible to conceive a child even though we hadn't completed the act?* His face flushed with shame. He didn't know how this had come about, but knew with certainty Maria was carrying his child.

. He sat down, lowered his head upon his folded arms and cried. *Will she ever forgive me for being so cruel to her?*

Swallowing his pride, he closed his shop and went looking for her. He found her working in the garden behind her parents' house. "Maria," he called out.

She looked at him "go away Joe. You made your feelings perfectly clear when I came to you, and I don't want to talk about this again."

Dropping to his knees in front of her, he wrapped his arms around her small body. She tried to push him away "Maria, listen to me. I am sorry. This is my fault. That day, the picnic, I took advantage of you. Please forgive me. I didn't mean to hurt you. We will go to your parents today and tell them we wish to be married as soon as possible. We will leave here. I promise I will protect you and the child with my life."

"My parents will wonder why the urgency. I don't want them to know."

"They are not foolish people. They know what it means for a young couple to be in love."

She stood up, and offered him her hand, then reached down to pull him to his feet. They stood there, with arms wrapped around each other. She was sixteen, he was not yet nineteen and the custom of the times threatened their happiness.

"Joe, I am afraid. What if my parents say no? When they find out I am with child? They will have no choice but to force me out of the village and disown me."

"Then I will leave with you."

They had cause to be afraid. It was the custom of their village that any unmarried woman who became pregnant was banished. First she was called by the Elders in front of the church and forced to describe her indiscretions in full detail. She had to publicly name the man involved, and then she was banished from the church. Her family was forced to stand up and denounce her. After that, the church destroyed every record of her – it was as though she never existed. The woman could remain in the village, but most chose to leave and were never heard from again. Those who chose to stay lived a life of shame. Nothing was done to the man in question.

That same evening Joe and Maria went to her parents to ask for permission to marry. Her father was very angry.

"You and I will go outside and speak to this man to man. This is one conversation I don't want my wife to hear."

Once outside he snapped to Joe, "what is going on here?"

"Sir, I love your daughter and she loves me. I will provide for her for the rest of my life."

"You are too young to know what love is," Maria's father snarled back. Then he paused and looked at Joe in the eye and asked, "What's your hurry, she is only sixteen, and you are barely nineteen. Are you sleeping with my daughter? Have both of you disgraced me?"

"No sir, I am not sleeping with Maria, but I want to very badly," Joe answered honestly, his face turning a bright red. "She doesn't want to disappoint you. I have a job offer in another town, and I want to take her with me."

"I see. If that's the way it is, then perhaps you should be married. I wouldn't want to have to denounce her in the church. Until this is done, you keep your hands off her, do you understand?"

"Yes sir," Joe agreed readily.

The next Sunday the first of the marriage banns was posted in the church. Three weeks later they had a quiet wedding without the usual celebration. Joe remained true to his story, that he was offered a job in a distant town and wanted to be married, so he could take Maria with him.

The next morning after the wedding, Joe, Maria accompanied by their parents went to the train station. Maria was in tears. For the first time she realized she was leaving her home and family. They had very little to take with them – their clothes, some money and a wooden box containing Joe's tools. Maria's mother was heartbroken that her daughter was leaving.

Several days before the wedding, she had taken Maria aside to explain what her husband expected of her. Maria began to cry.

"It is not that bad my child. If you love each other you will overcome and face all of the hurdles. On your wedding night Joe will want to make love to you. I am sure he will be gentle the first time."

Maria started to cry. "It's not that mother; I am already carrying his child."

Gathering Maria into her arms she replied. "I suspected as much when you were in such a hurry to get married. I hope your father never finds out, it will break his heart."

"I don't know how this happened. We haven't been together like a man and wife." She told her mother about the incident under the tree, and how Joe spilled his seed on the top of her thigh. "Mother, please don't tell father. I can't bear the thought of disappointing him."

Her mother also wondered. *How can this be? How can she be carrying a child, and still be going to Joe as a virgin on her wedding night?*

Joe was a talented carpenter, and his reputation preceded

23

him. He knew he would be able to find work even if the promised job did not materialize. After all, the offer had been made several months ago."

As the train pulled out of the station Joe kissed her, and asked, "Are you happy Maria?"

She smiled back at him, "Yes. Our wedding night leaves me happier than I thought could be possible."

The child was three months old when they sent a message to their parents informing them that they had a grandson and had named him Jesse. Secretly, Maria sent a message to her mother when the child was actually born, letting her know all was well. If Maria's father ever suspected otherwise, he never said anything.

CHAPTER THREE

Jesse was a precocious child, small for his age with blond hair and blue eyes. He walked and talked early, never cried, was undemanding, and never got angry.

Even at a young age he was serious, thoughtful and giving. At two years of age he carried on complete conversations with adults. By the age of three he challenged the Elders with his questions. Who is God? Where is he? Why can't I see him? Why do we believe in him?

By this time, Joe and Maria had been away from home for nearly three years, and both were homesick. They had received word that Joe's mother was ill and wanted to see her son one last time before she died.

Yet they were undecided. Joe had a good job as a carpenter, they had a decent home and Maria was expecting their second child. Still, in the back of their minds, was the fear that someone would find out Jesse's true age. If this should happen, how would they make people understand his conception when Maria was still a virgin the day they were married. Joe wasn't worried for himself, but the gossip would be devastating for Maria and her family.

. Often Joe's nights were filled with dreams about Jesse. The worst was when he was forced to watch the death of his son, and was powerless to intervene. He would wake up sweating and trembling. Sometimes he shared his dreams with Maria, but the nightmares he kept to himself.

Then one night, he had a dream of a different sort. An old man in a white shimmering robe came to him. "Joe, the time has come for you and Maria to return to your village. Jesse will be called upon to be 'the light of the world.' The time has come for him to prepare for his journey. Much will be demanded of him, but know this, he will never be alone. When you can no longer protect him I will be at his side. I have entrusted his care to you and Maria, but now the time is fast approaching when you must share him with others. Troubled times are coming, and Jesse has been chosen to lead the people out of the darkness."

This dream unsettled Joe even more. What did it mean?

He thought about the dream for several days and then told Maria. "It is time for us to go home. I had a dream. An old man came to me saying Jesse was old enough now to learn about, and begin living his purpose. I don't know what that means, but Jesse should get to know his family, and be properly schooled in our religion and traditions. I am sure it is safe to go home now."

After speaking these words to Maria he stared at her; her face seemed to glow. Joe gave her a bewildered look. "Joe, I too have had a dream. An angel visited me and told me that Jesse is 'a leader among men'. I don't know what that means either."

Joe thought quietly, and then replied, "I will finish the tasks I am working on, and you can begin packing." Putting his hand on Maria's swollen belly, he declared "this one will know its family."

"Joe I am afraid. What if someone finds out about us and figures out that Jesse was born before we said he was? What will happen then?"

"Maria, you are worrying too much about nothing. Jesse is

small for his age, but wise beyond his years. The old man in my dream assures me we have nothing to fear." Then giving her a wink he said," we are not the first, nor will we be the last to be caught up in this situation."

Once they returned to their families there were no questions. People were drawn to Jesse, adults and children alike. The Elders of the church were equally impressed, especially Elder John, who often sought his opinion on matters concerning the church.

And so it was, Joe, Maria and Jesse returned to their home village and began their new life.

*   *   *

After his mother's death Heinrich, who was named after his father, was raised by his grandmother. She was a bitter woman, broken down by life, and too old to be responsible for raising a young child.

. Husky and tall for his age, Heinrich was intelligent, but born with a mean streak. Throughout the years he lived with his grandmother she constantly berated him. "You are just like your father; he was born mean, as was his father before him. You are no good, you will never amount to anything," There was little, if any, love directed toward him

From as far back as he could remember Heinrich felt inadequate. His only friends were the imaginary ones he conjured in his mind. In order to cover up his feelings of inadequacy, and to get the recognition he craved, he became a bully. Even then, at an early age others in the village were afraid of him.

The other children frequently teased and laughed at him

27

because his clothes were ragged, and he was never completely clean. He did whatever he pleased, because his grandmother was old and often sick.

There was a softer side to Heinrich that he never allowed others to see, in case they thought he was weak. Often at night, he crept out and listened to the music coming from the taverns or from the church. Sometimes he went into the hills and sketched pictures of the trees and wildlife. These were the few times he was completely at peace with himself and dreamed of becoming a great artist.

At an early age, he learned that if he got the upper hand, the other children would do whatever he asked, because they were afraid. He learned power was control, and this became the code which would govern the rest of his life

Heinrich and Jesse began school in the same class. Both were eager learners, and a rivalry quickly developed between them. Jesse had a gentle way about him. He accepted his fellow classmates as they were, rich, or poor, their differences didn't matter.

In return, the other children showed their support for Jesse in small ways. He was always the first picked for a team, often given the role as captain. Heinrich was usually the last chosen because he hated losing.

Because Heinrich perceived Jesse as being weak he bullied Jesse unmercifully. He targeted Jesse on the sports field, called him names, stole his lunch and waited for him when the school day was over.

No matter what he did, Jesse didn't retaliate; usually he turned and walked the other way. This infuriated Heinrich even more. No matter what he did to Jesse, Heinrich always came out looking second best. His hatred for Jesse festered.

By this time Heinrich had a group of boys who tagged along wanting to be like him. In his own way Heinrich was also a powerful leader. Finally the day came when Heinrich accosted Jesse on the street. His friends formed a circle around the two of them, and encouraged them to fight.

"You are a coward with a yellow stripe down your back a mile long," Heinrich taunted Jesse. "Fight me, so that once and for all I can prove that I am better than you,"

Jesse looked at him and calmly replied, "I have no reason to fight with you Heinrich, and I don't intend to. That will prove nothing." With this statement he turned his back and walked away.

Heinrich became extremely angry. Jesse's actions caused him to lose face in front of his friends. He could hear some of them snickering behind his back. This made him more determined to get Jesse to fight.

He ran behind Jesse, pushing him face down onto the ground. "I hate you Jesse, and someday I will make you pay for being such a coward, and not standing up to me. Just you wait and see," he sputtered.

Jesse picked himself up, walked past Heinrich as though nothing had happened and continued on his way. The first action in the future show down between the two of them had taken place, and the result of that day would change the world forever.

CHAPTER FOUR

At the age of twelve Jesse was forced to leave school. His father was ill with a lung disease which came from working in a closed environment and inhaling too much sawdust. Forced to become the man of the family, Jesse took over his father's work in order to provide for his brothers and sisters. Joe helped as much as he could, but tired easily. Jesse's work was nearly as good as his father's and the business prospered.

Joe sat on a chair at the front of the house enjoying the beautiful day, and with rest, his health slowly improved. Jesse saw his father sitting there, and sat down in front of him on his haunches.

"Father, may I speak with you? The elders have approached me about becoming a minister in our church. They say I have the ability to bring the young people and their families back to our faith. I agree with them on that. They also tell me that one day I could become a great leader in the church."

"They do, do they. What else do the say?" asked Joe sarcastically.

The Elders had already approached him the week before to get permission to talk to Jesse. At the time he told them it was Jesse's decision and they hadn't wasted any time going to him. That alone made Joe suspicious about their intentions.

"They say I will become a rich and powerful man."

"Is that what you want, to become a rich powerful Elder of

the church?"

Jesse stared straight ahead. "No father, I have no wish for riches or power. Many times I disagree with what the Elders believe. I believe in a benevolent God but every day I see the injustices in our village; the rich favored over the poor. It should be the other way around, the rich helping the poor. I believe in a God that forgives and offers second chances. I believe we should love and look after one another.

"Is that what the Elders will teach you?"

"Father, I believe that is the very basis of our faith, but the message is getting lost. If I become a minister, I can return to the original teachings and scriptures. I hope I can change things and, at the same time, make a difference. "

"Jesse, what do you think you would be able to change?"

"I don't believe we should have to pay for God's favour. The Elders charge the poor for special prayers. Every time the Elders are asked to do something they need to be paid. That doesn't seem right to me."

"You are right Jesse; the system is broken and has been for a long time. I fear that this will be too great a challenge for you. Rarely can one man alone bring about the necessary changes."

"Father I know what you are telling me is probably the truth, but I have to try."

Joe looked at his son's earnest face and felt a stab of sorrow pass through him. The whole village knew the Elders were greedy and corrupt. That was not the life he wanted for his son. Yet another part of him was saying *and so it begins, just as the old man had predicted.*

"Have you talked to your mother about this?"

"Yes father, I have."

"What did she say?"

"She said that each of us is called to a purpose, and that I must do whatever I feel called to do."

"Jesse, my son, you cannot save the world. The task you have chosen is nearly impossible; the church is very powerful and unpopular. The people will oppose you. Some may see you as manipulating them for the benefit of the Elders. Those who directly benefit from the way things are now will feel threatened."

"I know father, I have thought about that, but first I must learn what is wrong before I can teach what is right. I can accomplish both of these by choosing to become a minister."

"In many ways you are right. Until you know what needs to be changed, you can do nothing. Let me think on this. Come help me finish this chair. I promised to have it ready for tomorrow and my strength hasn't fully returned yet."

Jesse and his father worked side by side late into the evening; each was lost in his thoughts.

Joe watched his son sanding a piece of wood to remove all trace of the glue used to make the repairs. *I don't want him to follow this path, but I know he must. I can't bear to lose him to the Elders and their corrupt ways.*

As he was sanding, Jesse wondered. *Do I really want to become a minister? Which is more important? My family or what I feel called to do?*

"That's good for tonight Jesse. We are finished for now. I will deliver this chair to Mrs. Schwab in the morning. I have been thinking if you feel so strongly about becoming a minister, you must follow your heart. All I ask is that you do it for the right reasons."

Jesse looked at his father and said, "I understand what you are telling me. But father you must understand my destiny is to change what I can in this world. Surely, this isn't the way it is supposed to be?"

"No Jesse, you are right again, but this is the way it is. How, may I ask, do you plan to accomplish this mighty feat? Have you given that much thought?"

"Yes father. I will do this one person at a time."

For the first time Joe realized that Jesse had known all along what path his life was to take. He felt relieved, but sad, *such a heavy burden for a young man to carry.*

Later that same evening as Joe and Maria were preparing for bed he said to her, "Why this? Why now? I don't want him involved with the Elders. What kind of a man will he turn out to be – a money mongering fool like the rest of them? I would rather see him remain a carpenter; at least it is an honest way to make a living."

Maria listened patiently as Joe ranted. When he paused long enough to take a breath she said, "Joe do you remember your dream about the old man? Jesse is here for a purpose, he has been given a promise he must fulfill. That is his destiny."

Angrily Joe retorted, "Why ours. Why can't somebody else's son fulfill that promise? He will get no thanks or support for

34

whatever he tries to do. I gave my permission, but I don't agree with the whole idea. You know that if the Elders can't corrupt him, they will turn on him."

"Joe I know this and so does Jesse. We have talked about this many times. It's almost as though he knows in advance what hardships he will face."

"I will let him go, but the minute I don't agree with what they are teaching him, I will take him out of there so fast his head will spin, and I won't care if he agrees with me or not."

Maria didn't reply. She knew Jesse's future was predetermined from the moment he was conceived, but she also understood why Joe was finding this difficult to accept. He was afraid for his son. She was too, but Jesse must be given the chance to do what he must. Every night, from then on, she prayed that offering Jesse the support he needed was the right thing to do.

Jesse worked extremely hard. By day he worked as carpenter alongside his father, in the evenings he studied with the Elders. Elder John, a wise old man, often took Jesse into his study and went through the scriptures and beliefs of their church. Jesse was an eager pupil, and quickly grasped the basic concepts.

Many times their ideas clashed, and they argued late into the night. A fondness developed between them. Jesse looked up to the man and respected him for his teachings.

Sometimes in the night, Maria would wake up and see a light coming from the kitchen. When she investigated she often found Jesse asleep, his head resting upon a book. She was worried about him most of the time, but he thrived.

For three years Jesse continued to maintain this difficult schedule. Young people and their families flocked to the church to hear him speak. His message was always the same. "Love and forgive one another just as the Lord has forgiven you. Treat people the same way you want to be treated."

The Elders were growing increasingly distressed with Jesse's teachings and his growing influence on the villagers and the church. Other ministerial candidates were beginning to follow Jesse's example rather than the established teaching of the Elders.

Jesse continued working hard with his father and for his church, but as the time approached for his ordination, he began to have second thoughts. He questioned some of the practices of the Elders – like their preoccupation with money, their excesses in food and drink, the closed meetings with the rich, and their neglect of the neediest in the village. Although most of the Elders were married, the frequent comings and goings of the unsavory women who lived in the village disturbed him.

He began to see that many of the Elders were self-serving, the opposite of what they were teaching. Many nights he lay awake wondering what he should do. He felt isolated. He couldn't talk to his parents or Elder John about his concerns. Reaching a decision felt impossible.

CHAPTER FIVE

Heinrich's life followed a different path. When Jesse was forced to leave school he became the prize student which gave him another opportunity to lord his achievements over the other students, but still that failed to provide him the respect he craved. Almost every day he found himself being compared to Jesse in some way.

He stayed until all of his grades were completed, and then convinced his grandmother to move to the city, so he could attend the University to study art. Twice he applied to the University, but each time was told his art didn't meet the standards required.

After his third rejection Heinrich went into a deep spiral. *This is Jesse's fault. He was the one who held me back in school. Because of him I don't have the top honors that are required.* He refused to believe the professors when he was told he didn't have enough talent to warrant further training.

Adding to his confusion his grandmother passed away from a stroke, leaving him beside himself with grief. She was the one constancy in his life and now he was alone. This, on top of his University rejection sent him searching for answers. He was a lonely man with no friends and most people avoided him because of his over-bearing attitude.

For several years he drifted around the country moving from one hostel to another, existing on the small inheritance his grandmother had left him,. As a last resort he joined the Army. He was tired of always being alone and feeling as though he didn't belong.

Here Heinrich excelled. It wasn't so much the routine and discipline of the army but the acceptance of his fellow soldiers and officers. Soon they looked up to him as their leader and spokesperson. He was offered officer training, studied hard, excelled in what all he was asked to do and quickly advanced up the ranks. More importantly, he honed his sense of being in the right place at the right time, which he used to his full advantage.

As the war progressed, he began to feel that he wouldn't get the opportunity to join the fighting before it ended. Refusing an officers commission he volunteered for flight training school with the vision of becoming a decorated war pilot.

If not for one unfortunate life changing incident the Army would have been Heinrich's life. He was up in the air with his instructor, approaching the airfield for a practice landing, when the motor quit and the plane plunged to the ground, bursting into flames on impact.

Heinrich dragged himself out of the plane onto the grass. When he realized his instructor was trapped inside the burning plane, he went back and dragged the unconscious man to safety. For this brave act he was awarded a medal for heroism.

What frustrated him was the fact that his country was losing the Great War and he had lost all opportunity to fight. Instead of becoming a bomber pilot and inflicting as much carnage as possible against the enemy, he spent months in the hospital being treated for the burns to his arms and a broken back. That was followed by several more months of rehabilitation. By the time he was ready to be released, the war was clearly being lost.

He spent most of the time wondering what he was going to

do. Because of the severity of his injury he knew he wouldn't be allowed back on active duty, and that left him with one of two options. The first was to take an honorable discharge and a pension from the Army, the other to accept a desk job which would limit any chances of advancement, neither of which appealed to him.

A small voice continued to blame Jesse for his misfortune. *This is Jesse's fault. If I had gone to art school I wouldn't be walking around with a broken back. Yet, I am a decorated hero for bravery, which should be good for something.* The closer the day came to when he would be leaving the hospital, the more depressed and despondent he felt. At one point, he had considered, but rejected, the idea of taking his own life.

On the morning he was preparing to leave his hospital room a messenger from the Army found him. "Sir, I have a letter from your commanding Officer for you. I am to wait for your reply."

This is it, he thought, *my walking papers. They certainly didn't waste any time getting rid of me.*

He was greatly surprised to see the note was actually a request for him to meet with his commanding officer at 1600 hours that very day.

"Tell him I will be there," he replied to the messenger. His spirits quickly lifted. *Maybe there is hope yet.*

Previously he had arranged for a taxi to pick him up. A porter helped him carry his bags to the waiting vehicle and he breathed a sigh of relief as he walked out the hospital door.

"Grenwald Army base," he told the driver, then sat back to enjoy the ride.

CHAPTER SIX

At precisely 1600 hours Heinrich was sitting outside his commander's office. He had walked too much that day and was in pain, but was reluctant to take one of the pain pills the doctor prescribed. He needed a clear mind when he spoke with his commanding Officer, confident that any sign of weakness would be used against him.

He didn't wait long. Within minutes of his arrival he was ushered into the office. Wiping his sweaty palms on his pants, he straightened his shoulders, mentally preparing himself for the bad news he was sure to receive.

"Heinrich, how good to see you looking so well," the Major complimented.

"Sir," Heinrich replied, saluting briskly.

"Sit down, Heinrich. How is that back of yours holding out? Much improved I hope?"

"Much better sir," he replied lowering himself onto the chair in front of the desk. Although the visible wounds were healed, and he was able to walk with a slight limp, his back ached if he walked or stood too long in one place.

"Heinrich, I'm not sure if you're aware that our beloved country is descending into political chaos. Between you and me, this war is going to end soon, and the people are disheartened. Not only are we in danger of losing this war but, for the soldiers returning home there will be no jobs, nor prospects of any.

On every street corner somebody is speaking out about

forming a new political party. The Nationalists are still governing the country, but other parties are growing in strength and challenging what our country has always believed in. Most of these will disappear, but there is one we care deeply concerned about, the People Workers party, which is here in Grenwald. We thought that if a decorated hero, like you, showed interest in their party they would have a difficult time refusing."

"Why would you want that? From what I have read in the newspapers they stand for the exact opposite of the Nationalist party."

"True, they do. What we want is for you to infiltrate the party, keep us apprised of what is going on, as well as who the leaders and the financial backers are. When we have enough information we will shut them down, and arrest everybody in one swoop. Does my proposition interest you Corporal?"

This is too good to be true Heinrich said to himself. *I would be a fool not to accept. An opportunity like this only comes once in a lifetime. This is certainly an option I hadn't thought about.*

"What's in it for me?" Heinrich asked.

"Always to the point aren't you?" the Major replied. He got up, walked over to the sideboard and poured two snifters of brandy. Handing one to Heinrich he continued, "How much time would you need to reach a decision? Of course we will make sure you are well provided for if you accept."

Heinrich sat there sipping his drink. Then putting the half empty glass on the desk he rose from his chair, snapped to attention and saluted. "Done. It will be my honor to serve you and our country this way,"

"Good. I thought you would say that. Return here tomorrow morning and we will go over the details. I will arrange for transportation and accommodation for you in town."

"Yes sir," Heinrich said, "I am at your service, until tomorrow morning then." He saluted again and left.

Heinrich was given a shabby second floor one bedroom apartment, an old Volkswagen to drive and unlimited amounts of money. He went from beer house to beer house, buying beer and cultivating friends. Whenever he allowed himself to be drawn into a discussion of politics he voiced the sentiments of the Workers Party.

At first his new friends were wary of him. The war had ended and the country was in complete disarray. The economy was flat, and the harsh terms of the peace settlement forced upon the country added to the discontent.

During this time a group of discontented army officers formed a new political party for the purpose of shaping a new right wing government, - one that had the interests of the citizens in mind. Political loyalties shifted quickly. Within a short period of time this new party became a bigger threat than the Workers Party to the current government. Heinrich's orders remained unchanged except now he was expected to find a way to infiltrate this new party.

Always the opportunist Heinrich aligned his arguments in the beer houses with their policy. All he needed was the right connections. That opportunity came faster than expected. As usual he was sitting at a table in the beer house down the street from his apartment when a man slipped into the chair across from him.

"Allow me to introduce myself - Ernie Rohm, will you allow me to buy you a drink sir?"

Heinrich looked across the table. In front of him was a short, balding heavy set man wearing a rumpled army staff uniform. Heinrich had never seen him before.

"If you wish," he replied. He was used to men coming and sitting with him, asking questions, most of them seeking the same kind of information he was.

"Served in the war did you?" Rohm inquired. "I see you have a military bearing, but I also noticed that you were limping when you came in."

Heinrich was prepared. "Yes, I was training to become a bomber pilot and hurt my back in a plane crash. The Army gave me a medal for bravery one day, kicked me out the next because I was no longer of any use to them. No wonder they lost the war."

This question gave Heinrich an opening. "The Army uses people to get what they want and then spits you out. They don't care what happens to a person after that. Now that the war is over the government can't seem to get its act together. After fighting so bravely for our country, there aren't any jobs available for those who want to work. What we need are people in power who care about the little guy."

The two of them spent whole evening talking and then Rohm excused himself. "It is getting late. My wife will be angry with me for not getting home sooner. Perhaps we could continue this conversation tomorrow evening?"

Heinrich smiled to himself as he watched Rohm stagger out

the door. *Finally I am getting some place, and will soon have valuable information to report back to my Commander. There was no doubt in my mind that, after tonight, I will be invited to join their party.*

When Rohm failed to show up the next evening, and the one after that Heinrich was extremely disappointed. Once again he felt he had been tested and left wanting.

CHAPTER SEVEN

Under the direction of his Army Superiors Heinrich turned his attention back to the Workers Party, making every effort to find out who the principle financial backers were. The party was poorly organized, and the mere fact that he was willing to speak out on their behalf, and volunteer for whatever task came along made him more than welcome.

With his sharp mind Heinrich targeted their propaganda policies as an area where he could quickly move up the party ranks. He wrote letters to the newspapers, developed slogans, drew and put up posters denouncing the current government around the city, quickly making himself indispensable to the party leaders.

As he became more trusted he was introduced to the men who were providing the money for the party to operate. He was invited to their homes for gatherings and social functions. Women made themselves available to him at every opportunity but he wasn't interested. Long ago he decided women were too demanding, and in this situation not getting involved meant there was less chance of getting caught. Besides his demands were different from than those of the average man, if he felt a need for a woman he paid for what he wanted.

In a bold step he appointed himself Chief of Propaganda and nobody objected. This gave him increased access to the inner workings of the party, which he used as an opportunity to begin shaping party policy. Each step of the way he dutifully reported to his Army superiors. In the meantime, he was making a strong political name for himself.

Late one evening he was surprised to hear a loud banging on his door. He had just sent home the prostitute he had in his home. Her refusal to entertain him with certain acts had incensed him so he exercised his demons by beating her and making her beg. Although he paid her well, his first thought was that she reported him to the police.

Seething with rage he put his robe over his naked body and opened the door. There were three men in suits, their black hats pulled down low over their faces.

"Heinrich Mollen?"

"Yes"

The first man pushed himself into Heinrich's apartment, grabbed him and slammed him against the wall. "You are under arrest."

"What for? That bitch is lying... I didn't hurt her."

"You are under arrest for conspiring against the government. Go put some clothes on and make yourself decent. You are coming with us now."

One of the men followed him into the bedroom and watched as he dressed.

"It stinks in here," the man said turning up his nose. "You must have had quite a party."

Heinrich ignored the comment. Once dressed, his hands were handcuffed behind his back then he was taken outside and forced into an awaiting police car. He was roughly pushed into the back seat, barely getting his feet out of the way before the door was slammed shut. He could see his neighbors peeking out from behind their curtains.

"Are you taking me to the police station?" Heinrich inquired

"You will see when you get there," one of the men snapped at him "but for now keep your mouth shut."

Heinrich was surprised when he was driven to the Army base instead. Upon his arrival the handcuffs were removed and he was escorted to the General's office.

. "Just what do you think you are doing, arresting me like some common criminal? What will my neighbors think?" Heinrich snarled.

"Now now, Heinrich, don't get so upset. How do you like my little charade? Earlier tonight we arrested the leaders and financial backers of the Workers Party. Right now the police are searching their offices for their records. The financial backers and the minor officials are all in jail. It would look suspicious if we allowed you remain free. This way they will think you received the same treatment as they have."

Although he was still angry Heinrich retorted. "You could have let me know ahead of time so I could have been prepared for your flunkies to come pounding on my door. I don't appreciate being arrested and treated like one of the dregs of society."

"We couldn't, it had to be this way. I wish though I had been able to see the look on your face." The General chuckled, and then added, "Don't allow your ambitions to control you. Because of your actions, the party was becoming stronger and a force to be reckoned with. We had to put a stop to the activities before you became too powerful. After tonight the party will fall apart. The backers will be given the option of going to jail for a very long time, or withdrawing their support. Without money, the party will fail."

"What about the others?"

"We will make an example of them to discourage those who might have the same idea. They are to be executed for treason."

"And me?"

"You are free to go, but I would lay low for a few days. You have completed your task. Now you will wait until we have need of you again. This is closed and you are dismissed."

"What do you mean dismissed?"

"We no longer need you. You have served your purpose. I will do what I can to find you a spot in my office, but as of today we are revoking your income and taking back the car we have allowed you to use. If you wish to keep the apartment, your rent is paid for several months. After that it is up to you."

Heinrich knew arguing would do no good. He saluted, turned and let himself out of the office. He was seething with anger. *I have been duped. They used me to achieve their political ends and now cast me aside without any means of supporting myself. Just what am I supposed to do now? I will make them pay for this.*

The next day Heinrich handed in his resignation to the Army, and accepted his meager pension. From then on he spent his time drinking himself into a stupor every night. When he ran out of money, the owner extended him credit which he repaid by cleaning the beer house in the morning before it opened for the day. He became the target for jokes and jeers. The regular customers laughed at him when he stumbled out the door every night, but he didn't care. As   far as Heinrich was concerned he had nothing left to live for.

CHAPTER EIGHT

While Jesse struggled with his decision about completing the final steps to becoming a minister, the world around his village was changing. The entire world was caught up in a depression. The crops had failed because the spring rains did not come. Those crops that did grow shriveled up from lack of moisture. Many men left the village seeking work to support their families, but most came back disheartened. There were few, if any jobs, to be found in the cities and towns.

The landscape and fabric of the government was also under siege. At first the people of the village laughed when they heard Heinrich Mollen was seeking election as Chancellor of the governing party. They remembered him as a child and the bully he had been. They watched as he rose in the ranks of their country's leaders and shook their heads.

As so often happens in difficult times, the rich prosper. One by one the families of the village moved away, seeking a better life. The Elders purchased their land for a fraction of its true value. For those who were moving, leaving with a little money was better than none at all.

The rich in the village became even more powerful. They dictated church and local government policy. Most of the money the elders used to buy the properties was borrowed from those in powerful positions, and the church was forced to pay a high interest rate for the use of the borrowed money.

As the church expanded its holdings, fewer and fewer

villagers were left to feed the ever hungry collection plate. Many of those left in the village were now working the land for the church and barely able to survive on the meagre sum they were paid.

To combat the loss of funds, the church imposed a tithe of ten percent of the monthly earnings of the villagers. A tax collector was hired to go from door to door once a month, to collect the money. In order to fulfill the demands of the church, many villagers starved. The babies and elderly were the first to die.

Those who could not pay the tax collector when he came around were charged an exorbitant rate of interest for each day they were delinquent. For those unable to pay after three months the church confiscated their property, and gave it to the rich as part of their debt repayment. Those working for the church to feed their families had their tithe seized before they were paid.

Jesse watched silently as this happened around him. Any extra money he earned he used to buy food for the widows and orphans in the community. In the village tavern, which he rarely frequented, he heard hair raising stories of hunger and poverty.

The one question which kept running through his head was why? Up until the last few years their village was prosperous. The more he listened, the more confused he became.

One morning, when his father was in his workshop, Jesse went to him. "Father, do you have time to talk? I am deeply troubled about something and I wish to get your opinion,"

Joe put aside the door he was repairing and said "of course. Come and sit beside me and tell me what is bothering you."

"I am weeks away from being ordained as a minister in our

church, but now I'm not sure. This isn't what I thought it would be. I see many of the villagers are suffering from hunger, but instead of the Elders helping the poor, they continually seem to take advantage of them.

I overheard a conversation the other day that bothered me, and I don't know what to make of it. I was in the library reading a particular passage that I didn't understand, when I heard Elder John speaking with someone in the hallway. I don't think they realized I was there. They were discussing increasing the church tax. What does that mean?"

"Jesse," Joe replied, "do you honestly not understand what has been happening around you, or have you been deceiving yourself? The church has become land rich and cash poor. As people moved away the Elders bought their land with money borrowed from the rich. The villagers became fewer and poorer with less to donate to the church. A tax was imposed on every household in the village. If one couldn't pay the church would take your property. Most of the shop owners no longer own their businesses, they worked for the church."

Jesse's face filled with sorrow as he listened, "father I know about the tithe but I don't understand why it is necessary. The church is not lacking, it has more than enough. Is that why the villagers are hungry and discouraged? Do the villagers think I am part of this scheme?"

"Yes, it is possible but I have never heard it said. They understand that you are only a student, and that you are not privy to the inner workings of the Elders council, They appreciate the efforts you make for the widows and orphans because they have no one to look out for them. I am afraid that once you become a minister, their feelings will change toward you."

Jesse's face was filled with anguish when he walked away. Joe could hear him muttering *how is this possible?*

Joe could see Jesse was badly shaken by what he had been told. Now the   father watched his son pace back and forth in the yard. Joe wanted to help, but he couldn't. He could see Jesse was struggling, but there was nothing he could do. Jesse had to make his own decision about whether he stayed or left the church.

Finally Jesse turned and walked back, "father," he asked "what should I do? I cannot, in good conscience, be a part of what the Elders are doing. It is wrong."

Joe looked at his troubled son, "You are the only person who can decide. You have to follow the dictates of your heart and head, but know that whatever decision you make, your mother and I are here for you. We will stand behind whatever you decide."

Later that night when Joe climbed into bed Maria asked, "What going on Joe? Why is Jesse so distraught? Why is he outside pacing and talking to himself? Have you two argued?"

"No Maria. He is a man, with a man's decision to make. He is questioning his calling to the church. He didn't know that the church had become the largest land owner in the village. He came to me wanting to know why the people were suffering, and why the church wasn't helping them. He accidently overheard a conversation about increasing the tithe. I explained to him how the rich and church were in collusion, each of them growing richer on the backs of the poor. That upset him very much."

They lay there for a minute, Maria's head resting on his shoulder as it had every night since they were married. "Does he know that you have been unable to pay the tax collector?'

"No, I didn't tell him. I was going to, but he was already so upset I decided it would be better to wait until another time."

"He needs to be told before they come back."

"I know my dear. I know, and I will find a way to tell him tomorrow."

Joe lay awake most of the night as Maria slept beside him. *What am I to do? How will it look if Jesse is a minister of the church, and his own father cannot keep the tax collector at bay? If I receive dispensation because he is my son, it will not be fair to the others in the village. It is best if I tell Jesse first thing in the morning, before he commits himself one way or the other.*

As the sun was coming up he finally fell asleep. *Thy will be done O Lord,* he prayed.

In the morning Jesse was gone. When Jesse failed to preach his morning sermon for several days the villagers began to ask about him Even Elder John came to their home to find out if he was sick.

Maria became deeply concerned. This wasn't the first time Jesse had left to think things out, but the longest he stayed away.

"Joe, do you know where he is? This is the longest he has been gone and I am worried about him."

"No Maria, I don't know. He is probably wandering in the hills. He told me he finds peace there. When he has made his decision he will come home."

Maria believed what Joe said was true, but her heart ached for her son. From the time he was born they always knew Jesse would be forced into choosing his own path, but as a mother, she never thought it would be so hard to stand by and watch.

While Jesse was away the tax man returned "you are now two months behind Joe. Either you pay the money you owe or I will confiscate your workshop and tools."

"You know I can't pay. I barely earn enough to feed my family. Those I have done work for have promised to pay, but so far they haven't. I have nothing to give you."

"You know what this means. As of this minute I proclaim your workshop and tools to be property of the church."

"You can't do this," Maria screamed, lunging at him. "What will you do, have us starve? Joe has worked very hard to build this business. You don't have any right to take it away from him."

The tax collector knocked her to the ground with his fist. She fell into a crumpled heap weeping. Joe knelt down beside her. "Take what you want," he said bitterly.

As Joe helped Maria to her feet, the tax collector picked up a board, and taking two nails from his pocket nailed the board across the workshop door, Maria wept as she watched him walk away.

"What are we going to do now?" she cried, tears streaming down her cheeks. "They have taken everything you need to make a living for us."

"It will be fine Maria. I will find a way to start over. I have faith that our God will lead the way. He has given me these two hands to work with and, I trust, he will show me the way."

The next day a very distraught Jesse walked into the kitchen.

Joe and Maria seemed to have aged overnight. Maria's eyes were red from crying. "Is it true," he demanded "that the tax collector confiscated your tools and your business? Why didn't you tell me that you were having a problem? I would have tried to help."

Maria jumped up from the table. She had never seen Jesse so angry. "Sit down Jesse, I will make some tea, and we can talk about this."

"Father, tell me, is it true?"

"Yes Jesse, it's true. I didn't tell you because you are becoming a minister in the church. After the first month I thought I would have the money, but nobody has paid me for a long time. I couldn't go and ask for money from those who have less than I do."

"How are you going to make a living? How are you going to feed mother and the children?"

"I don't know yet, but I will find a way. I suppose I could make a deal with the Elders and work for them. A little money is better than none."

Then Jesse walked over to his mother and touched her cheek. "How did you get that bruise on your face?"

Maria swallowed trying to decide whether to tell him or not. Joe saw the doubt in her eyes. "Tell him the truth Maria." he urged. "He will find out anyway."

"I attacked the tax man. He pushed me down and I hit my cheek on a rock."

He looked at his parents scrutinizing their red eyes and deeply lined faces. The injustice overwhelmed him.

"This is madness," he said "I cannot be part of this any longer."

"Jesse, calm down," Maria begged, placing a freshly made cup of tea in front of him. "We will figure this out somehow."

Sweeping his hand across the table he knocked the tea cup to the floor. He stood up, his eyes filled with steely resolve. "This is wrong. They have no right to treat you like this."

Maria dropped to her hands and knees and picked up the pieces of the broken cup. "There is nothing you can do."

"Oh yes there is," Jesse replied, heading for the door. "I am going to go to the Elders and try to talk some sense into them. This madness must stop. They are hurting good people. They are stealing their livelihoods; their reason for living. I will talk to them and convince them that this is wrong on every level."

"But your interview for completing your ministry is tonight, and that is more important than what is happening to us. You must go to your interview. Don't bring this up; you can talk with them another time, after you have an official position in the church. Please Jesse, calm down. If you confront the Elders, and they see how angry you are, you will lose all you have worked for. Your father and I can start over. The tax collector only took his tools, he didn't take his talent. The tools can always be replaced."

"Mother," Jesse replied "I have to do what I think is necessary."

As he stomped out the door he could hear his mother begging, "Jesse please don't say anything. Stop and think about what you are doing."

He heard his father say, "Maria, leave him. He must do what he knows and believes is right. This is in God's hands now."

CHAPTER NINE

It was near dusk when Jesse arrived at the church. The evening service was over, and the only visible lights in the building were in the upstairs meeting room. Barely keeping his anger in check he climbed the front stairs and opened one of the heavy front doors. His long legs carried him quickly down the aisle. He stopped at the front of the knave, bowed his head and then crossed the knave, went through the side door and took the steps to the meeting room two at a time. He burst into the meeting room without knocking, and slammed the heavy door shut behind him. Then he stopped short, his mouth open.

Five of the Elders, including Elder John, and the tax man were huddled around a table. In front of each was a pile of coins, and the tax man was shuffling coins from his hand onto the growing piles as though he was dealing a deck of cards. They were all laughing, and he heard one of the Elders say "well done. You made us rich today."

When he heard the door slam Elder John jumped to his feet. "Jesse what are you doing here? It's not time for your interview yet. You have arrived too early."

In three steps Jesse was at the end of the table. Reaching down, he tipped the table over scattering all of the coins on the floor.

Elder John ran towards him. "Jesse stop," he cried out

Still in a rage Jesse grabbed him by the throat, and backed

him against the closest wall. The tax man was crawling on his hands and knees trying to scoop up the coins on the floor. The other four Elders sidled toward the door looking for a means of escape

Jesse tightened his grip on Elder John's throat. "You thieves, you hypocrites, how can you do this? Your people are homeless and hungry, yet you take their last penny to line your pockets."

Looking toward the other Elders he shouted. "Stop or I will hurt him. Get back here."

In a group they edged back toward the upended table.

Elder John, his face bright red, struggled to breathe. "Let me go Jesse. Don't do something you will regret forever. We will give you a share. We will return your father's property and never bother him again."

"No," Jesse roared in his face. "How dare you offer me those terms. Who do you think I am?" He loosened his grip on Elder John's throat and threw him to the floor. "I want no part of this. Our duty is to serve and protect our people, not rob them blind."

Looking down at Elder John lying in front of him he said, "I believed in you. I trusted and respected you. I loved you as though you were my own father. How could you do this? The villagers are good people, why are you doing this to them?"

Using the table for support Elder John pulled himself to his feet. "You think that you are better than us. Once you are ordained, you will be standing in line with your hand out for your share - just like the rest of us. Money gives you power and it won't take you long to figure that out."

'Do you honestly think I would be part of this?" Jesse replied,

"That I would stand by and let you steal from our own people?"

"You would have come around sooner or later." Elder John stated. "We all did, and you would have been no different."

Jesse paused, and then looked into the eyes of each Elder, "You disgust me. I denounce you, your church and your faith. I am going to spread the word in the villages about what despicable people you are."

Elder John replied sarcastically, "They don't want to know what happens to their money as long as they are left alone to wallow in their poor pathetic lives."

Still angry Jesse walked toward the door. With his hand on the ornate metal door handle he said, "from now on I will teach the people about the God I believe in, one who loves and forgives. I will teach them of the God I thought we all believed in. I will carry my message far and wide to all people and tell them the truth."

Elder John moved in front of Jesse. Pointing his finger at Jesse's face he said, "If you walk out of here now you will be sorry. You will never be allowed to step inside this church or any other ever again. I will make sure of that."

Jesse paused as though he were truly considering Elder John's threat and its many implications. Then stepping around Elder John he replied, "So be it" and he walked through the open door letting it close on its own behind him.

CHAPTER TEN

Maria and Joe were sitting at the kitchen table when Jesse returned. She was watching for him to walk down the road, all the while hoping he regained control over his feelings before he faced the Elders,

"What is taking so long?" she asked Joe, "he should have been home hours ago. The interview with the Elders should be a mere formality. They know Jesse and how committed he is. They know how hard he has worked."

Joe looked at his wife. "Maria, you worry too much. I am sure he will be along shortly,"

For now it was easier to let her think Jesse was going for his interview. To say more would needlessly upset her. He had seen something in Jesse's eyes that he had never seen before. Anger? Disgust? Despair? Although he seemed relatively calm when he left, Joe felt the rage emanating from him.

He had no sooner spoken those words when the door opened and Jesse stumbled in. He looked grief stricken, his face ashen, his cheeks flushed red and his eyes filled with sorrow.   Maria rushed to his side, and taking him by the arm led him to the nearest chair.

"Jesse, what is it? What has happened? Did you not pass your interview?"

Jesse looked from one parent to the other, and with tears filling his eyes he replied softly, "I didn't know. I am so sorry. All this time they were using me for their own benefit."

He sat on the chair rocking back and forth, his arms tightly crossed across his abdomen like he was in pain "Please forgive me, I didn't know"

Maria looked at Joe, "what is he talking about – using him for what? What didn't he know?

Joe, what is going on here?"

"He will tell us when he is ready. Let him be Maria, something very serious has happened."

Suddenly Jesse jumped off his chair, sending it crashing to the floor. He went out the door, slamming it behind him. Joe and Maria ran out behind him. Jesse had one of Joe's new hammers and smashed it into the board the tax collector nailed across the workshop door. He pounded at it, sometimes missing and smashing holes in the door behind it. Finally the board cracked and Jesse tore at it with his hands until it was in two pieces. Then he yanked on each piece until the nail gave way and the workshop door open. His shirt was soaked with sweat; his hands bleeding.

"There," he said, "they will not bother you again."

"Jesse, what are you doing?" Maria screamed at him bending down to pick up the two pieces of wood and desperately tried to push them back on the twisted nails. "The tax collector sealed that door until we could pay him. If he sees what you have done we will be punished."

Jesse looked at his father. "No," he said, "they will not bother you anymore. If they return and make a fuss, tell them to talk to me." Still angry he stormed back into the house.

"Jesse stop," Maria called out to him. She started to follow him into the house, but Joe put his hand on her arm to stop her.

"Whatever this is about, he must deal with it his own way, and we must be patient."

"But Joe, I have never seen him this way before. He is so angry, so hurt…"

By now Jesse's shouting and slamming of doors awakened the other children. They were standing in the doorway, their eyes as big as saucers. "What's wrong with Jesse? Why is he crying?" Elizabeth asked.

"I don't know my little one. He hasn't told me. Come, back to bed with you. He is upset, but I am sure he will calm down in a few minutes."

Maria took the children into the house and tucked them back into bed. While she was soothing them Joe went into Jesse's room. She could hear their murmuring, but was unable to hear the words.

She checked the house before turning the lights off, making sure the curtains were closed and the fire in the cook stove safe to leave. When she crawled into their bed, Joe was laying there, his face turned toward the wall. He didn't roll over when she lay beside him. She could tell by the sound of his breathing he was still awake. She curled up beside him and put her arm across his chest.

Joe said to her softly, "Go to sleep Maria. He will be okay."

Later in the night the sound of Jesse crying woke Maria up. She wanted to comfort him, hold him in her arms like she did when he was a child, but didn't. Eventually he became quiet. Once again Joe whispered in the dark, "He will tell you when he is ready. He needs to work this out for himself." Neither one of them slept well that night.

Joe arose early and went outside to check on the damage from the night before. He knew he would have to make a new door for his workshop, but was surprised to see Jesse was nearly finished building the frame. Rather than say anything, Joe picked up a board and handed it to him. The two worked in silence.

Finally Jesse put down his hammer and said. "Father, I am done with the church and religion. I don't believe any more, and I am never going back."

"Perhaps you can go to the next town or village and the Elders there will help you complete your ministry."

"It's not that father."

Joe put down the board he was holding. Looking at Jesse he said "perhaps you should tell me what is bothering you. Whatever passes between us will be private."

Staring off into the distant hills, Jesse told him what had taken place the evening before. "When I saw Elder John with that pile of coins in front of him, I wanted to hurt him as much as he was hurting me. I looked up to him. I aspired to become the learned man that he was. I nearly killed him. It was all I could do to stop from chocking him to death. I wanted to wipe that stupid smirk off his face.

They lied to me. "You will bring younger people back to the church Jesse," he mocked, "you will be doing a wondrous thing and this will help improve the continuation of our faith. Do you know why? So they could get more money."

They are dividing the tax money between themselves and

70

stealing the land and businesses. It had nothing to do with the church. Our people are poor, some are starving, and others are bankrupt, and they are getting richer and richer. What kind of a God lets this happen?"

"That is not the work of God Jesse. That is the greed of man."

"What will the villagers think when they find out? Will they think I was one of them, that I prospered while they lost everything? Father, you must believe me," he pleaded, "I had no idea. I wasn't allowed to go to the Elder's meetings until I was a full-fledged minister. Now I understand why."

Joe was speechless. Rumors frequently circulated this was happening, but until now, that's all they were.

"I have been such a fool," Jesse continued, "How can I believe in a higher power that allows or even condones these actions? Is money the God we worship?"

Still Joe said nothing. He hurt as he watched his distraught son pace back and forth in front of him, disillusionment written on his face. He wanted to speak words that would help ease Jesse's guilt, but he knew that Jesse had to come to his own conclusions. Was this a test of his son's Faith to affirm what he truly believed in?

Soon Jesse stopped his pacing. He went over and gathered his father in his arms, "I cannot stay here. I must leave. I have a few dollars saved. I have been thinking about this all night. It is not up to me to destroy the faith of others because I am questioning my own. I pray you can understand this."

Joe hugged his son back and then asked, "Where will you go?"

"I don't know –maybe to the city." Jesse replied. "Father you know I need to do this. I must go. I need to find out who I am and what my purpose is. I can't do that here, not now. How can I look our neighbors in the eye and say nothing?"

"Perhaps you are right Jesse. I will tell your mother you are leaving and that I have given my permission. After you are safely away, I will tell her what you have told me, if you approve."

"Yes father, she has every right to know. I hope the Elders don't take their anger out on you."

"Don't you worry about that? In my own way I will let them know what you have told me. I can't give the people back their land or business, but I can, and will, encourage them to fight for what is rightfully theirs, and not give in so easily. The Elders will not try to stop me."

Jesse went into the house and gathered his few belongings. He kissed his mother, brothers and sisters goodbye and began walking down the road with everything he owned in the knap sack on his back. . He turned, waved once and slowly disappeared from view.

Maria whispered, "Go with God Jesse."

Joe went back to his workshop. He didn't want Maria to see that he was crying. Soon Maria came to him with her hands on her hips and stood in the doorway. Joe knew she was angry. "How could you let him go? You need him to help you here; you can't do all of this work alone."

"Maria, go back into the house. I will explain everything to you later," he replied gruffly. His hands shook as he went back to hanging the new door on his workshop.

When the children were outside playing in the yard and they were alone in the house, he took Maria's hands in his, "Maria I have something important to tell "you, but you must tell no one in the village. To do so will cause nothing but trouble among the villagers." Then he proceeded to tell her what Jesse had told him.

"Maria, our son is man of honor. He is right; the villagers would have lost their faith in him. He must find himself first, before he can be of any value to others. Remember how we were told Jesse was born for a special purpose? He cannot do his work until he is strong and confident in his calling. He will be tested many times in his beliefs, this being the first." He gathered her in his arms and held her close to his chest when she began to cry.

"I will miss him terribly." She said.

* * *

The Elders were in a panic, unsure about what Jesse was going to do. Would he rally the villagers against them? They were relieved when they began to hear rumors that he was seen leaving the village.

In the meantime, unknown to the Elders Joe met secretly with a few of his most trusted friends. He told them what Jesse had said, and together they formed a citizens committee. They agreed to try to keep Jesses' part quiet, to approach the Elders themselves and demand that they stop their illegal practices.

When the day came for the next scheduled Elder's meeting, Joe and his friends walked in unannounced, disrupting the meeting. When Elder John looked up and saw who walked through the door he turned pale.

"What is the meaning of this?" he roared. "You have not been invited to be here. Get out. Joe, what exactly do you think you are doing?"

Very calmly Joe looked at the old man then at the others sitting around the table, "you know why I am here," he said. "I have spoken with Jesse." Then, slapping his hand flat upon the table he added, "This ends today. No more."

"I don't know what you are talking about," Elder John declared, but the look on his face spoke otherwise.

"Yes, you do," Joe said, "and we know what you have been doing. We are going to reach an agreement tonight, and if we don't, by tomorrow morning the whole village will know.

"First", he added, "stop the tithe you are stealing from the people. Next, fire the tax collector and stop the confiscation of any more property. Third, increase the wages of the people working for you so they have enough to feed and clothe their families, and lastly provide enough for the widows, children and elderly so they have decent clothing and sufficient food."

One of the other Elders stood up, "and how, if I may ask, are we going to pay for all of this?"

Joe looked at him coldly, "Use the money you stole from them to line your own pockets."

The Elders mumbled among themselves and then Elder John spoke up. "We have no choice; we will do what you say. Now about Jesse…"

Joe looked at him with disgust, "he left," he replied.

The six men turned and began filing out of the room. Joe hung back and heard the Elders arguing among themselves.

Several days after their confrontation, Elder John approached Joe while he was working in his workshop. "I am ashamed," he said. "I ask your forgiveness for the hurt I have caused Jesse and your family. Where has Jesse gone? Perhaps I can go and speak with him."

Joe stopped what he was doing. Turning to Elder John he replied, "He has gone to the city. Even if you could find him and apologize, it won't do much good.

Elder John, you took everything Jesse believed in and destroyed it. Your words, no matter how sincere they are, will never give him what he once had."

Elder John reached out to touch Joe's arm but Joe pulled away. "I am deeply sorry," he said to Joe. "I didn't mean to turn Jesse against his faith."

Joe looked at him. "Go away. Your words won't fix what has already happened. It is too late for that."

Elder John turned and walked away head down, his eyes fixed upon the ground. He looked like a dejected shell of the man he used to be and Joe almost pitied him.

CHAPTER ELEVEN

Heinrich was intoxicated, his head resting upon his arms on the table when Rohm slipped into the booth across from him. "You look like hell," he remarked. "I heard you were spending your time getting drunk and feeling sorry for yourself."

"Leave me alone" Heinrich answered in a drunken slur. "Get your fat ass out of here and leave me alone." Then looking at Rohm through red, bleary eyes he said "What am I supposed to do now? I have no money, no job. The Workers party has completely fallen apart, and they have the audacity to blame me. Too obvious, they say. If not for me, they would have disappeared a long time ago."

Rohm signaled the waiter to bring two more beers. "What are you going to do now?"

"How the hell do I know? There's not much out there for a used up soldier with a crippled back – a political has been."

Rohm sat there for several hours, buying Heinrich drinks and plying him with questions. When a man was as intoxicated as Heinrich, he would be telling the truth.

Finally Rohm said "let me take you home. When you have sobered up, come see me at this address." He tore off a corner of a paper napkin, wrote on it, and then tucked it into Heinrich's shirt pocket. "If you show up we will talk some more."

He half carried a stumbling Heinrich to his room, and left him there lying face down on the floor, curled up like a child.

77

It was mid-afternoon when Heinrich finally awoke. He was sober, but had a raging hangover and felt sick to his stomach. Stumbling to his feet, he began searching his pockets for a coin to buy more beer. When he emptied his shirt pocket he pulled out the napkin with an address on it. Vaguely he remembered Rohm being with him, then helping him home. The address was for a café in a middle class working area on the opposite side of the city, but he couldn't remember why Rohm had given it to him.

He washed, shaved, put on his cleanest set of clothes and walked across town to the café. Upon entering he looked around for Rohm, but he was nowhere to be seen. He had managed to find enough change on his dresser to buy a cup of coffee. He ordered, but when his coffee came, his hands were shaking so badly he could barely lift the cup to his mouth without spilling it. He sat there waiting for Rohm to show up, trying desperately to remember what they had been talking about.

About an hour later the waiter came over to him and asked, "Sir, are you waiting for somebody? Perhaps I could call him for you."

"Yes I am waiting for a Mr. Rohm. He told me to meet him here." Pulling the piece of napkin out of his pocket he showed it to the waiter. "This is the right address isn't it?"

"Yes," the waiter replied, "That is correct. I will check to see if there is a message for you. What is your name?"

"Heinrich Mollen."

The waiter didn't return, but ten minutes later Rohm himself appeared beside the table.

"Good day Heinrich. You look a little worse for wear. I trust you slept well on the floor? At least that was the last place I saw you."

Heinrich glared at him and stood up to leave. "I didn't come here to be insulted." He hated to be reminded of his short comings.

"Sit down and stop being so touchy. I have been watching you for some time. I know you were a spy for the Army, and they dumped you as soon as they got the information they needed. I am also fully aware that is why you accepted your pension and discharge. In your drunken state I'm surprised that you haven't been thrown into jail for what you have been saying. Those were pretty strong words lad, but you are lucky that most of it sounded like the ramblings of a drunk, not worthy of anyone's attention."

Heinrich wasn't so quickly mollified, "so what do you want?"

"We saw how effective you were as the Chief of Propaganda for the Workers party and we want you to come and work for us."

Heinrich senses went on full alert. *Is this some kind of a trap?*

"If I maybe so bold as to ask, who is us?"

"I'm sure you have heard of the Nationalist Socialist Party. We have every intention of forming the next government. We want change and to see this country recover the glory it once had."

"Why me? How do you think I can be of use?"

"Actually before we go any further, the bigger question is can we trust you? That's the one thing we aren't sure about. Tell me Heinrich, are you still working for the Army?" he asked staring right into Heinrich's eyes.

"No," Heinrich replied. "On the other hand how do I know I can trust you? As a condition of leaving the army, I am forbidden to align myself with any political party. How do I know that you aren't trying to trap me? Maybe," he added "you are really a spy sent by the Army to figure out how much I know, and how much danger I pose."

"My offer is legitimate." Rohm declared, lighting his third cigarette from the tip of the second. "I can work with mutual distrust, which will keep us both honest."

Rohm ordered two beers for each of them, and they sat talking for several hours. Finally Heinrich stood up, put out his hand and replied "I will be pleased to join you." The two men shook hands.

"Thought you would be," Rohm replied. "Meet me here tomorrow at four and we will discuss this further. Oh, and Heinrich, we have men positioned in the Army, and we will know if you betray us."

That night Heinrich stayed away from the beer house in an effort to get sober. As always his main question was *how can I make this opportunity work to my advantage?*

CHAPTER TWELVE

With Rohm as his sponsor Heinrich was welcomed into the National Socialist Party. As a former Army officer, armed with his new hatred for the Army and the current government, he quickly became a catalyst for change.

In his own right he was already a powerful figure head, and the NSP was a perfect fit for him. The first thing he convinced Rohm and the other leaders of was that they needed a strong security force to protect them.   Then he proceeded to hire a violent group of men who would to answer only to him. Their duty was to attack and break up the meetings of the communists and any other political parties. Their acts of violence made the party appear stronger and more dangerous than it was.

From his previous association with the Workers party, Heinrich knew who had money, and who was opposed to the current government, thus making his contacts invaluable. Heinrich was a passionate man and a strong communicator and, as a result, was put in charge of party fund raising. He was a frugal man and kept the rooms he lived in for years. His office was the table in the beer house he frequented.

One day Rohm came to him. "Heinrich, you need to be more careful. You are developing enemies within the party that don't agree with the amount of force your men are using. Some have gone so far as to demand your resignation."

"Can't they understand that all of this and much more is needed to overthrow the government?"

"They prefer to bring candidates forward to run in the upcoming election and be voted into office. They feel that will provide a broader representation for the public. To defeat the current government in an honest election would be a great victory."

"And you Rohm, what do you think?" Heinrich asked, drumming his fingers on the table, a clear sign that he was becoming agitated.

"If there are enough people willing to run and enough money to pay for the campaigns, I believe it may be possible."

Heinrich was crossing and uncrossing his legs and chewing on his bottom lip. Rohm sensed the anger building in him.

"They are stupid foolish men – all talk and no action. We need people who are willing to do whatever is necessary," Heinrich raged. "They are stupid men and have no idea how politics work. You have to make the people afraid to vote for anyone except you, that is how to win."

He got up and started pacing back and forth in front of their table. It was a good thing the beer house was fairly empty, and those present paid no attention to him.

"Damn it, if that's what they want I resign as of this minute. I will form my own party. Without me and the funds I raise, you will amount to nothing. I will take my powerful influential friends and backers with me. They are idealistic, and with very little persuasion, will follow me."

"You can't do that."

"And why not?"

"If you take the backers we won't have money to field enough candidates in the election. We would have no hope of winning."

Heinrich sneered at Rohm. "Exactly my point, now go back to them and tell them what I just told you. Make it plain that if I leave they will have nothing. If they disagree with me, my resignation will be effective as of today."

Rohm got up and left. He didn't like dealing with Heinrich when he was angry. That very night he called a meeting of the NSP leaders, and they argued into the early morning hours over the best course of action.

The next morning Rohm and Heinrich met again. "I have been instructed to ask you to withdraw your resignation. We argued bitterly but, in the end, we decided it was more important to replace the government. Without financial backing we cannot succeed."

Heinrich wasn't surprised. He knew all along that the party leaders would capitulate to his demands. He had them exactly where he wanted them.

Over the course of the next few months he cajoled and bullied his way into becoming the undisputed leader of the party. Those who opposed him disappeared, or met with fatal accidents.

Heinrich also understood that he needed the support of the general population to achieve his goals. He began holding public meetings to convince others that under his leadership the country would once more become prosperous, and there would be work and food for all. His guards quickly dealt with those who heckled or opposed him at the meetings.

Rapidly he gained a following. Even his most radical ideas were approved. He was treated like a movie star – anything he wanted was laid out before him.

As he grew stronger, so did the party. Behind the scenes he had a group of men plotting to assassinate the Chancellor which would throw the country into total disarray. While this was going on, the party would start moving their followers into various public positions. This group also decided that Heinrich would take over the role of Chancellor on a temporary basis.

The evening before the assassination attempt, a squad of policemen arrived at Heinrich's door and arrested him. There was a traitor in their group. Other important members of the party were also arrested and convicted, but the main leaders, including Rohm escaped.

Heinrich failed to recognize that in his journey for power he made many enemies- some of whom were connected to very influential people and opposed his line of thinking.

In the middle of the night he was tried in secret, and although he was allowed a lawyer to defend him, his guilt was a forgone conclusion. Subsequently, he was sentenced to five years in jail and hauled away to prison.

Those who supported Heinrich faded into the background. Each decided, in his own way, to leave the situation the way it was, and to wait and see what the final outcome would be.

The NSP party was demoralized. Without Heinrich's presence and leadership, they were back where they were – secretly meeting in back rooms. Any hopes of winning and election and forming the nest government vanished.

CHAPTEER THIRTEEN

Heinrich was shocked when the cell door slammed shut behind him. At least, for now, he was alone in his cell.

The only light entering the eight by ten foot cell came through a dirty window and a dim light bulb in the ceiling. There were four bunks in the space and he took the bottom left, so he could watch the corridor just beyond.

The thin mattress stunk of sweat from the men who had been there before him. The guard gave him a pillow and a threadbare blanket to use. In the far corner were a dirty sink, and an even dirtier toilet. He smelled the fear emanating from his own body.

"This is the most disgusting place I have ever seen – I don't know if I can stand five years of this." He gagged, and then ran to the toilet and vomited.

Heinrich was used to order. He had a place for everything as he had learned in the Army. . His room was always clean and neat. In comparison his cell was a pig sty

Feeling shaky after vomiting, he lay down on the narrow bed covering his shoulders with the thin blanket. For the first time in his life he was truly afraid. He heard the stories about what went on in the prisons.

I will kill any person who tries to touch me he vowed. *My lawyer assured me this wouldn't happen because I am a political prisoner, and would be placed in a special section. Instead here I am, in general population with the dregs of society – rapists,*

85

child molesters and murderers. I was sure one of my so called friends would bail me out before I ended up here. I find it hard to believe that I have been condemned to live in this stinking place for the next five years. As soon as I get out of here, I will get even with them.

He quickly fell into the routine of prison life. He was released from his cell four times a day, three times for meals with the other prisoners, and then for an hour in the exercise yard. He kept to himself, discouraging the other prisoners from approaching him. His first act was to convince a guard to bring him a bucket of water and some rags. He scrubbed until his cell was clean. He remained alone in his cell and was grateful for that.

Every day Heinrich spent hours writing letters to his influential backers begging them to use their influence to get him released. When he wasn't thinking about that, he plotted different ways to kill whoever was responsible for putting him in prison. He also spent time plotting and planning what he was going to do when he did get out. *Obviously the current government thought I am a danger to them or I wouldn't be in prison now.*

With so much free time on his hands he evolved a plan to become the head of the government. He would no longer be at the mercy of the actions of others because he would set the policy and dictate the rules. The longer he remained in prison the more self-centered he became.

Over time he began to realize that he should be looking at this experience from a different point of view. Here were the people he needed, people who didn't care about anyone or anything. He began to cultivate the friendships of the most influential, and made rash promises he had no intention of keeping.

He also began talking to the other prisoners about the NSP party and his plans for the future of the country. Many scoffed at him, but others believed him. He roused them into taking action against the ruling party – that if it weren't for the unjust rules they wouldn't be in prison. He encouraged them to become vocal. Others, with shorter sentences, he promised lucrative positions in his government when he formed it.

Nine months into his sentence he received word that his influential backers were making progress in getting him released. This news prompted him to begin writing his ideas in the form of a handbook. He often worked late into the night writing down his grandiose ideas and plans for the future.

Gradually he came up with a seven point plan, his Manifesto he called it.

1. **I will declare myself leader of the church as well as the state.** *My grandmother forced me to go to church with her everyday but, where was her God when I needed him? I saw the Elders getting rich, and if I was the leader, they would have to listen to me and forced to share their wealth. Those who oppose me will be killed.*

2. **In order to achieve this indoctrination camps would be built and forcible change would be achieved. Any person who speaks out against me or my ideas will be moved to these new locations.**

3. **I will thank my backers by providing free labor from the camps. Their businesses would prosper, and, when the time comes, it will be easy for them to switch to building weapons and machines.**

87

4. I will form a large military presence loyal only to me. I have a good idea who I will put in charge.
5. I will surround myself with a strong group of men whose duty is to protect me. I also know who I will put in charge of this force.
6. I will begin in the schools by indoctrinating the children from kindergarten to my way of thinking, which will insure a steady group of followers as the years pass.
7. When I have complete control over my country I will begin assimilating the neighboring countries into my own. If all works as I have planned I will be considered the most powerful leader on the continent, maybe even the world.

While formulating his plans he began writing and smuggling out a series of communications supporting the NSP party. For a price, the guards would do whatever he asked. Even as he sat in jail his party became stronger, and his influence grew. He found ways to keep his ideas in forefront of the party and the public.

The political climate was becoming more and more volatile with the NSP being targeted. His messages were passed secretly from hand to hand, and more people joined the party. Heinrich knew that time was of the essence - that to fulfill his plan he had to get out of jail. He increased the pressure on his supporters, to some he promised a seat in parliament; each promise was specifically tailored to their desires, still others he threatened to destroy their businesses taking away all they had worked for. He swore to unearth their scandals and sexual deviances and make them public. He would turn them into the laughing stock of society.

Eighteen months later from the day he entered, Heinrich walked out of prison a free man, with a pardon in his pocket. The powers that be hoped that as soon as Heinrich was released from jail, his power would diminish. Part of his allure was the fact he was in jail, and still finding a way to speak out. He was now more popular than ever. The current government asked him to promise that, upon receiving the pardon, he would refrain from holding public gatherings. Of course all parties concerned knew this wasn't going to happen, but they had to show accountability to the public in some form.

Within days of leaving jail he began receiving messages from those who secretly continued to support him. He resurrected the strong arm of the party putting those he knew believed in him in control. Because of the uniform – brown shirts, caps, pants and boots they became known as Brown Shirts.

While languishing in jail Heinrich realized something else. Assassinations and armed revolution were not the answers to achieving power. He needed to be elected as the leader by the public and gain the confidence of those who voted for him.

CHAPTER FOURTEEN

Upon his release from jail, the leaders of the NSP Party welcomed Heinrich back, unanimously appointing him as their party leader. In amazement, and almost single handed, he achieved his original goal. When he inquired about Rohm, nobody seemed to know where he was. He escaped capture and disappeared. Some thought he left the country, others that he was dead.

He was disappointed. Most of the old guard from the party was gone, but the new members were young and enthusiastic and eagerly accepted him as their undisputed leader.

Once again they spoke of him leading a revolt as a means of overthrowing the government, but he quickly discouraged that idea. At a special meeting, he told the party executive, "The only successful way to overthrow the government is by election. We have to run candidates in every major riding all over the country, placing our strongest members in the most important places then do whatever is necessary to win.

We need to discredit the current government by making them look weak and ineffective. We don't need to win every riding, only the majority. Once we have the support of the people, it will only be a matter of time before the opposition from the other parties disappears. We will endeavor to help that along as quickly as we can."

Immediately he put his plan in motion. He began a campaign of intimidation, knowing that even the strongest person would buckle when threatened. He appointed Sig Rotter, one of his new acquaintances from jail, as Commander of the Brown Shirts and gave him free rein to do whatever was necessary to insure his party won the election.

Over the next four months, Heinrich worked tirelessly to attract the public to his cause. He promised jobs, free education, and renewed prosperity and freedom. In the meantime, the Brown Shirts waged a campaign of terror against the other parties. They tore posters down, had rallies in the street, disrupted meetings and verbally abused the other candidates.

The Brown Shirts used every opportunity to denounce and defame the other candidates. Their campaign of terror also included destroying their offices and beating up their workers. Candidates from all parties were given the choice of withdrawing or dying. Their families were threatened and their homes burned. Several of the more prominent candidates were found dead under suspicious circumstances and the police, already infiltrated by Heinrich's men, found no blame.

By the time the day of the election came around, there was no doubt the current government would be defeated. In many places, the NSP candidate was the only candidate left to vote for. Heinrich waited until the polls were closed then broadcasted on the radio declaring himself as the new leader and Chancellor of the country. Now he was free to do as he pleased.

Victory dances and parades were held in the streets. Whenever Heinrich appeared in public, the crowds chanted his name over and over. In the first days he replaced the heads of the Army, Navy and Air Force with his chosen leaders. Those who opposed him were jailed; others disappeared and were never seen again.

Essentially the country was now in the hands of a dictator, yet because of his charisma and skill at manipulating people, the number of his supporters grew. He forced the church Elders to teach his doctrine and sing his praises. He also began systematically arresting every person heard speaking against him. Quickly they were rounded up along with their families, and sent to build indoctrination camps.

He had chosen a deep valley surrounded by hills on three sides with only one way in for his camp. There he built guard towers and a black wrought iron fence at the entrance. The area was heavily guarded by armed men day and night. Miles of electrified fence were built around the camp and foot patrols regularly patrolled the rocky hills.

At first the prisoners were housed in tents until they constructed huts to live in. They had little protection from the elements; by day the hot sun beat down on them and by night they froze.

Other prisoners were put to work building a railroad spur to the camp entrance. Several miles from the camp a small city was built to accommodate the guards, and the officers and their families.

Inside the camps water and food were rationed, and soon the prisoners became ill and many died from hunger and exposure.

Heinrich kept his promises to the big companies. The prisoners not used for building the camps were forced to provide free labor. The company's paid Heinrich large sums of money each month to cover the room and board of their workers, but instead of providing the proper accommodations he had promised, the men and women were given a set of clothes, a pair of shoes, a blanket and a pillow, a wooden bunk to sleep on and one meal a day. It was also clearly understood by all parties that the women and girls could be used for any form of sexual exploitation. If a worker died, for a small fee another was provided in his or her place.

Heinrich was proud of his achievements. He had a goal and all of his careful planning was paying off. He had everything he had ever wished for – power, money and respect.

At a party fundraising dinner party Heinrich was surprised when he overheard a group of men talking about the Believers and their leader Jesse.

"Who is this Jesse? Where does he come from? Why haven't I heard from him until now?" he asked.

"You must know him Heinrich; he comes from the same village as you."

Suddenly, he felt as he did when he was a child. No matter how hard he tried, or how well he did, he always came out second best to Jesse.

He started to laugh. "That Jesse? He is nothing but a lily livered coward. The last I heard was when the Elders refused him to ordain him as a minister, he skulked off to the city, and was drinking and whoring himself to death. Do not fear my friends; he will be no problem for us. At the first sign of intimidation he will turn tail and run."

That evening after he returned home, he poured himself a drink and sat in front of the fireplace thinking. *At last, I am better than him. I need to show the country how much of a coward he is. If that fails, I will have him taken care of. There isn't room for both of us. I will squash him like I would a*

94

common bug.   The next day he instructed Rotter to send several of his more trusted Brown Shirts to infiltrate Jesse's group. Within a week, Rotter returned with a report.

"You are right Heinrich, they will be impotent. They are severely disorganized and not much of a threat. I am sure that if you threaten them, they will quickly disband. Their leader, the man named Jesse doesn't appear strong enough to build an organization that will threaten you."

Heinrich smiled as he listened to Rotter's report. "I guess I will show him once and for all who is the greatest. Keep an eye on him and report back if there are any changes in his activities."

"Do you want my men to pay him a visit?"

"No, I don't think that is necessary. Jesse and his followers will never be a threat to us."

CHAPTER FIFTEEN

As he walked away from his village Jesse felt hurt and disillusioned, but what hurt the most was the fact that he had loved and respected Elder John. He still wanted to believe he was a pious man who had faith in the church and its teachings, and struggled to admit that he was as human as every other person, and that greed was a human frailty.

What kind of a man am I that I could put my hands around the neck of another and want to kill him? I put Elder John on a pedestal, forgetting that he was just a man and would act as one. How could I have been so naïve? I knew what the Elders were doing, but looked the other way. In essence I am no better than they are. In fact I am worse because I thought I was different. My family will be better off without me.

Jesse was desperate to put as many miles as possible between him and the village so he could disappear forever. Unconsciously he walked toward the capital city of Bern. He slept where he could, sometimes under a tree at the side of the road, or in a stranger's barn. Sometimes he accepted the rides offered to him, but mostly he walked the one hundred and fifty miles. He had very little money and was often hungry. Rather than feeling sorry for his situation, he chose to believe he was paying penance for his stupidity.

Other than when he was a baby, Jesse never travelled more than twenty miles from his village. For the first time he became aware the world was larger than the area around his village.

The closer Jesse got to the city, the more congested the road became. Several times he was forced to jump from the side of the road into the ditch to avoid being run over by a passing vehicle.

The further he ventured into the city the more his senses were assaulted by the smells and cacophony of sounds. He felt bewildered and uneasy. People were rude, pushing him out of their way when he stopped and gawked at the ornate buildings surrounding him. Already he was longing for the clean air and green hills of home.

He couldn't go back. Village life was centered on the church and the Elders, and he didn't believe anymore. What hurt the most was that everything he had trusted and believed in turned out to be a lie.

Using the few coins he had left in his pocket, he stopped at a bakery and purchased a loaf of bread and a small piece of cheese. This was going to have to last for several days, at least until he could find work as a carpenter.

As evening approached he came across a park. *This looks like a good spot to spend the night;* he muttered taking his small blanket out of his knapsack to cover himself. He ate part of his bread and cheese then put the rest back into his knapsack to save for the next day.

Because there were a lot of people in the park, he found a secluded spot under a bush. He used his knapsack as a pillow and laid down to rest. Covering his shoulders with the small blanket he fell asleep

Suddenly out of nowhere something thumped him hard across his legs. He woke up with a start.

"You can't sleep here," a deep voice said.

Jesse looked up to see two men dressed in brown shirts standing over him. One of them raised his arm and struck him on the side of his head with his truncheon.

Slowly he got to his feet, gritting his teeth against the pain from his head and legs "I'm sorry," he said "I didn't know."

"Beggars and bums aren't allowed to sleep in the park. This is for the law abiding citizens of Bern. Get out!" one of the brown shirts said, lifting his arm to strike Jesse again.

"I am new to the city. I had no place to sleep," Jesse replied, gathering his blanket and stuffing it into his knapsack.

The other man pointed, "head west over the bridge and keep walking. You will find more of your kind there. There is a soup kitchen where you can find something to eat tomorrow. My best advice is to go back where you came from. There are already too many of your kind here."

Jesse slung his knapsack over one shoulder and headed in the direction pointed out to him. His head ached from the blow he received and he could hear the two men laughing at him as he left.

As he walked down a badly lit street a woman sidled out of the darkness and approached him. "Are you looking for a good time?"

"No," Jesse replied, feeling embarrassed. He heard other men talking about the kind of women who made themselves available to men for a price, but had never seen one.

"Bastard," she called out as he walked away. "How am I

supposed to feed my children tomorrow?"

He shuddered. *Is this what the world is coming to? Women should not have to sell their bodies to feed their families?*

He kept walking, and passed many drinking establishments. The noise was loud, the air smelled of stale beer and cigarettes. Both men and women were vomiting in the streets. In one dark corner he saw a man and a woman, her skirt above her waist, the man deep inside her pounding her back against the wall. She was crying. "You are hurting me," she pleaded, "Please stop," but the man ignored her and kept on. As Jesse continued down the street, he was accosted by more women, some no more than children. He felt himself begin to gag.

Jesse was relieved to see the bridge the man in the brown shirt told him about. He hurried toward it; the slight breeze off the river cooled his face.

When he reached the middle of the bridge he stopped and took a deep breath. It was quiet and he stood there for a long time soaking in the cool breeze. His mind was reeling from what he had seen so far. *How can people live like this? What has happened to bring them to this point in their lives? Now I know for sure God doesn't care about the poor. If he truly cared, people wouldn't have to spend their time drinking and whoring.*

He continued to walk across the bridge and, in the darkness, didn't see the man lurking in the bushes. As Jesse walked past the man stepped out and hit him with a board across the back of his head. When Jesse came to his knapsack was gone. When he touched the lump on the back of his head his hand came back bloody He was dizzy and his head ached.

. Why would anyone steal from me? I have little enough as it is

100

but, if they had asked, I would have gladly shared what I had.

Not knowing what else to do, he continued stumbling forward. In the distance he saw a fire burning and heard the sound of men's voices. He gravitated toward the spot. *At lease I will not be alone. Maybe they will let me stay with them until daylight, and then I will see if I can find some kind of work.*

Several men stood around the fire burning in a garbage can trying to keep warm. Their clothes were threadbare and ragged, and many had several days' worth of beard on their faces. He saw others milling about, still others leaning against a building, talking in quiet voices. Some were lying on the ground sleeping.

Tentatively he walked toward the fire, hoping that no one would notice him. "Hey you," a voice out of the darkness inquired, "are you okay? Come; stand by the fire with us."

Those are the first kind words Jesse heard for several days. A figure emerged from the darkness. Extending his hand to Jesse he said, "My name is Peter. What happened, you don't look well?"

Jesse looked at the man speaking to him. He was a full head taller than Jesse, with a tangled beard which fell to his chest. His dirty clothes hung from his gaunt frame, yet Jesse noticed his kind eyes.

"First two men in brown shirts hit me, and then as I crossed the bridge, some one hit me from behind and stole my belongings. I saw the light of your fire, hoping I could join you until morning." For some unexplained reason he wasn't afraid of this man.

"You are bleeding, come over here and let me take a look at

101

that cut," Peter said, taking Jesse by the arm pulling him closer to the fire. He inspected the wound on the back of Jesse's head. "You will live," he pronounced very seriously.

Jesse laughed. That night Peter shared what little food and drink he had with Jesse. He let Jesse sleep in his spot by the wall, and covered him with his own ragged blanket.

An instant bond of trust and acceptance formed between the two men. From that night on Peter walked by Jesse's side.

CHAPTER SIXTEEN

Jesse dozed in intervals. His head hurt, the ground was cold, and the slightest noise made him jump. Usually at times like this, when he felt troubled and afraid, he would pray. When this idea came into his head he banished it quickly. *If there was any truth in the teachings, I wouldn't be where I am.*

When he awoke in the morning there was only the two of them, Jesse and Peter, everybody else was gone. "Where are the others?" Jesse asked, looking around.

"I'm not sure," Peter replied. "We go our own way during the day, but at night rely on the comfort and safety of being with others"

"Who are these people? Why are they here?"

"I really can't say. Some are destitute, some are mentally ill, others have fallen on hard times and still others are in hiding. I don't ask questions. The less we know of each other's business the better off we are.

"What brought you here Jesse?" Peter asked, "You aren't like the rest of us."

Jesse evaded his question. "That's not important. I have other more pressing problems. I have no money, no food and no place to stay. I am a carpenter by trade and I need to find work."

Peter looked at him. "Come," he said "let me show you around." Peter took his blanket from Jesse and tucked it into his own knapsack. "If you leave things lying around they disappear," he commented.

When they exited the alley Jesse was shocked to see the squalor around him. Last night, in the dark, he hadn't paid much attention to his surroundings. All he had been interested in was finding a degree of safety with a fire and other people.

They walked for several blocks until they came to a place where there was a long line of people. "I come here once a day to get food. It isn't that good, but is better than doing without." Peter told Jesse, "Come, we had better get in line."

As they made their way to the end of the line, Peter spoke easily with the other men inquiring about their health and other concerns. Others sought him out. Jesse was quiet; he didn't know what to make of the situation.

At first he was angry. *Why don't these people clean up and find a job?* Then he realized because of circumstance beyond his control, he was now one of them. *If the Elders were who they were supposed to be, I would be at home with my family. They are the reason I have nothing.*

When they got to the front of the line each was given a bowl of watery soup and a thick slice of bread. Because he didn't have his own bowl, Jesse was given a battered tin mug. He ate his soup, but put the bread in his pocket for later.

"Come," said Peter, "I will show you where you can apply for a job." They crossed the street and walked several more blocks. Once again, they came to a line of men, although this one was much shorter.

"This is the employment office." Peter said. "It is best to

come early in the morning because that's when the best jobs are available. Also, the first in the line get the jobs. There is always some kind of work available although much of it is disgusting. As a carpenter you may fare better than some. A word of advice, if you see any groups of Brown Shirts coming towards you, turn and walk away. They don't need any excuse to beat you. They consider it a sport."

Each day Jesse got up before dawn and stood in line for work. Some days he was lucky. He ate the simple meal provided by the soup kitchen. With the money he made he bought a few articles of clothing and several warm blankets which he shared with others.

Late at night, he told Peter his story. His anger burst forth in a tirade as he paced back and forth. "They lied and took advantage of me. It if wasn't for them, I would be at home with my family.

"What choice did I have? I couldn't stay there. The villagers would begin asking questions, and come to the conclusion that I knew what was going on, and was a part their scheme the whole time. What else could I do but leave?"

Peter let him go on for a while, listening attentively, but finally had enough. "Listen to yourself Jesse. It doesn't matter what the Elders did or didn't do. There is corruption in every facet of life. Nobody is perfect, but isn't what you believe more important? You are a hypocrite, and no better than the Elders you blame. They took the easy way out and so have you, because that's what you learned from them. Take who you are, what you know, and use these talents for those who need you, but you are no good to them unless you truly believe what you are teaching."

Jesse was angry. He laid awake most of the night thinking about what Peter had said and came to the conclusion that he was right. They never spoke of that night again.

Chapter Seventeen

As the weeks passed, Peter watched Jesse struggle. He saw the torment written on his face, his eyes vacant, as though he was a lost soul. He had given so much of his young life to the church, now he was like a ship adrift without an anchor.

Jesse started drinking with some of the other men and was rarely sober enough to go to work. He let his appearance go; his hair became long and stringy, his clothes filthy, and he needed a bath. He began taking his anger out on others, and was always looking for a fight.

One day, as Peter was walking to get soup for Jesse and himself, he saw a poster about a revival meeting nailed to the side of a derelict building He had heard others talk about this speaker, Jean Baptiste, and was curious. He knew he was the leader of a small group of people who called themselves the Believers.

That evening when he and Jesse met back in the alley he commented to Jesse. "Jean Baptiste, the revival leader, is in town and I am going to go listen to him. Why don't you come with me? We can go together to hear what he has to say."

Jesse was in terrible shape. He had no money, and had nothing to drink for several days. He was shaking and constantly fidgeting.

Jesse turned on him "No, I won't go with you. Shut up and leave me alone. You know how I feel about religion and God.

Look what he has done to me. I am sick and tired of you trying to tell me any different."

Peter, tired of Jesse's whining and complaining said, "I didn't ask you to come with me because I am trying to change you. I asked because it is safer for two men to walk down the street rather than one man alone."

By now he was angry. "Who do you think you are Jesse? Night after night you crawl into camp so drunk you can't stand up. You are not the same man who joined us. That man was hurting, but he had a sense of who he was, and what he believed in.

You have become nothing more than a pathetic drunk always blaming others for your problems. The truth is you have given up on yourself, and I am not going to stand by and watch you continue to destroy your life. I turn my back on you. You are no longer my friend, and I am sorry I asked you to go with me."

Jesse was stunned at the depth of Peter's anger. He was the only friend Jesse had. He watched as Peter picked up his knapsack and walked out of the camp.

"Go with him," a voice whispered. Jesse looked around. He was alone. At Peter's outburst the other men drifted away. "Jesse, I command you to go with him."

Jesse picked up the tattered brown knapsack he found in the garbage and walked quickly to catch up to Peter. When he joined him Peter said nothing. They walked in silence.

When they arrived at the meeting place a huge white tent had been erected. Jesse looked around in surprise. There were many who were homeless like him, but there were also many more that were rich and well dressed.

Jean was a charismatic speaker. His eyes shone as he spoke. "In troubled times such as these, we must pray for guidance and courage. We must look out for one another - become you are your brother's keeper. We must love and respect who we are, and treasure the gifts we have been given."

After the meeting ended Peter and Jesse walked back in silence. Jesses mind was troubled. Jean had spoken of all the things he believed in. *Was what Jean preached the truth? His teachings are opposite to what I learned from the Elders.*

When they arrived back at the camp Peter went one way Jesse went another, and was not seen for two days. Sometime during the second night Jesse returned, drunk and belligerent. His clothes and face were bloody.

Barely able to walk Jesse staggered to where Peter was sleeping and kicked him. "Wake up I need to talk to you." Peter was awake, but pretended to be sleeping.

Jesse kicked him again. "Get up I said."

Peter continued to ignore Jesse. He knew from previous experience there was no sense trying to talk to him when he was like this.

Jesse kicked him a third time, even harder than the time before, nearly falling down in the process. "Get up you lousy bastard, I have something I want to say to you."

Peter had enough. He rolled over and jumped to his feet. "Go to bed and sleep it off." He walked over to Jesse and pushed him against the wall. Through clenched teeth he spoke in a hoarse whisper, "I am tired, leave me alone."

Jesse looked up at him through glazed eyes. "Why couldn't you leave well enough alone? But no, you had to try and fix me by taking me to that Revival meeting. This is your fault."

Peter looked down at him. "Go to sleep. We will talk about this in the morning." Jesse's eyes rolled back, and he crumpled to the ground.

Peter stayed close and watched over his friend all night. He heard Jesse stagger out of the alley, and get sick on the street. He listened to him moaning and cussing in his sleep. In the morning, when he awoke, he looked over to check on Jesse and saw he was lying in his own vomit and had soiled himself.

The other men left, each looking at Jesse with disgust. Peter remained and continued to keep watch over his friend.

When Jesse awoke around noon he was very ill. His body was covered in fresh bruises from being beaten up while he was gone. Peter helped him strip off his filthy clothes, found some clean water and washed him. He threw Jesse's clothes into the burning barrel and helped him dress in his last clean set.

Using the last of the water, he cleaned Jesse's vomit from the ground. While all of this was taking place, neither said a word to the other.

When Jesse looked half presentable again Peter laid him on his own blanket. "I will go and find us some food. Stay here until I get back."

An hour later, when he returned, Jesse was gone. Peter wasn't surprised.

As soon as Peter was out of sight Jesse got up and walked in the opposite direction. Slowly and painfully he made his way

110

back to the Revival tent. The afternoon meeting was just beginning.

He sat there listening carefully as Jean spoke. When the meeting was over, and Jean's many admirers had left, Jesse walked up to him and shamefully asked, "Please help me?"

CHAPTER EIGHTEEN

Peter was deeply concerned about Jesse's disappearance. Nobody had seen him for days. *Did something happen to him? I have searched every alley, every brothel and tavern, but he seems to have completely disappeared. I will probably find him in worse shape than when he left, if he is still alive.*

He was shocked the evening Jesse walked back into the alley. Peter greeted him, but didn't ask any questions, he knew Jesse would talk when he was ready. Jesse was clean, shaved and wore new clothes, but best of all he was smiling and happy. The men crowded around him and welcomed him back.

In the still of the early morning Jesse woke Peter up. Speaking quietly he said "I have been with Jean Baptiste. He has helped me see that the Elders didn't start out to become the way they were, but evolved that way overtime. Jean has shown me that we worship the same God, but in a different way. As we talked, I saw that his group of Believers follow the same principles I believe in.

Peter, I was lost, but I have found myself. I chose to become a Believer, and I am going to begin my ministry anew here.

I have known since I was a child that I had a calling. I have found my purpose, and I know what is to come. I will be reviled, hunted and probably, in the end, lose my life to the cause. I willingly accept all that is ahead for me.

I see what is happening in the city around us- how people are being treated. I refuse to accept Heinrich as our leader. We had our differences in the past, but someone needs to stop him. I know him well and what kind of man he is. We are from the same village and went to school together. When he finds out it is me opposing him he will do everything in his power to stop me."

"Why you Jesse? What makes you think and feel that you are the man chosen to stand against Heinrich? He is pure evil and won't be satisfied until you are dead."

Jesse replied, "I know that but, with Heinrich as our leader, there is no hope. That is my purpose – to offer hope. Hope for a better way to live." Then Jesse looked into Peter's eyes and asked "will you walk with me by my side?"

Peter replied "Yes," and it was settled between them.

* * *

At night the men often gathered to drink and gamble. Instead of joining them Jesse did what he could to ease the suffering of those who were sick. Some of the men would gather around him and he would assure them, "God forgives you. Whatever you have done or think you have done is forgiven as soon as you pray.

Love one another, look after each other, forgive others if they have wronged you, but mostly treat others the same way you wish to be treated."

As his message passed by word of mouth more and more people came to the alley to listen to him. For once there was hope in a community that knew only suffering and pain.

One day a young prostitute approached Jesse. "My name is Marika. Is it true your God will forgive me even though I sell my body to men for money?"

"How old are you?" Jesse asked.

"Sixteen."

"How long have you been doing this?'

"For five years. My father sold me to a man to pay for his drinking debts, and I have been here ever since."

Jesse looked at the waif like child who stood in front of him. The pain and sorrow in her eyes was more than he could bear. "This life has not been one of your choosing, or any fault of yours. Now that you know different, you must stop."

"That's easy for you to say. How am I to live if I stop? What am I supposed to do instead?" she replied heatedly, turning away from him

As she walked away Jesse remembered her voice from before. Then it dawned on him, when he first arrived he walked past a man and woman in the shadows, she was the woman begging the man to stop because he was hurting her. *I can still hear the sound of her being slammed against the wall. My heart breaks for what she must endure night after night.*

Even as he talked with the men and listened to their stories his anger grew. He was still bitterly angry with the elders; he didn't want to be a minister. Yet here he was, doing what came naturally to him.

One evening twenty Brown Shirts, carrying truncheons and sticks, attacked the group. They lashed out hitting and kicking indiscriminately at the men. Their sole purpose was to maim and injure Jesse. The men who remained bravely tried to defend

115

themselves, but in their weakened state were no match. By the time the fighting was over, one man was dead, and several seriously injured. The rest had run away when the trouble started, but these were the ones unable to. After the attack Jesse did his best to help those who were hurt.

"Jesse, Jesse," he heard Peters voice call out to him. Peter was coming down the alley carrying the child Marika in his arms. She was bleeding and unconscious. Jesse could see the blood running down her legs.

"Bring her over here," Jesse said, grabbing a blanket and laying it on the ground beside the building. "What happened to her? Is she alive?"

"Yes, she is breathing, but unconscious. She was attacked by five Brown Shirts. They took turns with her. I managed to get her away from them and came directly here, but I don't know what to do for her."

"Maybe I can help." A man, new to their group, stepped forward. He quickly checked Marika over and then made her comfortable. "She has no broken bones, but has been repeatedly raped. There is a large lump on her head, but I am sure she will awaken soon."

Peter stayed with her while Jesse and the man tended the others who had been hurt.

When they were finished, they stood beside the fire warming themselves. Marika began to whimper and Peter stayed by her side quietly talking to her.

"You seem to have some skills in this area and know what you are doing." Jesse said to the man standing beside him. "I haven't seen you here before."

"Yes," the man replied, "I used to be a doctor."

By now, Jesse understood that every man in their group had a story. This was a place of last resort- a place for hiding, a place for men seeking obscurity. He also learned not to ask any questions.

"I killed a child," the man continued, "it was an accident, but I couldn't live with myself. I had been drinking and gave her too much pain medication. She died as a result."

Jesse stuck out his hand, "My name is Jesse."

"Mathew," the man replied, shaking Jesse's hand.

Marika stayed with them. She helped with the sick and the hurt. In the mornings, Jesse took her to the soup kitchen for food and watched over her the rest of the day, taking her with him if necessary. All of the men understood she was under Jesse's protection and none of them bothered her.

One evening, Mathew, Peter and Jesse stood by the fire apart from the others. "Jesse, why are you here?" Peter asked for the hundredth time.

This time Jesse opened his heart to the two men. "I was nearly ordained as a minister in our church. The church was rich but many people in our village were poor and starving and I couldn't understand why. I found out the church had imposed a tax to make up the shortfall to repay their debt to the rich. When people were unable to pay, all they had was taken from them. When I saw the Elders dividing the tax money I left. I was so angry I almost killed my mentor, Elder John, with my own two hands. I couldn't stay there and be part of what was going on."

"And you Peter, why are you here?" Mathew asked.

"I was a successful business man, who was more interested in making money and had little time for my wife and family. I came home one day to find my wife gone and a note which said she had taken our son and left with another man."

"Did you try to find her?"

"No. She deserved to be happy because she was miserable with me. Frankly I didn't blame her."

"What about your son?"

Peter didn't answer. The three men stood there silently watching the flames in the garbage can.

Finally Peter asked," what do you believe in Jesse? Maybe your role wasn't there in your village but someplace else. Maybe it was meant to be here?"

"If the Elders were honest I wouldn't have abandoned my village and my family." Jesse replied bitterly.

"Did they drive you out? Did they force you to leave in any way?"

"No. I didn't tell them. I said goodbye to my parents and walked away."

"Then the truth is you left on your own accord. Instead of staying and doing what you could to help the villagers get their property returned you turned your back on them."

Jesse was quiet for the rest of the evening. *Maybe Peter was right, maybe I should have stayed. I let everybody down and deserve to be where I am.*

118

Jesse's reputation as a carpenter grew, and soon people asked him to work for them. He worked hard; taking every job offered, and then used the money he made to help the less fortunate. He bought food, and provided Mathew with money to buy medicine for the sick.

Soon more men from the surrounding camps came asking for advice. At night they gathered and listened while he spoke to them. "God forgives what you have done or think you have done As soon as you pray asking for forgiveness, it is done. Love one another. Look after one another, treat people as you want to be treated."

As his message of a loving God spread, the men began to call themselves Believers of a Benevolent God, which was later shortened to the Believers. Even Jean began to follow him.

From these humble beginnings Jesse's message spread and the crowds coming to listen to him increased. Slowly a band of trusted men surrounded Jesse – Peter, Mathew, Luke, John, Thomas and Judaea. Marika was always present at his side. In spite of all this attention he remained a humble man.

Soon Jesse began to leave the alley and ventured into other parts of the city to spread his message. The growing group of Believers attracted Heinrich's attention. When he realized it was his nemesis Jesse he began sending out squads of Brown Shirts to break up the gatherings. But that had little effect. The gatherings kept growing. The people wanted to believe Jesse's message because it offered them hope for a better tomorrow.

Life was harsh under Heinrich's government The Brown Shirts were indiscriminate and unchallenged as they bullied the citizens of the city. They took what they wanted, leaving misery in their wake. No one was exempt. The men were often beaten, and forced to watch their wives and daughters raped in front of them. Valuable articles were stolen, and their complaints went unheard by officials.

As Jesse's fame grew, he left the city and, with his inner core of Believers, carried his teachings to the nearby towns and villages.

When word of Jesse's fame reached his parents, they were worried. Heinrich was changing the politics of the country and his message was the opposite of Jesse's. He began taking out newspaper ads out attacking Jesse, threatening repercussions to any person who followed him. It was inevitable that at some point in time the two of them would meet face to face.

CHAPTER NINETEEN

Mathew was sound asleep when he heard Marika's voice begging him to wake up. "You must come quickly," she said, "Jesse is very ill.

Instantly he was awake. Physicians have an uncanny skill which enables them to become alert whenever they are needed. "Where is he?" Mathew asked, looking around and not seeing him in his usual spot.

"I moved him into the shelter, and then came to get you."

The shelter was in a corner between two buildings, out of the elements, and away from the prying eyes of the street. Jesse had helped the men construct a roof between the walls. Often he went there if one of the men wanted to speak to him in private.

"What seems to be the trouble?" he asked, as they stepped around the sleeping men. Life was getting harder in the city, and each day more men arrived to seek safety.

"He is burning with fever, and mumbling and moaning in his sleep. He complained of not feeling well for the most of the day, but refused to rest when I asked him to. I almost had him convinced, then that new group of men arrived, and he insisted he had to see to their needs."

"Marika, do you think you can find me a light so I can examine him?" Mathew asked. He went into the shelter and kneeled down beside Jesse, putting a hand on his forehead. It was very hot. He put his ear to Jesse's chest. His heart beat was very strong, but his lungs were filled with fluid, and barely any air was passing through them.

When Marika returned with a candle, he examined Jesse further. His skin was dry, his lips parched, his eyes were normal, but Mathew could see his chest heaving as he struggled to breathe.

"What is wrong with him?" Marika asked.

"He has pneumonia. We must try to get his fever down and get some water into him. Go get Peter. Ask him to bring any water he can spare and some clean rags if he has some. We must sponge him to get the fever down. In the morning I will send you to the Pharmacy for some willow bark for tea to help with the fever. Stay outside, and when Peter comes, the two of us will bathe Jesse to try and bring his fever down."

Marika woke Peter. "Mathew needs you. Jesse is very sick. He wants you to bring what water you have and clean rags, if you have any. He hopes that if the two of you bathe him with cool water his fever will come down."

By now the men sleeping around Peter began to stir. Peter picked up his battered canteen of water and tore an old worn blanket into pieces. Marika knew it was the only spare blanket he had and the nights were getting colder. She was deeply touched by the sacrifice he was willing to make for his friend.

Peter followed Marika to the shelter and went inside. Marika stayed outside as she had been told.

One by one the men approached her, asking about Jesse. Several of them pressed a coin into her hand. "He will need medication, maybe this will help," each whispered to her. "It isn't much, but is all I have." Marika was amazed and grateful that they were willing to give what little they had for Jesse.

Peter came out of the shelter several times and spoke to one of the men who stood close to the rekindled fire. Marika stayed where she was.

At one point Peter came to assure her. "He is young and strong, try not worry about him."

Several hours later Mathew came out of the shelter, looking tired and defeated.

"How is he?" she asked.

"I can't get his fever to come down, but he seems to be breathing easier." Reaching into his pocket he pulled out several coins. "It is not nearly enough, but go to the pharmacy and see how much willow bark and camphor ointment you can get for this."

Marika opened her hand showing him the three coins she had been given. "That will help. Go quickly now."

Marika looked up and saw the tears in Mathew's eyes. "Is he going to die?" she asked.

"Not if I have anything to do about it," Mathew replied gruffly, and then turned and went back into the shelter.

She ran all the way to Daub's Pharmacy. When she arrived, he was with another customer and she was forced to wait. The other customer seemed to be full of questions about the items he was purchasing. After several long minutes, he was satisfied and left.

123

Turning to her the Pharmacist asked, "And now young lady, what can I do for you?"

Putting her coins on the counter she replied "I need as much willow bark and camphor ointment this will buy."

"This is only enough for one, not both." he said kindly. "Who sent you?"

"The doctor Mathew. Jesse is very sick and needs this medicine. This is all the money we were able to scrape together."

Mr. Daub knew of Jesse and had secretly followed his teachings for some time. He looked at the waif like child in front of him "what is your name child?"

"Marika sir," she replied.

"Well Marika, this is your lucky day. It so happens I am having a sale on camphor and willow bark today. Wait here."

He went into the back room then he returned with two small packages in his hand, and a round glass container of ointment. He picked the coins up off the counter and put them into his pocket.

Marika looked at him in surprise. She had not expected such large packets.

"Go now" Mr. Daub said, "Tell him to put this in Jesse's water and make him drink. It will help bring the fever down."

"Thank you sir," Marika said. She started to leave the store and then turned. "You know of Jesse?" she asked.

"Everybody knows who Jesse is. Stop asking questions and go," he replied

She stayed by Jesse's side for the next two days feeding him water containing the willow bark by spoon and wiping his forehead with a damp cloth. When he was shivering, she lay down beside him and held him in her arms to keep him warm.

On the morning of the third day he opened his eyes. "I knew you were here," he rasped.

She started to cry, "You are awake. I will go tell Mathew and Peter, they have been very worried about you."

"Hurry back," he whispered.

* * *

Slowly Jesse regained his strength and Marika stayed by his side. The men brought them what food and water they could spare and chuckled among themselves. It was plain to all of them that Jesse and Marika were developing strong feelings for each other, but Peter was worried.

One evening Peter and Jesse stood alone by the fire. Marika was asleep in her usual place. "You are unusually quiet," Peter said in a low voice. "Is something wrong?"

"I am torn," Jesse replied. "I am in love with Marika, but I know it can't amount to anything."

"Why not?" Peter asked.

"She is impure. You know what she is - the number of men she has been with."

"There you go again," Peter said, "judging others. You stand up and preach that God forgives us for our sins, but the truth is you say one thing and do another."

Jesse looked at him. "This is different. Men give her money to have sex with them and she doesn't refuse it."

Peter was suddenly angry. "Her father sold her into that life when she was eleven years old. She didn't have a choice. You tell me, has she done anything to bring shame upon herself since she joined us? Do you think she enjoyed what those men did to her day after day? They pawed at her, used her body and then tossed her aside. They didn't care if they hurt her as long as they got what they had paid for.

Are you aware that the man who bought her raped and beat her, and took the money she earned? Did you know this is the first time in her young life that she has been treated with dignity and respect? If you cast her out, she will have no choice but to return to the only thing she knows how to do. Jesse, you are the biggest hypocrite I have ever met."

Jesse stared at Peter, his hands balled into fists ready to strike out. Abruptly he turned and walked away from the fire into the night.

Then Peter heard a weeping sound behind him, suddenly aware that Marika had overheard most of their conversation. Going over to her, he gathered her into his arms. "I am sorry you heard that."

"No, it's true. I am nothing but a whore, and that is all I will ever be. I will leave first thing in the morning."

"Marika please," Peter begged, "give him another chance. He is young and has much to learn about the world we live in." He held her close while she cried herself to a sleep.

CHAPTER TWENTY

For two days Jesse walked the streets of the city. For the first time since arriving he saw the lives of the people as they were, not as he wanted them to be. Up until now he thought only of himself and how he ended up here. It was a harsh reality. In his village he was loved and protected, but this was an entirely different world.

Thinking he was another beggar, the rich treated him with distain. He was targeted and chased by the Brown Shirts, and barely able to escape from them.

He saw fear and hopelessness in the faces of the average citizen as they scurried from one place to another; afraid to look into the faces of people they passed on the street. He saw the locked churches. In the park, he listened to the orators speak against Heinrich and freedom. He watched as the Brown Shirts broke up gatherings, beat the speakers and dragged them away.

At one point, he found himself on the edge of a large crowd as Heinrich spoke of all the wonderful things he was going to accomplish.

He remembered what his parents and what the true church tried to teach him, and recalled the words he had spoken to his father not that long ago, 'I believe in a God who forgives and offers a second chance. I believe we should look out for one another." He remembered his father challenging him when he spoke of his destiny to make the world a better place.

"How are you going to do that," his father asked.

He remembered his answer, "one person at a time."

He began to understand that Peter was right, he truly was the biggest hypocrite of all – all talk no action. *If I can't forgive Marika, whom I love and cherish, how can I teach others to do the same??*

Slowly he made his way back to the alley and his friends. He stood across the street watching and seeing for the first time that, although they were ragged and hungry, they cared for each other. He watched as Marika spoke with each man, hugged Peter and began walking away from the group.

She was crying, her shoulders slumped in defeat and she carried a small bundle in her hands. He didn't need to be told she was leaving, and the only recourse she had was to begin selling her body again.

As he watched her walk away a deep sense of shame overwhelmed him. *I did this to her with my cold, unbending, hypocritical attitude.*

As she walked deeper and deeper into the seedier, more dangerous part of the city he followed her. He crossed the street hurrying to catch up to her and just as he was ready to call out her name, a man approached her. He didn't hear all of the conversation, but he heard Marika's reply "two marks."

The man disappeared into the nearest alley. When she turned to follow him, Jesse saw the pain and despair on her face.

"Marika," he called out. "Stop, don't go there." He ran to her side. "Please," he begged, "you don't need to do this."

"I have no choice Jesse," she replied sadly, "this is what I am and all I know. Even you, whom I trusted with my life, rejected me. I heard you and Peter talking the other night."

The man appeared at the opening of the alley, his hand rubbing his crotch. "Hurry up, I don't have all day."

Jesse realized this was Marika's choice to make. The three of them stood there staring at each other. Then Marika took Jesse's arm and pulled him away. He heard the man cussing behind them, "Come back you little whore, we aren't finished yet."

In silence they walked back to the bridge and down a small footpath to the water. There they sat on the side of the river bank - both quiet for a long time. Suddenly Jesse pulled her into his arms, "Marika, I am sorry I have hurt you, but I never meant to. Why would you leave a place where you were safe to go back to that?"

Marika looked at him, a sad expression on her face, her eyes filled with unshed tears. "I am a whore Jesse. That is all I have ever been, and what I will be thought of. I heard it in your voice, and saw in your face. You will never be able to see past that."

"Yes," he admitted, "you are right. That is what I thought that night, but over the last two days, my eyes have been opened. I spent hours, walking around the city and for the first time I see life as it actually is. Instead of accepting responsibility for my own actions I blamed others for my misfortune."

When the sun went down, and for many hours after, they were still sitting there talking. Marika told Jesse about her father, and the cruelty she suffered at the hands of the man who bought her. Jesse told her of his broken dreams and disillusionment with the Elders. He spoke of his purpose, his calling and his desire to help others.

Eventually, she fell asleep in his arms. He sat, holding her and watching the river flow past until the sun came up.

When she awoke he said, "Marika I want us to get married".

"Oh Jesse," she replied, placing her hand on his cheek "I can't, you know that. I can't change my past and neither can you. We are what we are – you are still a man of God, and I am still a whore.

"Marika," he replied gently, placing his hand on top of hers "No one is perfect. All of us have a history we are not proud of, but it doesn't matter. We can put that into the past where it belongs, and move into the future together."

Then he surprised her. He got down on one knee in front of her and took her hand "Marika I love you. From this day forward I will cherish and honor you. Will you marry me?

"Yes," she replied, tears streaming down her face. "When? How?"

"Now," he said, "come with me. I know of somebody who will be more than willing to do this for us."

Jesse took her hand and helped her climb the river bank. Together they walked across town until they came to where Jean's large white revival tent stood.

The prayer meeting was still in progress so they waited outside until it ended, When Jesse thought everyone was gone he said. "Wait here, I will go inside to see if we can speak with him."

Jesse went into to the tent and returned in a few minutes. "Come," he said. Hand in hand they entered the tent. A large man, with a long white beard, stood at the front.

"Good to see you again. Jesse. What can I do for you today?" Jean asked.

'This is Marika we have come to ask you to marry us."

"When?"

"Now, if you will."

Jean studied the young couple in front of him. Marika wore a thread bare, yellow, print dress and her long hair was braided. Jesse wore a pair of pants that were above his ankles, a blue shirt that was mended many times, and days' worth of beard.

"I know who you are," Jean said to Marika. "Jesse has told me much about you.

Her face turned red and she hung her head in shame.

Jean walked over to Marika, put a finger under chin, and lifted her head. "Do not be ashamed. You were a child when your father gave you away. It was not your choice, but I also know you have been forgiven and work alongside Jesse. Do you love him?

Marika nodded yes. Then he turned to Jesse he said "Do you love Marika?"

"With all my heart," Jesse replied.

" Are you sure this is what you want? Marriage is a life time commitment to each other."

"Yes," they replied in unison.

"Did you get a license from the court house?"

The couple looked at each other. "No," Jesse replied, "we didn't know one was necessary."

When he saw the stricken look on their faces Jean teased them some more. "Did you bring witnesses?"

"No, we didn't know that was necessary. Do we need all these things before we can get married?' Jesse asked.

Jean laughed "Don't' worry about that. I will find somebody. As for the license we will forget about for now. One of Heinrich's latest edicts is that nobody can be married unless he approves. When I am finished you must go to the court house and register your marriage. I will give you a certificate stating that I performed your wedding."

Jean left, and returned within a few minutes with a man and a woman and a document in his hand.

"Shall we proceed?" he asked.

In a brief ceremony, witnessed by strangers, Jesse and Marika became husband and wife.

Jean handed Jesse the marriage certificate. "You must understand, in the eyes of God you are now man and wife, but you must register your marriage at the court house. Only then will your marriage be recognized by the government."

The young couple thanked Jean and left. In their excitement they forgot about filing the certificate. This small error prevented Heinrich from finding out Jesse was married, and provided protection for her in the future.

CHAPTER TWENTY ONE

Many hours later, Jesse and Marika, grinning from ear to ear, walked into the alley holding hands. All traces of doubt and worry gone from Jesse's face. Peter was alone, although the other men would be returning soon.

"Jesse, Marika", he acknowledged with a nod of his head. They stopped in front of him.

"I wish to move mine and Marika's things to the shelter for a couple of days," Jesse said, still grinning.

"Why?" Peter asked, still not paying too much attention. His mind was caught up in other problems.

Marika spoke up. "Jesse and I got married this afternoon. This is our wedding day."

Peter stopped what he was doing, turned, and looked at the smiling couple. "You can use it until we need it" he answered gruffly. He didn't seem the least bit surprised at their announcement.

They moved their few belonging into the shelter and put up a torn blanket for a door. When the men returned they were excited about the news.

That night, after they went into the shelter, they lay down side by side. Jesse rolled onto his side and kissed his wife. "I don't know what to do. I have never been with a woman before," he whispered.

Marika blushed. Looking at him she replied "I don't know what to do when love is involved."

They lay face to face, her head on Jesses shoulder. He kissed her again, and sometime during the night, they figured it out.

In the morning, when they arose, they found an array of gifts on the ground outside the door – a coin, a crust of bread, an apple and a red ribbon for Marika's hair. The men were bunched together close by the fire in an attempt to give the two the privacy they needed.

Hand in hand they walked over to the fire and thanked each man for their gift. Jesse was changed. It was though he walked through the fires of hell, and emerged on the other side a different man -one filled with love and purpose.

After his marriage Jesse settled down. He was no longer the young man filled with anger, but a man who knew what he had to do, and did it. Marika was always at his side, tending to his needs and those of his followers.

As Jesse's popularity grew so did the danger. Heinrich began to send large groups of Brown Shirts to attack his gatherings and Jesse began to worry about Marika's safety. If Heinrich learned she was his wife she was in danger. Often, he saw the fear on her face when the Brown Shirts showed up. It was difficult for him as well, because he kept remembering what one small group had done to her.

One evening he drew Peter and Mathew aside. "I am concerned about Marika's safety. We can't be with her all the time and she is having nightmares about being attacked by the Brown Shirts."

"I agree with you" Peter replied. "We must find a safe place, for her, but where? Perhaps with your family Jesse?"

"I've thought about that, but I would still worry about Heinrich finding out. He is from my village and as soon as she arrived he would be told. I don't want to take that chance because he still has friends in the village.

"I have an idea," Mathew said, "I could see if I can find a position for her at the hospital in Ardanna, the town I am from. She is a hard worker, and a fast learner, and they always need more help."

Jesse thought for several seconds, "Yes, that's a good idea. See what you can do. She will be safe there and no one will suspect she is one of us."

Two weeks later Mathew came to Jesse. "It is arranged. Marika can stay with of my sister, and help care for the patients. They are expecting her."

"Thank you Mathew. I will tell her of our plan tonight, but I know she isn't going to be happy. This was the easy part. You know how stubborn she can be when she doesn't want to do something."

Jesse was relieved. The violence at the gatherings was escalating. Several days ago two men were killed defending him.

That night, as Marika lay in his arms, Jesse said. "I have made arrangements for you to go Ardanna to live with Mathew's sister. He was able to procure a position for you at the hospital there."

She sat up abruptly, "I am not going. As your wife, my place is by your side."

"Marika, please don't make this any harder than it is. You must understand that you are in danger. If Heinrich learns about you he will use our marriage against me. I couldn't bear to have you fall into his hands."

"Is it because I was a whore? Are you ashamed of me?"

"No, that has nothing to do with this. Heinrich hates me and he would use you as a way to hurt me. I love you. I want you to be safe."

Marika thought for a moment then said, "I know you are right, but I am not afraid. I'm not going and that is final."

They argued back and forth, Jesse pleading with her to be reasonable, Marika insisting she was staying. Finally they ran out of words.

"We will talk about this again in the morning," Jesse said. He turned his back to her and moved as far as possible to the other side of their pallet.

"I am not going," Marika said defiantly, doing the same as Jesse. They both lay awake for a very long time.

After what seemed like hours, Marika turned to Jesse and put her arm across his body. She knew he was still awake.

"I know you're right Jesse, but I can't bear the thought of not lying beside you every night."

"Nor can I," he replied, "but I must know you are safe. I don't want to give up my ministry again, but I would for you. Please, don't force me choose between the two most important things in my life?"

She was crying. "I will go. I realize you are sending me away because you love me. Please Jesse; don't stay away too long at one time."

Jesse cried too. He kissed her, and taking her into his arms he shared his love for her the way a man does with his wife.

In the morning he went to Mathew, "she is willing to go, but how are we going to get her there?"

"I have arranged for James to take her, He has a friend who owns a car and will drive them most of the way, after that they will need to walk." Mathew replied. "James trusts his friend and he will keep her safe. He knows how important Mariska is to you.

I have also asked him, on his way back, to approach the Believers in that area and arrange for you to meet with them. That way you and Mariska will be able to spend some time together."

So it was.

CHAPTER TWENTY TWO

Through past experiences Heinrich learned his greatest ally was fear. The people in the towns and villages didn't understand politics, but they understood threats and shows of force.

The first and most important step in Heinrich's plan was to seize control of the church and the men in charge. When the Elders spoke in his favor, he knew the people would follow.

He knew just the man for the job. – Sig Rotter, a sadist and a man who liked power. They joined the Social Activist Party, and were in jail at the same time. Before that, Rotter was in charge of the Brown Shirts, and within a short period of time turned them into a fierce fighting unit, willing to obey any command given to them. He handpicked his squadron leaders carefully and the ranks were filled with men like him. They were men he knew and trusted, men willing to do whatever was necessary, and enjoy it.

After his release from jail Heinrich, once again, put Rotter back in command of the Brown Shirts. He knew all he had to do was issue an order and then sit back and watch it executed. How was no concern of his. He knew Rotter's actions would be precise and effective.

Sig Rotter's headquarters were located in Dufenvald prison – a name that struck terror in the hearts of the country. Heinrich knew the stories of torture, rape and death in the prison, and that pleased him. The more terrorized the general population became, the more confident he was that they would not oppose him.

Heinrich had carefully considered all aspects of his plan and knew, beyond a doubt, Rotter was the only man capable of carrying them out. He was mean, sadistic and enjoyed his job

Picking up his telephone he spoke to his secretary. "Find Commander Rotter and tell him to meet me at my home this evening at eight o'clock. Make him understand that it's important he be there. Accept no excuses if he says he has a previous engagement."

At precisely eight o'clock Commander Rotter knocked on Heinrich's drawing room door. When he entered Heinrich was standing, looking out the tall windows, with his hands behind his back

"Sir," he saluted. "It is good to see you again Heinrich." Looking around, he added "you have done well for yourself since leaving prison."

Heinrich turned and said "good to see you too" then the two men hugged patting each other on the back. "It is good of you to come on such short notice. Can I pour you a drink my friend? Cognac? Come we will sit over there," indicating two chairs in front of the fireplace.

"Why am I here Heinrich?"

Heinrich poured two drinks and handed one to Rotter then sat down on one the chairs, motioning to Rotter to sit on the other.

"I have a special job for you. The time has come to put the next phase of my plan into action. We are safe here, nobody can hear us. I plan to take over the church and put the Elders under my control. I want them to acknowledge me as the Supreme Leader of the church and state.

Rotter nearly chocked on his drink, "That's a tall order Heinrich. If I may be so bold as to ask, just how do you plan on accomplishing this big dream of yours?"

"That's where you come in. I am going to put you in sole charge of the Brown Shirts, answerable only to me. Then I want you to develop this group into a special kind of police force answerable only to you. Like yourself, these men must be willing to do whatever is necessary, if you get my meaning. You will have everything you need at your disposal.

It is a well-known fact that the Elders have become greedy old men. They feel comfortable and secure in their positions, and that's what makes them vulnerable. The easiest way for them to protect what they have is to go along with me. So, we allow them to keep doing what they have been in return for acknowledging me as the church's leader and teaching what I tell them. They need to understand that they must do as they are told. Failure to do so will result in death.

There is also a faction growing in our country known as the Believers led by that coward Jesse. He is their self-appointed leader and people are flocking to listen to him. I know Jesse for what he is - a sniveling coward, but a very charismatic speaker. He has a way of persuading people that his gospel is the truth."

"Still up to your old tricks I see."

"You might say that, I have big plans and I need men willing to stand up against those who dare to resist me and change their minds."

Rotter chuckled. "There is nothing I would like more than to settle a few old scores myself."

"The first ones to go after will be those who publicly speak out against me, and the shop keepers. They carry too much influence over the people who come to their stores. Your purpose is to spread terror, not kill. We need the people to be afraid of me. Break up public meetings, and attack the speakers. I am sure you get the idea. Injuries are fine, but I don't want anybody killed unless it can't be helped. Any unnecessary deaths will turn the people against me. Do you understand what I am saying?"

Rotter smiled, "very much so."

"The most important thing is that we need to get rid of Jesse. If we can convince the majority that he is the cause of all the dissention, and following me is a better alternative, he will lose his followers. They will pull away in droves."

"Tell me," Rotter asked, "how are you planning to convince people they should follow you? Heinrich, this is one of the craziest ideas I have heard you come up with."

Heinrich turned to him with an icy stare. "Don't ever say that to me again. I know exactly what I am doing."

Sig thought to himself *he really believes what he is saying. Crazy or not, it just might work.*

"I apologize, I wasn't thinking. Tell me how you are going to make this happen? "What do I have to do?"

They talked into the small hours of the morning, developing a fool proof plan to take over the church. Heinrich would then have the position he desired as Head of the church and the state, with a population of three million people forced to obey him.

"Let me get this straight," Rotter clarified, "On New Year's

Day you want my men to attack the businesses and homes of those we know are involved with the Believers. We are to drag them out into the street, denounce and beat them. The windows of their shops are to be broken and the businesses destroyed. That same day you will issue a notice that all Believers must now wear a yellow cross on their clothing. Those who refuse, or fail to do so, will become fair game for my men. We will have the authority to seek them out and punish as we see fit. My men will want to know what to do about the women?"

"They can do whatever they want. If they need to protect their women, especially their daughters, the men will be easier to convince. A few rapes will add to the terror you will inflict. Another thing, most of the people won't have time to be accustomed to the idea of wearing a yellow cross on their clothing and you explain that if they were wearing the yellow cross they would be left alone. Word will travel fast that I am not to be taken lightly."

"To continue, on January second you will announce a tax levy of two hundred percent on all property owned by the Believers. My men will start collecting it immediately. Those who refuse to pay will have their possessions confiscated, and they, and their families, will be sent to help build the indoctrination camps. I am hoping some of the camps will be ready by then."

"What are these indoctrination camps you speak of?"

"I don't want a Believer left to follow Jesse. I want them removed and kept separate. I am building places to move these Believers to. When and if, they change their minds, they can return home, but they will have to make a choice, their life, Jesse, or death"

"How are you going to feed and clothe that many people?"

145

"To tell you the truth I don't care what happens to them. Some of the healthiest will be given jobs; the others will stay in the camps. I want you to find someone you trust and put him in charge of this."

"I am still somewhat confused Heinrich. What will wearing the cross prove?"

"Nothing! The point of this exercise is to force the population into acknowledging me as their leader. They need to see the difference. Those who choose to follow Jesse will be held responsible for making life hard for the others. My promise is that the terror will stop when Jesse is eliminated. Those wearing the cross are to be considered traitors and will be treated as such."

"I could also take some to Dufenvald and make examples of them," Rotter exclaimed. "If I took some of the mayors and chiefs of police, who will surely speak out against your actions, we can put our people in their place. Next we can march on the newspapers, shut them down - once again use them for our own purposes."

"Now you are getting the idea. Don't forget the whole purpose is to have me acknowledged as leader of the state and church. I will be the one in control."

Rotter continued, "Then on January sixteenth you are going to call all of the Elders to a meeting. Attendance will be compulsory. Those who choose not to attend will be dealt with harshly and made examples of. At this time you are going to offer them half of the tax increase if they begin to denounce Jesse and his Believers. They are to convince those attending their churches that you are now Head of the church and are to be worshiped as such. I think you are developing a God complex

146

Heinrich," Rotter added, teasing Heinrich.

"On April eighth, during the Easter celebration in the cities, my people will infiltrate some of the churches. Just before the services conclude we will march in, with guns drawn to display a great show of strength. The Elders, who have done as you proposed, will be congratulated, and those who have not, will be arrested in front of their congregations and taken to Dufenvald."

"Yes."

"Am I free to assume that any Believers who happen to be in the church or on the streets can be immediately be arrested, taken to the transport cars and confined in the camps?"

"Yes. When you are in front of the congregations, you must tell them why this action is taking place and declare war on the Believers. This will mark the beginning of an official campaign to eradicate Jesse and his group."

Rotter shook his head. "You know Heinrich, this is so crazy it might work. Do you really think people will be gullible enough to fall for this charade?"

"That's where you come in Sig. It is up to you to make this work. Jesse must be destroyed. In the meantime I will give a speech to declare my position as head of the church and state. The radio and newspapers will hail me as the leader. I am going to close the borders to our neighbors, which will keep the Believers in one place. Only those who acknowledge me and what I stand for will be able to leave. The people will be left with no choice but to recognize me. Then Sig, your job becomes one of making sure those who oppose me are dealt with severely. You do whatever you have to do from now on."

"I am curious Heinrich, why me?" Rotter asked.

Heinrich turned and faced him. "Because you are a sadist and like to hurt people. Don't ever question me again. I told you what I want, now look after it. If you don't want work with me on this say so now. I can always find somebody to replace you, and you will spend the rest of your days in Duvenvald prison. It's up to you."

The meeting concluded shortly after that. They agreed to meet several more times before the plans were put into action.

That man is crazy. He has delusions of grandeur and power. If I play my cards right, it will be a simple matter to dispose of him and take over. Sig you are brilliant. This works perfectly into my own plans. When the time is right, I will be the leader of the country with full benefits, and I can make it look like I am actually saving the people from a mad man

CHAPTER TWENTY THREE

"Commander Rotter is here to see you sir. He says it is important." Heinrich's aide announced opening Heinrich's office door.

Heinrich was tired. Sleep often eluded him, and some nights were worse than others. "Show him in."

Sig Rotter entered the room and saluted, "Sir I have news of Jesse."

Heinrich looked up from his desk with a grin on his face. His jacket was unbuttoned, and he was in his stocking feet. "Where is he?"

"He will be in Gia at the end of the week. My informant in the Believers reports there is much panic among them. They are afraid, and many refuse to wear the yellow cross. They are waiting for Jesse to tell them what to do. That would be the perfect time to capture him and his main followers and get rid of them once and for all."

"Let me think about this," Heinrich replied He walked around his desk to a cabinet and removed a bottle of liquor and two glasses. He filled them, and handed one to Rotter.

"I am of two minds on this. The first is to agree with you and be rid of him once and for all. Heaven knows that would make my life easier. The problem is that his followers could make him a martyr, and then the Believers would become stronger. Someone would step into his place and his name would become

149

a rallying cry. The second is to put on a show of strength, humiliate him, and show his followers what he really is."

"I understand," Rotter replied as he watched Heinrich pace the floor in front of him. Then he stopped with a smirk on his face.

"What about this idea." Heinrich said, "We will find out for sure where he is, when he will be there and we will be waiting for him. Your Brown Shirts will surround the group and attack the followers from behind. When Jesse sees what is happening he will slink away like a rat."

"What about Jesse? What will we do with him?"

"You confront him and charge him with holding an illegal gathering. Your men will have the group surrounded, and then you step up and charge Jesse for not wearing the yellow cross, as I decreed. They will see for themselves how brave he is when he begs for your forgiveness."

"And if he is wearing the cross? Then what?"

"You will think of something. I am the true leader of the church and of this country. He has to be breaking some kind of law. Make one up if you have to. No one will know the difference. If they find out later there is no such law, it won't matter. It will be your word against theirs.

Once he acknowledges me as the Leader of the church and state let him go. He will be of no more use to us. Let his followers go. He can't admit I am the leader of the church and preach about a different God. Word will travel fast enough. If he slinks off at the first sign of trouble you will denounce him as coward, urging those attending to rip off their crosses and follow my true church."

"You know Heinrich this might work, up until now he has felt relatively safe. There have been no attacks on him or his group. This action will put him on notice. Sir, I do not wish to argue with you, but, I personally think, we should use this opportunity to get rid of him."

Heinrich, who was now sitting in a green velvet armchair with his feet on a matching foot stool relaxed and smiled

"Sig, you know what to do from here. Try to keep in mind our objective is to publicly humiliate him. I want to see him crawl before we kill him, and trust me, that day will come.

* * *

In the middle of the night before the planned action against Jesse, Rotter moved a group of twenty men to a staging area close to the town. Each man was issued a baseball bat. When all was ready, he called his field officers to his side. "Heinrich doesn't want Jesse hurt. His goal is to humiliate him in front of his followers."

Pointing to one of his officers he added, "Once Jesse starts to speak, move your men in behind him in case he tries to run away. If he does, grab him forcibly and bring him to me. Gustave, do you have the yellow paint I asked you to get?"

"Yes sir."

"Good. Make sure to bring it with you. Andre, you and your men block all the exits around the town square, and don't allow anyone to leave. Dieter, when I give the signal, you, and your men come in on three sides, using your bats on anyone who gets in your way. Women or children, it doesn't matter who you hit, nor does it matter how hard you hit them, if you know what I mean. If they are wearing the yellow star you have my permission to use as much force as you wish. I leave that to you."

"If they are not wearing a star, what do we do then?"

"Leave them be, that is the whole point of this. Those not wearing the star are safe for now."

"What do we do with Jesse, if he doesn't turn tail and run?"

"Leave him to me. I have plans for him." Rotter chuckled.

Throughout the morning a steady flow of people arrived in the town and began to gather in the town square. There was a holiday atmosphere – vendors selling food, ale, and trinkets commemorating Jesse's visit. By noon, hundreds gathered, with more arriving every, minute. People visited with friends, children ran around and squealed, some of the men staggered from drinking too much ale. A feeling of excitement filled the air.

Peter watched the crowd grow larger than they had anticipated. "I don't like this Jesse. There are too many people. I have been told that the Brown Shirts are conducting a field exercise close by, and that can't be a coincidence. I think we should cancel this gathering. Something doesn't feel right to me."

Peter and Jesse had arrived early the previous evening and taken shelter in the home of one of the Believers. Jesse looked out the living room window, "I agree with you, but what can I do? Many have travelled a long ways to hear me speak, I can't disappoint them."

152

"Please Jesse reconsider what you are doing. I have a bad feeling. If something goes wrong there aren't enough of us to protect you. It is sheer lunacy to go out there."

Jesse looked calmly at Peter, "I must do what I must do. Stay close to me."

As the church bell struck noon Jesse, surrounded by his men, began to walk through the crowd making his way to the platform the town had hastily erected for him.

He could hear the whispers in the crowd, "its Jesse. Make way, let him through." Women held out their babies for him to kiss.

Peter pleaded with him once again, "Jesse please don't do this. It's not safe."

Jesse smiled at him then climbed the three steps to the platform. The people were cheered and chanted "Jesse, Jesse . . ."

After a few minutes he held up his hands and the crowd became silent.

"My people" he began holding his arms out in front of him. "These are difficult times and a new kind of madness is taking over our cities and our country. There is total disregard for the rights of others. Neighbor is being asked to turn against neighbor; brother against brother, friend against friend, and for what?

.   "We are supposed to wear this," he said, raising a yellow cross in his hand. Peter stepped forward and pinned the cross on the front of Jesse's coat.

"The first infringement to our right of free thinking is this. It divides us further against one another Wearing this cross will separate those of us who believe in a benevolent God from those who follow Heinrich. Our God loves us all and forgives our sins. He wants us to love one another; to treat others as we want to be treated. He wants us to be compassionate, help the poor and the widows. He alone offers us hope for a better tomorrow."

While Jesse spoke, the crowd was transfixed, hanging on to his every word.

Suddenly from the back of the square the sound of women and children screaming filled the air. Jesse looked up to see the square surrounded with Brown Shirts. Men were indiscriminately swinging their bats. People pushed each other trying to get out of the way. Jesse was stunned to see what was happening in front of him.

Peter said, "Quickly Jesse we must get out of here. If we leave during this confusion I think we can get out through the back." Grabbing Jesse's arm he tried to pull him away.

"No Peter, I can't leave now. This is happening because of me. I can't expect others to do what I'm not willing to do myself."

Just then Jesse heard a voice. In front of him a man he did not recognize dressed in the uniform of a Brown Shirt spoke. "Aah Jesse, We meet at last. Heinrich has told me much about you. Allow me to introduce myself; my name is Commander Sig Rotter."

Jesse looked at him "Why are you doing this. Stop your men at once. These people have done nothing to you."

Rotter laughed as he mounted the three steps of the platform and stood facing Jesse. A group of Rotter's men formed a tight circle around the platform. In the front the crowd became silent as they became aware of the drama being played out in front of them. At the back people still screamed and cried out.

"I came to see what kind of a man you are. From what I have been told, you are a coward, and your followers need to see you for who you really are."

"I see you have been listening to Heinrich. When it comes to me you do realize that he is delusional. He has been bearing a grudge against me for years, and for no reason. This is about a petty childhood competition."

"Enough," Rotter snapped. Taking his gun from his holster, he fired a shot into the air. The noise was so sudden, so unexpected, that everyone, including his own men, turned to look at him. All that could be heard were the moans and cries of the wounded.

"Now that I have your attention," he said, "this is an unlawful assembly. You are no longer permitted to hold large gatherings without permission. Furthermore, Heinrich is head of the church and state, no other beliefs are allowed. You are forbidden to worship in any other place except the church."

The people whispered amongst themselves, afraid of what was going to happen.

Then, turning to Jesse, he shouted to the crowd. "This man is a coward and a fake. Did you notice that he didn't come in here wearing a yellow cross? He came in, put one on, and then declared he was one of you. To me that means he is afraid of what people will think of him if he wore one on the street. Isn't

155

that true Jesse? You feel safe with these people, but behind their back you are afraid to admit you are one of them."

Jesse looked at him with pity. "No it's not true, but no matter what I say, you will twist my words to suit you."

Rotter gave a signal and one of his men approached the platform with a can of yellow paint. Two guards grabbed Jesse, one on each arm, and forced him to his knees in front of Rotter. The crowd watched in silence. Some who moved to help Jesse were held back by the Brown Shirts in front of the platform.

Rotter drew back his arm and slapped Jesse across the face. Jesse did not react. He slapped him again and again, but still Jesse did not cry out. Then, in a fit of rage, Rotter took the can of paint and dumped it on Jesse's head. The paint ran down his face, into his eyes and onto his clothes, forming at puddle on the platform in front of him.

The two men yanked Jesse to his feet and Rotter, taking a club, slammed Jesse in the stomach. He doubled over in pain. Rotter laughed and hit him again across the back of the neck and Jesse fell to the floor into the puddle of paint.

Rotter turned to the crowd and sneered. "See what did I tell you? This man doesn't even have enough guts to fight back and try to stop me, and you believe he will protect you? Now you can see him for what he is, a coward."

He signaled his men to leave and within minutes all of the Brown Shirts were gone. The crowd stood there not knowing what to think. Peter helped Jesse to his feet." Come, let's get you cleaned up. We must go before this crowd turns on you."

Peter took Jesse by the arm and led him into the house.

Quickly he got a cloth, and wiped off as much paint as he could.

Jesse didn't say a word, but the pain of what had taken place was etched in his face.

"Take off those clothes." Peter pleaded, "I will fill a bath for you to remove the rest of the paint and then we must leave.

Jesse held up his hand to Peter. "No Peter, I am going back outside as I am. No one will harm me. How can I expect others to believe in my teachings if I run away at the first sign of trouble?"

The crowd, waiting outside was chanting "Jesse, Jesse ..."

"Why? Haven't you given them enough for today? You are hurt; surely they will understand why you are leaving."

Jesse looked at Peter. "Stop, they are worried, that is all. They are afraid I have deserted them."

Slowly Jesse got to his feet and made his way to the door. His head ached from the blows he had received, but that did not deter him. He stepped outside, still in his paint filled clothes, and when the crowd saw him, they began to cheer.

Holding both hands above his head he waited until the crowd became quiet. "I am asking each of you to go home while it is still safe to do so. Go, and spread word of what happened here today. Tell every person you meet that I am not afraid of the Heinrich and his threats. There are times to fight back, but this was not one of them. This is one of those times when our actions needed speak louder than our words."

The crowd began to murmur among themselves. Peter stepped to Jesse's side. "Jesse must rest. He is hurt. Go with

God."

Peter tried to lead Jesse back into the house but he refused to go. Instead he walked through the crowd touched and spoke softly to each one who was injured. To those more seriously hurt he knelt beside and kissed their forehead.

The crowd could see the compassion in his eyes. His tears washed the last of the yellow paint from his face. He hugged the children, and touched the women on their cheeks.

"Jesse, Jesse," the crowd began to chant again. People reached out to touch him. He stopped and spoke to, or touched every person in the square that day.

When he was done, Peter came to his side, took him by the arm and led him into the house where they were staying. Jesse sobbed openly.

"I have failed my people," he cried.

"I don't understand," Peter replied, "why didn't you fight back?"

"Because that is what he wanted. If I fought back I would be no better than they are. This way my followers can see for themselves the difference between us, and they must choose who they are going to follow."

Peter replied, "I don't understand your thinking, but you must have your reasons."

Peter helped Jesse undress and washed him to remove the paint. There was a large purple bruise on his abdomen where he had been hit. His lip was cut and one eye was nearly swollen shut.

They stayed in the house until dark and then slipped away. With Jesse gone it was safer for the villagers, if the Brown Shirts returned.

Many of the people who were there claimed miracles took place that day: broken bones spontaneously healed, cuts and bruises disappeared, and those who were close to death lived. Word of Jesses' bravery and compassion spread like wild fire, and more chose to follow him and his teachings.

* * *

Late the next afternoon, Commander Rotter joined Heinrich for an early supper. He was enjoying himself as he related what he did to Jesse. "You should have seen him - yellow paint running down his face and onto his clothes. It was so funny. I am sure his followers walked away in disgust. An ordinary man would have fought back. He didn't even try to stand up to us. I am sure those who were beaten will reconsider following him. Why take a beating for someone unwilling to fight? You are right Heinrich that should be the last we see or hear of Jesse."

Heinrich sat in his easy chair with a drink in his hand. He laughed at Rotter's description of the events. "I wish I had been there to see it with my own eyes. You did a good job, and you shall be rewarded. It sounds like Jesse hasn't changed much. Even as a child he didn't have enough guts to stand up for himself."

CHAPTER TWENTY FOUR

When Heinrich received word from Rotter that one of his informants saw Jesse at the home of parents, he couldn't resist the idea of facing off with him one more time. Hastily he put together a plan to make a triumphant entrance into the village, and show the villagers how powerful he was.

Heinrich knew for some time that the Elders operated as they always did and paid little heed to his declarations. This gave him the perfect excuse to enforce his edicts about being the head of the church and force Jesse to acknowledge the fact.

The village of Norenberg, like so many in the area, was built around the village square. The church, located along one end, was the most prominent feature. At the other end, was the town hall stood and along the sides were the shops. The houses of the rich and prominent were built on the side streets just off one side of the square. The homes of the residents were neatly lined up along the other side streets, the main highway passed behind the village.

The convoy of vehicles entered the village - like conquering heroes. Heinrich stood in an open jeep, waving at the people on the streets. Behind him, three trucks filled with Brown Shirts shouted and waved their guns in the air.

The military parade drove across the village square, and stopped in front of the Town Hall. One truck of Brown Shirts turned around and went back to the east end of the village setting up a roadblock, which stopped other vehicles from entering. The second truck proceeded to the west and blocked the street coming from the other direction.

When Heinrich got out of the jeep some of the Brown Shirts from the third truck guarded the doorway of the town hall. This meant no one could enter or leave. The rest marched toward the church. Heinrich and two of his personal body guards walked through the front door of the town office.

Once inside, while taking off his gloves, he looked around, "nothing has changed," he announced. "Why is there no picture of me at the entrance?"

In the meantime, a secretary for the Mayor burst into his office. "Come quickly. Heinrich Mollen is here."

The Mayor grabbed his jacket from the back of the chair, and ran his fingers through his hair. "Why is he here? What does he want?" He was still doing up the buttons when Heinrich walked into his office,

"Welcome Heinrich, how good of you to visit our village today," the Mayor said bobbing his head up and down. "What a surprise. If I had known you were coming I would have prepared a celebration. It has been a long time since you have graced our village with your presence."

Heinrich ignored him and walked to the front windows overlooking the square. "I see little has changed since I left."

The mayor walked over and stood beside Heinrich, "you have done well for yourself," he continued, "Who would have thought the greatest leader in our country would come from our humble village. What an honor it is, and we are proud to call you one of our own."

Abruptly Heinrich turned and leaned forward, his face only inches from the Mayor's face. "You say these things to my face, but behind my back you disobey me. Do you think that my rules and edicts don't concern you?"

"I don't understand. What do you mean?" the mayor blubbered. "I have done my best. You can ask anybody."

"Then why is the church still open? I decreed all churches were to be barred and shuttered. The only ones allowed to remain were those who acknowledge me as head of the church. I haven't heard a word from you on this matter. I am the head of the church, and I will be respected as such. As of today I am closing your church."

"But, you can't do that. What will the people think of me, if I allow this to happen?"

"Who cares what they think. At this very minute the Elders are being arrested and the sacred relics destroyed. They are traitors and will be punished as such."

The mayor tried to reason with him. "Surely that isn't necessary. Let me talk to them, and to the villagers, I can make them understand."

"It is too late for that, you had your chance. Instruct someone to ring the church bells to call the villagers to the square. I will tell them they can no longer worship or pay tribute there. From now on, they will salute and pay tribute to me, and only me."

Then he added, "I understand Jesse is here. Send someone to find him and bring him to me. There is no use closing the church if he is going to continue to turn the villagers against me. Tell them to bring him to the church steps in one way or another. I will send two guards to make sure he doesn't turn tail and run."

The mayor scurried out of his office. "Go get somebody to ring the church bells, and summon the villagers to the square." he shouted to one of the office workers.

To another he said, "Go find Constable Jacobs and tell him to take two of Heinrich's guards, fetch Jesse, and bring him to the church steps."

"Do you think that is a good idea? We all know how Heinrich feels about Jesse." The worker replied.

"Don't argue with me; just do as you are told."

Minutes later the church bells rang with an urgency never before heard in the village. People immediately stopped what they were doing and ran to the square to find out what was wrong. Usually such an alarm indicated an emergency.

When he was satisfied that all was in place Heinrich marched out of the office and across the square. The mayor, flanked by the two guards, trudged behind him. He couldn't look into the faces of the people. He was confused about what was going on and why.

As the small procession marched across the square the crowd parted, and made a path for them. Fear and anxiety were written on their faces, even the children were silent.

Heinrich walked directly to the church, mounted the steps, and stood in front of the massive wooden doors. He could hear the crowd murmuring "its Heinrich!" The Mayor was manhandled up the stairs by the guards and forced to stand beside him.

Heinrich turned to one of the guards standing in front of the doors and barked, "Bring out the Elders."

As the doors opened the crowd gasped, and the Elders were forced out at gun point. Their robes hung in tatters, their hands were bound and their feet were shackled. All had been beaten, some worse than others. Elder John had blood running down the side of his face.

"These men dare to disobey me," Heinrich roared at the crowd. Pacing back and forth, with his hands behind his back, he continued, "they did not listen to what I told them and now they will pay. I am the head of this church and of this country. I will be acknowledged and respected as such. My orders will be followed. If you don't listen to me, you will be punished as they are."

He motioned to the guards, "Shoot them."

The Elders were forced to stand in a line in front of the solid wooden doors of the church, and one at a time was shot in the middle of the forehead. Every one of them seemed too dazed to realize what was happening to them - blood and brains smattered against the door and dripped down. The church steps turned red.

The crowd was stunned. Many of the women began wailing. Others stood shocked, unable to believe the carnage taking place in front of them.

The Mayor stepped forward. "Heinrich, you didn't have to do that. They would have listened to me if you had given me a chance to explain."

Heinrich walked over to the mayor and slapped him twice across the face, knocking him to his knees. "Shut up you

165

sniveling pig. Count yourself lucky that you are not one of them. This is your fault. If you had obeyed my orders I wouldn't have needed to come here."

Then, turning to the crowd, he demanded, "Where is Jesse?"

"I am here," Jesse replied.

Once again the crowd parted and Jesse, with a determined step, walked up the stairs and stopped in front of Heinrich. "What do you want?"

"I understand you are going against my rules and preaching a different kind of religion. They say you teach about a merciful God who forgives. Is that right?"

"I am, and I do," Jesse replied, his voice even and unafraid.

"Call to him, in front of all of us, and beg him to forgive these people for not listening to me."

"I can't do that. Forgiveness comes through the heart of each person."

The crowd gasped as Heinrich slapped Jesse across the face. "I am the head of the church, and from now on you will believe in me and obey my orders."

"No," Jesse replied, not backing down, "I will not because you are not my God."

Heinrich slapped him again, even harder. "I order you to get down on your knees and bow to me. You will disband your followers and follow my teachings. Do you understand that?"

Jesse staggered from the force of the blow, but remained standing. "I will not," he replied, wiping his hand across his
166

bleeding mouth.

Heinrich slapped him again. This time he knocked him down to his knees on the bloody steps, Jesse's mouth and nose bled, and one eye swelled. Pulling himself to his feet, Jesse stood defiantly in front of Heinrich - just as he had done when they were kids.

Heinrich continued to scream in Jesse's face. Spittle dripped from his chin and his eyes were crazed like those of a mad man. "You will do as I command from now on. If not, you and your group of Believers will end up just like them," he screeched, pointing to the dead Elders. "Now what do you say?"

"Go to hell" Jesse replied then turned his back to Heinrich, and staggered down the stairs.

The crowd stood in shock. Maria, his mother, ran to Jesse, and put her arms protectively around him. She was sure that Heinrich was going to order his guards to shoot Jesse in the back.

Then Heinrich began to laugh, in a maniacal sort of way. "You haven't changed a bit, have you - still a coward; still afraid to fight me. This is going to cost you and those who follow you. Why people want to follow a yellow dog like you is beyond me. At least now, they will see that you are a fool as well as a coward."

Then he looked at the Mayor and said, "Change his mind. If you don't, you and every person in this village will forfeit your lives."

Heinrich walked down the stairs and approached Jesse again. "One day you will kneel at my feet, and beg for your life, and my forgiveness."

"Never," Jesse replied.

Unobtrusively Heinrich's driver moved his jeep, with the top still down to the front of the church. As he climbed in, Heinrich tipped his hat to Jesse and said "until we meet again."

That day a line was drawn between them. For both men it became personal. There could only be one winner. Jesse knew that Heinrich was more determined than ever to make him back down and give in- at any price.

He stood watching as the jeep and trucks drove away. Turning around, he looked again at the bloody bodies of the Elders lying on the step. "I must stand against him mother."

"I know Jesse," she said sadly, "I know."

Then Jesse said to her, "I pray God will give me the strength and courage to do what I must do."

The villagers were in shock. The mayor got to his feet, hurried down the stairs and went from person to person and cried out, "this is not my fault." I didn't know he was coming." One at a time they turned their backs to him.

Four men opened the doors of the church and moved the bloody bodies of the elders inside. The square became deathly quiet. The only voice heard was that of the mayor going from person to person begging for their absolution.

CHAPTER TWENTY FIVE

Jesse continued his work, but with a new degree of caution. The murder of the Elders and closing of the church signaled an escalation of the terror tactics against him. He confided in Peter and his few trusted men his biggest fear was that Heinrich would find out about Marika. As long as he stayed away from her, she was safe.

One evening he took Peter aside. "If something should happen to me I am asking you to look after Marika and Maria for me and keep them safe."

"Nothing is going to happen to you Jesse. I don't know why you are worrying about this."

"Promise me Peter. I will not always be here to look after them and I need to know that you will do this for me. I don't know what Heinrich would be capable of if they fell into his clutches."

Without hesitating Peter replied, "Of course I will. I would have done so anyway without you asking."

When he was near home, Jesse refused to stay with his parents. Just the fact he was in the same town put them in harm's way. Instead, he chose to stay in a cave in the hills with Peter and the other men he trusted. If the Brown Shirts raided the village again his family would be safe. He worried about whoever Heinrich hired to chase him down was unscrupulous, and would stop at nothing to get to him.

Sig Rotter had spies in the most unlikely places. Most were good people who, in ordinary times, would never think of turning on their friends and neighbors. Now, the culture of the times encouraged even praised these actions

Late, the night before, Rotter had received a message that Jesse, along with several of his most trusted men, were seen in his home at Norenburg. He realized this was the opportunity he had been waiting for, a chance to get rid of all of them at one time.

The next morning he forced a meeting with Heinrich. "Jesse and his companions are in the village of Norenburg. This could be our opportunity to wipe them all out with one stroke. I don't know when we will ever get this chance again. We must act right away."

"You seem very excited at the prospect," Heinrich replied, "What's in it for you?"

Rotter was flustered by the comment. Usually Heinrich was not so perceptive, and he knew he had to be careful about giving away his deepest thoughts.

"I don't know what you mean by that sir," he replied.

"It's easy, if we capture Jesse and his men what will you

170

expect from me? I know you well enough to understand that everything you do is for a reason. So what is it?"

Rotter visibly relaxed. "Sir, if we capture Jesse I expect nothing less than a promotion."

Heinrich chuckled, "I figured as much. If this is the end of Jesse, you will receive that promotion. That man is like a thorn in my side. You have my permission to go capture and bring him to me alive, I don't care what you do with the others."

Rotter saluted and left the room. *This is going to be easy.*

Within hours a company of fully equipped men in trucks moved toward Norenburg. Their .orders "do whatever is necessary to eradicate Jesse and his followers."

* * *

"Jesse, come quickly," Peter shouted as he ran up the hill to the entrance of the cave. "The Brown Shirts are attacking the village. They are killing every person they see."

When Jesse was home, he sought refuge in a large cave in the hills above his village. Here he could meditate, rest, and meet with his "Inner circle" of followers. His following around the country was growing larger and this was the one place he could relax when he needed a break from his demanding schedule. Many times he was tempted to move Marika to the village to live with his parents, so he could be with her more often. He was sure she would be safe here, but Peter had talked him out of it.

In desperation, they ran down the hill, staying away from the road. If the Brown Shirts were in the village, they could be in the hills too.

171

Jesse and Peter cautiously entered the village from an alley, on the backside of the village, a route they frequently used to move unobtrusively to Jesse's parents' home. Mark and Luke were waited for them. Both were sobbing and covered in blood.

Jesse strode past them. Acrid smoke filled the air. The pungent smell of gun powder and blood wafted on the gentle breeze. Arriving at the town square, Jesse could barely comprehend what appeared in front of him. The square was littered with bodies – men, women, children and dogs. There was blood splattered everywhere.

Some of the bodies held old army rifles in their hands and still others shovels and axes. Plainly they had tried to fight back, but were no match for the guns of the Brown Shirts. They lay where they fell.

Jesse felt sick as he looked at the carnage. The shops were looted, their windows broken, and their contents dragged out into the streets. "Believers die." was written in blood, on the door of the Village office.

He ran to the church, spurred on by the dark smoke that rolled out of the broken windows. When he arrived, he stood in disbelief. The front steps were littered with the naked corpses of women and girls who had been mowed down by a machine gun.

When he stepped through the front door his senses were overwhelmed by what he saw in front of him. A two year old little girl lay on top of the altar, her blood dripping down onto the marble floor, and a knife sticking out her chest. The bodies of several young girls lay in front of the altar. Plainly they had been raped and suffered terribly. Jesse felt as though he could hear the scream of the women in the silence.

He ran from body to body, checking to see if any were alive, but soon realized that none survived. He vomited onto the floor, but not before noticing the pews were covered in blood. Then he screamed at the lopsided figure on the cross. "My God, how could you allow this to happen? Where were you while this was going on? Why? These are simple people who trusted and served you. Sweeping his arms in a circle he cried out, "they didn't deserve this,"

"Jesse…"

Jesse started; he hadn't heard Peter come up behind him. Taking him by the arm Peter said gently, "Come away. There is nothing you can do here. Men from the neighboring villages are arriving; let them take care of this."

"Oh my God, my family, I must find them." Jesse cried out, his eyes wild.

Peter quietly said, "I have just come from your home, they are all dead. We found a few survivors in the square, and Mark is caring for them now."

Jesse turned and began running toward the door, but Peter put out a hand to stop him. "I think it would be better for you to stay here. It is a horrific scene at your home. Please let us look after this for you."

Jesse pulled away from Peter's hand, ran down the aisle, out the front door, and down the streets to his parents' home. When he arrived, he saw the bodies of his father and brothers lying on the ground ripped to shreds by machine gun fire. His two youngest sisters had been repeatedly raped until someone had mercifully shot them in the forehead. He could only imagine their terror as the beasts took turns mounting them.

173

"Where are my mother and sister Elizabeth? I don't see them here." he shouted to the men close by.

"They must be inside." Peter answered, gasping for breath. "Jesse let me go in first. I beg you."

"No," Jesse replied, shoving Peter to one side, "I must be the one to find them."

The front door, hung by one hinge, and blocked the entrance. Jesse ripped the door off and stepped inside the kitchen. The place was a shambles, there was blood everywhere. The baby, only fourteen months old, was skewered with a bayonet; her small body left hanging from the wall. As he stood there he heard a faint moan which seemed to be come from a pile of smoldering broken furniture.

"Peter," he cried out. "Someone is alive."

With his bare hands, oblivious to pain, he clawed his way through the smoking debris.   The moaning came from underneath a heavy cabinet. .

"I see someone," Peter cried out. Using all of his strength, Jesse lifted a corner of the cabinet while Peter struggled to remove the person trapped underneath. It was his sister Elizabeth.

Gently, Peter lifted her into his arms and carried her outside. She was beaten- massive bruises covered her body. Both eyes were swollen shut, her left arm hung at an impossible angle. She was naked, and was clearly sexually abused.

"Her pulse is strong and she is breathing easily," Peter answered Jesse's inquiring eyes. "I think she is badly hurt. I will send one of the men go and fetch Mark." Jesse turned to go further into the house to find his mother.

He stood in front of his parents' bedroom door, fear gripped his insides, and his mind reeled from the carnage surrounding him. He was afraid of what he might find inside. Taking a deep breath he pushed the door open knowing that at some point he had to find out.

His mother lay face down on the bed, her arms and legs tied to the four corners of the frame. Somebody had carved the words "Die Jesse" on her back. Her head lay in a pool of blood, and a wine bottle stuck out of her vagina.

Grabbing a blanket from the floor he covered her. *Nobody must see her this way.* Using his pocket knife, he cut the bindings from her arms and legs, and carefully rolled her onto her back.

Kneeling on the floor, his arm cradling her body he cried, unaware of the passage of time. *What kind of animal did this to another human being? What is all this death going to prove?*

"Jesse, Mark is here. We are going to move Elizabeth to the make shift hospital he has set up." Peter said, coming to stand beside him. He placed a hand on his shoulder.

"Tell Mark to come in here. I need his help with my mother."

Mark entered the room, and Jesse showed him what was done to her. "Can you help her? Nobody must see what those animals have done."

"Wait for me outside Jesse. I'll see if there is anything I can do."

Why God why? Jesse fumed, the same words running over and over in his head. *Why have you taken all that I love and*

175

value from me? You are supposed to be a merciful loving God and yet you allow this to happen. I don't understand.

A few minutes later Mark came out, took Jesse aside and spoke to him. "Go to her and say your goodbye, I am sure she is no longer with us. I must get back to the injured some of them are barely alive."

Jesse went into the bedroom, knelt down beside her and held her in his arms. He cradled her head against his chest. He didn't believe she was dead, and needed a few private moments with her before he went back outside.

Suddenly he felt a movement in his arms. At first he thought he was dreaming, and then he felt it again. Her hand moved under the blanket.

"Peter," he shouted," she is alive."

Peter ran into the room. "Jesse, don't do this to yourself, Mark told you she is gone, and you are only imagining things."

"No, she lives," Jesse said emphatically. "We must get her to Mark. We must take her to his hospital."

He laid her back down on the mattress, wrapped the blanket tightly around her and tugged it toward the door. "Leave her there. We must disturb her as little as possible."

Peter shook his head. How was he going to make Jesse understand that his mother was among the dead? Going outside he motioned to four men. "I need help taking Maria to Mark. Even though she is dead, Jesse thinks she lives. It's best that Mark be the one to convince him, he won't listen to me."

Several of the men went into the bedroom, lifted a corner of

176

the mattress from the bed and dragged it outside. Somebody ran to get a cart. Placing her in it, they pushed it down the street to where Mark worked. Peter ran ahead to tell Mark what was happening.

"Bring her in here" he said to the men as they approached. He had turned the mercantile store into a makeshift hospital.

When Jesse arrived at the building he went inside. There were men and women lying on the floor. Some were heavily bandaged, others sat stared straight ahead. Elizabeth sat huddled in a corner, her heavily bandaged arm in a sling.

"Go outside Jesse" Mark commanded. "All you are going to do is get in my way."

Jesse felt like protesting but did as he was told.

Lifting the blanket Mark carefully examined Maria. Jesse was right; she was alive, but barely. Then he saw the bottle, "Dirty bastards" he muttered. Walking over to Elizabeth he touched her on the shoulder, "come I need your help with your mother. She is badly hurt."

She lifted her hand, and he helped her off the floor. He showed her the horrific act performed upon her mother and cautioned. "We must remove this very slowly because we don't know how much damage there is inside."

Using her good hand Elizabeth followed Mark's instructions. Suddenly Maria convulsed and screamed. The bottle came out, followed by a gush of blood and fluid. Jesse, who was waiting outside, cringed when he heard her screams. He paced back and forth, alternately praying to and cursing God.

An hour later, Mark came out to speak to him. "She is

177

conscious Jesse, but just barely. She was pregnant and lost the baby. Unfortunately she will be unable to have more children. There is too much damage.

I did what I could for her. She lost a great deal of blood, and if she doesn't get an infection, she will survive. Her other wounds are superficial, and will heal in time. Elizabeth is with her now, but she wants to see you."

Jesse went in and kneeled beside her. "They came to the house looking for you. Somehow they heard you were back." she whispered to him. "When we refused to tell them where you were, they did this."

"I will find them and kill whoever did this to you."

She placed her hand on Jesse's arm and begged, "No Jesse, you are called to a greater purpose. Go, your men need you," and then she closed her eyes and drifted off to sleep.

More men from the surrounding villages arrived. They gathered in the small cemetery and began digging a mass grave. They toiled long and hard using every tool they could find. Others went from house to house to load the bodies into truck boxes then transport them to the cemetery. Still others attempted to identify, and write down the names of the dead. Complete families, from grandparents to children, were laid in the huge grave that slashed the earth.

Jesse carried the bodies of his family to the grave site and laid them together. His face was etched with sorrow, and his eyes were red from crying.

"Jesse, let me help you," Peter offered. "This is too much for you."

"No. this is the last thing I can do for them." He laid the baby on his father's chest as tears coursed down his face. *Why? Why? I don't understand* he kept asking himself.

When all of the bodies were recovered and covered with dirt, Jesse stood at the head of the grave. He looked at the broken hearted men who stood in front of him and spoke, "The Holy book tells us that we should not kill, to love our neighbor and take care of them, but these were innocent men, women and children who were no threat to Heinrich."

Somebody from the crowd interrupted him, "are you saying we have to accept this? These were our friends, family members and neighbors. Are you trying to tell us to ignore what happened here? More than six hundred people died here today, and for what?"

Jesse calmly answered," I too lost all of those near and dear to me. My mother clings to life, and my sister struggles to come out of the darkness. I am repeating the words of the Holy Book "Thou shall not kill," but it doesn't say that we can't fight back. We will avenge the deaths of those who died here today."

The men cheered, some raised their shovels and waved them in the air.

"We will burn this village to the ground and leave the ruins to show others what took place here. We will spread word far and wide about the tragedy that occurred here and who was behind it. We shall poison the well and burn the crops. We will leave nothing that will benefit Heinrich and his Brown Shirts. Every time someone passes this way the scorched ruins will tell our story."

Jesse, his men, and those who came to help aided Mark move

the few survivors into vehicles transporting them safely to the next village. Each was hidden in a different home to be nursed back to health. If, and when the Brown Shirts returned they would believe all were dead. Any witness who could speak of the atrocities that had taken place would be tortured and killed.

Of a village of six hundred people not many were left– six badly wounded men, a small child, Maria and Elizabeth. The village was silent, even the birds were gone.

When Mark was finished, Jesse and his men fanned out into the streets, each man carried cans of gasoline, bottles and rags for wicks. They emptied gasoline into the bottles, stuffed a rag in, and lit the rag on fire. Jesse threw the first torch into the window of a house, His men followed suit, and soon the entire town was engulfed in flames.

With his words Jesse lit the flames of rebellion which would soon consume the country. At the same time he took an irrevocable step which would lead to him facing Heinrich down one final time.

PART TWO

THE RESISTANCE

CHAPTER TWENTY SIX

After lighting the fires Jesse and his men gathered at the graveyard. Their hearts ached with sorrow, the pain etched on their faces- six hundred men, women, and children, all dead and for what reason?

Once satisfied the raging fires would consume the village the weary men left, disappearing into the hills surrounding the village.

Exhausted and barely able to put one foot in front of the other, Jesse made his way to the cave in the hillside, and waited for his men to arrive.

"Peter, as the men arrive take them inside. Feed them and encourage them to get some rest."

Peter looked at him, "Jesse there is no food or water here. How do you expect me to do this?"

"Go to the back of the cave, and you will find all you need. There is also wood for a small fire."

"What about you Jesse? Come, you need to rest also. The men will want to talk with you about this terrible day."

Jesse looked into Peter's eyes. "Why Peter? Why butcher all of these people. They did nothing wrong, my parents, brother, sisters, aunts and uncles all gone, and for what?"

"I don't have the answers Jesse," Peter softly replied.

"Is this my fault? Was this village destroyed because of me?"

"I don't know Jesse." Peter bit back the sobs in his throat." *How is he going to be able to go on after this?*

"Look to the men first. I will be along later; I want to be alone right now."

Reluctantly Peter left. Jesse wanted to pray, but all he felt was anger. He stood at the entrance of the cave staring down at the smoke rising from the valley floor below.

The men, instead of resting, were angry and agitated. Their minds were having difficulty processing what they had witnessed - the savagery, brutality, but most of all the deaths of so many good people.

Thomas spoke out angrily. "Did you listen to him? He preaches to us that we should not kill. Are we supposed to stand by and let the Brown Shirts get away with butchering the people of this valley? Jesse buried his father, brother and sisters today. Does he really believe that we shouldn't retaliate? If it was up to me, I would kill Heinrich and every Brown Shirt who follows him with my bare hands."

Peter allowed Thomas to rant, and then stopped him. "Thomas, do you really believe that Jesse isn't beside himself with grief, and that he isn't angry beyond words. Do you think he doesn't want to kill Heinrich with his own hands? Today he lost more than any of us, but he is a man of God, a man of peace. His words are a warning to us- don't do anything stupid.

Didn't you see the look on his face as he carried the bodies of his brothers and sisters and laid them gently in the grave? After

184

what was done to his mother and sister, don't you think he is half out of his mind? Didn't you see him weeping as he laid his father beside the children? How many aunts, uncles, cousins and friends did he bury today? Unlike us, Jesse was born and raised here. Everything he valued in his life has been taken from him. His mother is dangerously ill, possibly dying. His one remaining sister may never recover. "Don't you think he wants revenge more than we do, but our God teaches "thou shalt not kill." For him to do so, would make him no better than the animals who butchered the people of his village."

Thomas and the other men shook their heads, and stared at the cave floor. They didn't seem to understand. One at a time they settled around the fire, some rested, others stared straight ahead, the anger palpable in the air.

After the men were fed and settled Peter went back to the cave entrance. Jesse had not moved. He still stood at the entrance staring out over the valley.

"I brought you something to eat. I sent Aaron and Remi to the nearest village to bring back more supplies."

"I'm not hungry,"

"You must try and eat something."

"Take it away" Jesse replied angrily, "Leave me be."

Peter had never seen his friend so despondent, so filled with rage. He stood with Jesse for a time, and then went back to the fire.

Several hours later Peter poured a cup of coffee for Jesse and took it to him. He still had not moved.

"Jesse, I brought you some coffee. You must be cold and tired. Come to the fire and rest for a while."

Jesse turned to Peter and the tracks of his tears showed on his face. "Peter I don't understand any of this. Why? What kind of beast does this? I feel like I did as a child every time Heinrich got the better of me. To fight him wouldn't have proved anything, it only would have made his bullying worse. Do you think Heinrich was behind this attack?"

"I don't believe Heinrich was directly responsible for this, but I'm sure he won't object to what was done. Jesse, don't you understand? You are the leader of the Believers. You are loved and respected. You speak and teach of love, forgiveness, equality; your message brings hope. Yours is not a religion, as much as it's a way to live a good life. You are a threat to him. Heinrich believes that by declaring himself head of the church, he is now better than you. Let's face it; the man has to be insane to believe any of this."

Jesse looked into Peter's eyes. "I hope you are right. If not, then all of this was unnecessary and for nothing. I wish that I was the one who died instead of all these people."

Peter didn't know what to say. The agony on Jesse's face was more than he could bear. He patted him on the shoulder as a gesture of comfort and then turned and walked back to the fire.

In the early morning hours, he went to check on Jesse, but he was gone. Peter stepped outside and looked around, but there was no trace of him.

Walking back to the fire he commented to the men who were still awake, "Jesse is gone. I don't know where he went."

"You were talking to him earlier, did he tell you he was leaving?" inquired Thomas. "I'm not surprised. When push comes to shove, and it's time to take action, he doesn't have enough guts to do what it takes."

Peter turned to Thomas, his fists balled up ready to strike, "I dare you to say that again. Jesse must have his own reasons for leaving."

"Stop it both of you." Aaron demanded, stepping between them. Aaron and Remi had just returned with supplies from the villages. "We have talked with the men in the villages, and they are prepared to fight back."

"What are you saying Aaron?" Peter asked as he lowered his fist, and turned his back to Thomas.

"Some want to fight back and kill the Brown Shirts. They are willing to sacrifice their lives to get retribution. They are very angry, and want some place to direct their anger."

Peter listened closely as Aaron continued, "I have been thinking about this. Jesse teaches us that we shouldn't kill, and in his own way he is right. We are outnumbered a thousand to one. If we go against the Brown Shirts we don't stand a chance, but it is also true that Jesse told us that we shouldn't fight back. There is more than one way to resist Heinrich. Because of what was done here and his foolish declarations he thinks we are afraid of him. He lives in his own little world. The generals and their men use Heinrich's new power to benefit themselves; their futures are tied to him."

"You sound as though you have a plan Aaron."

"I do, but I must wait until Jesse returns and talk it over with

187

him. In the meantime, we will gather what we need – guns, ammunition, explosives and money for bribes and supplies."

"Jesse won't go along with your idea. You know how he feels about killing."

Aaron smiled, "yes, but doesn't the Holy Book tell us an eye for an eye, a tooth for a tooth. Theirs is a campaign of terror, and Jesse didn't tell us that we needed to stand by and do nothing. Well, Did he?"

By now the men gathered around them nodded their heads in agreement. Plainly they saw that Aaron had a point, and they agreed with him.

"First though, we must wait for Jesse to return," Aaron cautioned." All we do from here on in is going to be blamed on him."

The men sat around the small fire, discussing Aaron's idea and waited for Jesse to return.

CHAPTER TWENTY SEVEN

Jesse's grief was incomprehensible, more than he thought he could bear. His father, all of his younger brothers and sisters lay dead in the mass grave. His mother and sister brutalized. *Heinrich was behind this, but why?*

After leaving the cave, he wandered aimlessly through the hills. Everything he once called his own was gone, taken from him in one cruel stroke. He talked and preached forgiveness, but this was too much. He didn't know if he could ever forgive the men who did this.

"Lord, what you expect of me?" he cried out. "This is too much. A whole village, every living relative I have – I don't know if my mother will survive, and then there is Elizabeth. What is going to become of her? If I could put my hands around Heinrich's neck, I would slowly squeeze the life out of him. I would make him suffer. I don't understand what Heinrich is thinking or trying to prove. He was born and raised in this village; some of those people were his friends. Even if he isn't directly responsible, he still hired the men who did this. I can understand his animosity towards me, but to murder more than six hundred men, women and children? That doesn't make any sense. It is said everything happens for a reason, but I can't see any rhyme or reason for this."

Exhausted he stopped by a large tree overlooking the valley. From this vantage point, he could see the fires still burning in the village. The air was thick with smoke. He threw himself on the ground, and wept under the branches until he had no tears left. Eventually, he fell into a troubled sleep.

"Jesse," a man's gentle voice awoke him, "do not weep for what cannot be undone."

When Jesse opened his eyes, an old man with a long white beard, dressed in a white robe stood over him; a soft glow emanated from his body.

"Who are you? Where did you come from?" Jesse demanded, as he jumped to his feet, his hands balled into fists ready to fight.

"I am the one you believe in."

Instantly Jesse was angry, "go away. I don't believe in you anymore. How could you let this happen? If you are as mighty and powerful as you say you are, why didn't you stop the massacre? All of the villagers, my family, friends, and my own father lay in that mass grave and for what?"

Jesse lunged toward the old man, but instead fell at his feet, his face bowed to the ground and his body wracked with sobs.

The old man let him exhaust himself. When Jesse stopped weeping he asked "Jesse, did you know you were conceived under this tree?"

"What has that got to do with this?"

"Bear with me Jesse. Your parents were young and innocent; neither of them had been with another. Your mother remained a virgin until her wedding night. I used that opportunity to bring you to life. You are my chosen one. You are the light of the world."

190

"You are nothing but a crazy old man. I'm not going to stand here and waste my time, listening to you." With that, Jesse got to his feet and began to walk away.

"Jesse, wait. A monster has been unleashed upon your country. His plans include conquering 139the world. He is ambitious. Nothing can stop him. He calls himself god, and has set out to destroy all who believe in me. You are the only hope of my people. Without you, all will be lost. You are my Son, the Savior of the world."

Jesse began to argue with him, "I have no idea what you are talking about, if this is your idea of being a chosen one you can forget it. After what happened today I'm not prepared to take on that role and it isn't fair of you to expect that from me. That doesn't account for all of those dead people down there – I couldn't save them from being killed. If I couldn't save my parents, my brothers, and my sisters, how do you expect me to save the world? You better go find someone else for the job. I want no part of it."

"I gave man the freedom of choice. Heinrich gives orders, and the people who did that to your village obeyed them. Jesse, can't you understand that if Heinrich isn't stopped, this is the way it will continue to be. I know the struggle in your heart. The faith you were taught as a child and as a youth offering his life to the ministry is my faith. The Elders knew this too, but they were greedy to make money, and possess power and prestige. They made that more important than my teachings. You are following the path of my word as it is written in the Holy Book. This is what will sustain you as well as those who choose to follow you."

Jesse stood there and listened to what the old man had to say

191

but he remained unconvinced. The smoke was still rising out of the village; nothing was going to change what had happened there.

"Just how am I to do this? Jesse asked. "I have seen with my own eyes what happens to those who believe. Wherever I go, Heinrich will follow. Is this what you want to happen to others?"

"Jesse, do you believe in my teachings? Are you a true believer, or do you merely go around paying lip service to what I say?" There was no hint of reproach in his voice.

"You know that I believe. Why do you ask? Do you doubt me?" Jesse questioned angrily.

"Then you must do as I ask. These are dangerous and troubled times. Much will be asked of you, but know that I am with you always."

Jesse stood and stared at the old man for a long time. "The Holy Book says, "Thou shall not kill". How do I obey this law, and do what you ask? Right now, if I could get my hands on Heinrich I would kill him, and think nothing of it."

"Trust in me Jesse. Go out and teach the people to love and forgive. Gather my people to you and your cause." Then the old man added "this is my commandment that you shall love one another as I love you. Greater love has no man than this, than to lay down his life for another." I love you Jesse, I will never leave you. Even in your darkest hour I will be with you. Trust me."

"That doesn't answer my question. Will following your course of action get me killed?"

"I think you already know the answer to that question Jesse."

192

They both stood in silence – the enormity of what the old man was asking was huge. *Am I up to this? Can I really accomplish what he is asking of me?*

Finally Jesse asked the one question that was troubling him. "Am I to die?'

"You will have everlasting life."

"I guess that is as good an answer as any," Jesse replied

They remained silent. Finally the old man asked, "Jesse will you do what I ask of you? For the sake of the world, can you do this, and not falter? "

"Yes Father, I can." At that moment, Jesse made a life altering decision, one that would change the course of his life and history.

They went and sat under the big tree and talked quietly. Soon Jesse fell into a restful sleep. The old man watched over him for a while and then smiled, put his hand on Jesse's head and blessed him.

"Do not doubt me my son. I will always be with you. And in your time of need, I will be there to comfort you." With these words he left as quietly as he had come.

CHAPTER TWENTY EIGHT

Exhausted Jesse slept under the tree until late into the evening. When he awoke, he stood overlooking the valley where plumes of dark smoke were still rising from the village.

Was the visit from the old man a dream? Whether it was or not, now I know what I have to do and how it will end. I understand Heinrich has made our differences personal, and that I am the only person who will be able to stop him. I still don't understand his reasoning, but knowing what is behind his motives is more than I can bear. What I still can't understand is why me? Then, squaring his shoulders he began to make his way back to the cave.

Surreptitiously he wandered through the hills. He couldn't risk the Brown Shirts finding him. If they were searching the hills, he had to be careful about leading them back to his men.

Approaching the mouth of the cave he stood quietly and listened for strange noises, but there were none. When the clouds covered the moon, he slipped inside.

Peter found him sitting near the entrance with his back to the cave wall. "When did you get back? I was worried about you, and the men didn't know what to think when you left. Some are concerned that you have deserted them."

"I have been back for several hours."

"I will go wake the men and tell them you have returned. That will put their minds to rest."

"No Peter, let them sleep. After yesterday they need the peace that only sleep can bring." Besides, I have much I wish to say to you."

Peter sat down beside Jesse and waited for him to begin speaking. "You are going to find what I am going to say unbelievable, but it is true. I fell asleep under a large tree and was awakened by a man in a white robe."

Peter jumped up and ran to the cave entrance. "Did you know him? Did he follow you here?"

"Come and sit down Peter, all is well. This man spoke to me. He told me I am the one person who can stop Heinrich."

Peter looked at Jesse. "Come and rest Jesse, the strain has been too much. You must be imagining all of this."

"Stop Peter, I am quite lucid. I am telling you what I saw and heard. I know what I must do now. I only hope I can prove myself worthy of the responsibility he placed upon me. Come, sit back down, we have much to discuss."

They sat quietly and talked until they heard the sound of men's voices from further back in the cave. "Go to them Peter but say nothing for now. Make sure they are well fed, and then when they have finished eating, I will come and talk to them."

"Jesse, are you absolutely sure this is the only way? You don't have to make defeating Heinrich your personal mission. People will understand once they know of the great tragedy you have suffered. There has to be another way."

"Peter, try to understand. I'm not out to defeat Heinrich. My role is to give the people hope – something to believe in. They are entitled to freedom, to worship as they wish and how they

196

wish. After the news of the massacre in my village gets out, many will be afraid."

"But, why you? There are others who can take up the fight and they will. Why must you sacrifice yourself?"

"Peter, this is what I am born to do. Now please stop trying to convince me otherwise. My mind is made up. I know what is coming, and I also know how it will end. I am afraid, but I can't allow my fear to stop me, there is too much is at stake. Now, I don't want to discuss this anymore. This is probably the last peaceful day we will enjoy for a very long time."

Peter returned to the back of the cave and helped prepare breakfast for the hungry men. They were a dispirited lot. After the men finished eating Peter told them "Jesse returned in the night. He has something of great importance to tell us."

Jesse walked to the fire, and looked at each of his faithful men in the eye. Some began to fidget under his scrutiny, others looked away. Finally he spoke, "A horrific crime took place in my village, and I am afraid this was the first of many. This act was against the Believers and me, because I am their leader. Heinrich must be stopped."

"How do you propose to do that Jesse? We are few, and they are many," a voice called out that Jesse didn't immediately recognize. "He has an army to back him up."

Jesse told them about his visit from the old man. "I must go away from here, and continue spreading the word that there is an alternative for our people to believe in. I must continue to speak the truth of a loving God, and not the one Heinrich and the Elders want us to believe in. Each person must choose how they want to live; under Heinrich's tyranny or as the world was before

197

– at peace with each other.

The Holy book tells us "This is my commandment, that you love one another as I have loved you. Greater love has no man than this, to lay down one's life for his friends."

"Jesse, are you talking about open rebellion against Heinrich and his Brown Shirts? If so, they will hunt you down like an animal," Peter stated.

"I am aware of that." Jesse replied.

Another voice spoke up "If you go away, where does that leave us?"

"Peter and I have spoken at great length. Each of you will go out amongst the Believers and search for those you trust. Find those who are willing to fight Heinrich. These groups will become freedom fighters for all of us, and will carry a heavy responsibility. I will reach as many people as I can, and convince them that there is a choice, and pray that our God will give us the courage and strength to take our country back.

This fight is not for us alone," he continued, "but for our children's children and theirs after that. Today each of you must decide for yourself which is the best course of action to follow. Heinrich will hunt you like an animal. You will be tortured, even killed if you go against him. If any of you wish to leave, that is your choice to make. No one here will hold that against you. I only ask that you don't speak of this morning. The rest of you must accept their individual choices, and allow them to leave with no hard feelings.

"I must leave now, and see to the welfare of my mother and sister. I will return later this evening. By then, each of you will

198

have had time to make your decision."

CHAPTER TWENTY NINE

After Jesse left, Peter went back into the cave, and gathered the men around him. They spent the rest of the day discussing ways to stand up to Heinrich. The task was monumental. They had no guns, explosives, ammunition, radios, vehicles, information or money to start with, but what every man had was a desire to avenge the massacre that took place in the village. They were all too conscious of the heavy gray pall of smoke still hovering over the valley. The wind seemed to carry the screams of the dead and dying as it howled across the doorway of the cave.

The nine men remaining divided themselves into four groups of two; one for each point of a compass, Peter was to form the center of the group. The men swore each other to secrecy, and to never reveal the leaders of the other groups.

Peter wished each group didn't know the identities of the others, but there was little he could do. They named themselves "Freedom Fighters". Each man offered his life for Jesse and the cause, and each privately swore that he would be the one to destroy Heinrich.

"My main concern," Peter told the men, as the discussion was winding down, "is that each of us knows the name of the person who leads each group. There are spies among Jesse's followers and they will try to infiltrate your groups. If you have direct contact with each other, you will be found out.

Appoint someone as your commander that you have complete trust in. Have a line of communication to them alone, but remain in the open as one of Jesse's followers. The Brown Shirts must not suspect you are involved in any way. You also need to be aware if you are captured and are suspected of being part of the resistance you will be tortured."

The men nodded their heads in agreement, then Remi spoke up "from here on in, it's safer that you don't know what our plans are. You are in greater danger than we are, because you are closer to Jesse."

"I agree," Peter said. Leaving the men, he went to sit at the front entrance of the cave. He felt torn. *There is nothing I would love more than to put a gun to Heinrich's head and pull the trigger, but I know Jesse needs me now more than ever. He is a broken man and I don't know if he will be able to keep on going. If he stops no, at least he tried, and that is more than a lot of others have done.*

He sat there for several hours while the men discussed a plan of action. He knew that if he tried to stop them now, it would be nearly impossible.

Peter met with each group privately and shared what information he had. Then he sent each in a different direction. The sign of the fish___ < >= was to be the secret identity code among their groups. In response, a cross + was to be printed above the sign. He instructed each group to do whatever they thought was necessary in their area. He knew Jesse probably wouldn't approve but desperate measures were necessary.

Peter hugged and kissed each man on the cheek as he left, "may God be with you" he said as each group walked out into the night, without telling the others which direction they were going. As he walked away, each man knew he had little chance of survival, but was willing to lay down his life to stop the evil from overtaking and destroying their country.

When Jesse returned Peter was alone. "Where is everybody?" he asked. "Have they all deserted us?"

"On the contrary Jesse, each man has left to stir up as much trouble as he can. They have scattered into the countryside to begin a campaign to stop Heinrich."

Jesse was angry. "You should have tried to stop them. How can they expect accomplish very much. They are poorly equipped and have no money. Maybe all of you should have thought this through a little more, and taken the time to develop a plan before going into action. This isn't what I wanted. This will only lead to more killing and more death. I don't want their blood on my hands too."

"Jesse, these are resourceful men, willing to do whatever it takes. If they falter all they need to remember are the bodies they helped bury in that mass grave. Their anger will fire them up again."

"I have also come to a decision," Jesse added, "I will leave my mother with Elizabeth and Mark, and leave here to continue spreading the word. The only way to defeat Heinrich is to offer the people hope for a better future. It distresses me to know that I will also have the blood of these good men on my hands."

"Jesse, there is no need to be angry with them. Each man knew when he left here that his chance of survival was small, yet each one made the choice to do whatever he could."

Jesse stopped and thought for a moment. "I shouldn't blame

you, nor do I have the right to stop them."

Running his fingers through his hair he added "for the life of me I can't understand what is happening, or why any of this is necessary. In the end, what will Heinrich accomplish? At some point he will have to realize he can't keep going on this way. What are you going to do now Peter?"

"For now, I am staying here to do what I can. I have men willing to work with me and we have a plan. You must leave as soon as possible because Heinrich's men will still be looking for you. As soon as I am able, I will join you. The two men embraced, and then Peter slipped out into the night.

"May God have mercy on our souls as we set out to do what must be done," Jesse prayed, and then he too stepped out into the night.

Within days a campaign of harassment began. In the countryside communication lines were cut; trains were switched to the wrong tracks and sent in the wrong direction, and vehicles left unguarded were vandalized.

When told of the incidents, Heinrich laughed them off. "School boy pranks. If we ignore them, they will stop. Besides, I have nothing to fear from these people. I am powerful and I am invincible."

CHAPTER THIRTY

Lieutenant Otto Schmidt entered Heimlich's office, snapped to attention and saluted.

"Well what have you got to tell me?" Heinrich asked, not looking up from the papers on his desk.

"Sire, we had a great victory. We struck at the very heart of the Believers. Now that the people know what we are capable of, I am sure there will be no more trouble."

Heinrich got up from his desk and looked out the windows, his hands behind his back, a scowl on his face.

"Tell me about this great triumph." he replied sarcastically.

"We took the village by surprise early in the morning. My men rounded up every person and forced each of them into the village square, most still in their nightclothes. I demanded they tell me where Jesse was hiding. I also sent a group of ten men to Jesse's parents' home to catch him if he was there, and to make sure he didn't get away."

"Was he there?"

"Well no sir."

"Then what did you do?"

"Sir?" The lieutenant seemed confused. "I tried to find out

where he was. Naturally I questioned the villagers."

Heinrich walked over and slapped him across the face.

"You fool. Let me tell you what you have done. You killed, looted and destroyed his home. Instead, you could have made an example of a few by killing them on the spot to force others to talk. You could have used them as an example to show what happens if they withheld information, but instead you murdered over six-hundred men, women and children. You gave Jesse and his Believers a reason to oppose us."

"But sir, our intelligence reported him there, in the village, the day before. Our informer spoke with him at great length."

"Now we have given Jesse a rallying cry." Heinrich roared, "instead of quietly capturing him and bringing him to me. The whole country will learn what you have done. I wanted him to go on trial, and publicly admit I am the true head of the church. I wanted him to admit that he believes in me and my teachings. If he didn't, he would die. His followers would have disappeared when they saw him sniveling and begging for his life. Now we must destroy him no matter what."

Lieutenant Schmidt was forced to stand at attention and listen as Heinrich launched into one of his tirades. He paced up and down his office like a caged animal, and shouted obscenities in the Lieutenant's face. He blamed him for the missed opportunity to punish Jesse. His face was dark red; spittle ran down his chin.

Then, as abruptly as he started, Heinrich stopped. He was exhausted. Pushing his face into the Lieutenant's, their noses almost touching he said, "The next time you are sent to do something important for me, do not fail. If you do, I will have you shot as a traitor. Now get out of here."

The lieutenant said nothing. He saluted, turned and walked out the door.

Heinrich stood and watched him leave. *Now I need to find another way to get Jesse. Hopefully now that my men have struck at Jesse's heart he will decide the time has come to give up his crusade.* Even as the thought crossed his mind, he knew that would never happen. Jesse was more like an angry bull, and he had the power alone to derail Heinrich's grand scheme.

My best hope is that Jesse will hold true to form, like the coward he is, and choose not to fight back.

.

CHAPTER THIRTY ONE

Anxiously Jesse approached the village. He was worried about his mother and sister and how he was going to explain to them that he would be leaving to continue what he was called to do.

The first thing he did was go to the house where he knew Mark was staying. As he approached he saw Mark on the street, talking to a man from the village.

As soon as Mark saw Jesse he rushed to him, the serious look on his face brightening. "Jesse, how good to see you. Have you come to see your mother and Elizabeth? They have been asking about you."

"Yes, but first we must talk. Is there some place we can talk without being overheard? It is hard to know who to trust anymore, and I would prefer nobody hear what I am about to say."

Mark thought for a moment and then said, "The villagers already know you are here and will presume you have come to see your mother. They know I brought her here, so it's natural for us to be seen walking and talking together."

"You are right. How are they Mark? I have been very worried about both of them."

"Elizabeth is doing well, all things considered. She has bad dreams, and screams out in the night. All I can do is sit with her until the dreams end."

"And my mother?"

"Physically her body is healing. She will always have scars from the knife wounds on her back. Fortunately, there are no signs of infection. Mentally she is in a dark place. She stares at the walls and talks to no one, - not even Elizabeth. She eats practically nothing. It's almost as though she has a death wish. Maybe she will talk with you."

"I don't blame her. Everything was taken away from her: her husband, her children, her home, and most of her extended family. I too would think it would be easier to die, and be with them rather than continue living. But, that is not why I am here. What is the talk in the village? I imagine as a doctor you hear most of what is being said."

"Heinrich's Brown Shirts claimed a great victory. They claim they were peacefully coming into the village and you and the Believers ambushed them and they had no choice but to fight back. They maintain they were lucky to get out alive. This was also a warning that the same thing will happen to anybody who stands up against them."

Jesse's face turned red from anger. "Do people believe this nonsense? Can't they see the truth for themselves? What more will it take?"

"They know Jesse, but they are afraid. These are humble people who have never had to face anything of this magnitude. They don't understand what is happening or why."

"Mark, I came to tell you I am leaving. If I remain here, none of you are safe."

"I agree. Heinrich sees you as a threat, and is on a mission to

210

destroy you. As the leader of the Believers, your ideas resonate with the people and they are willing to follow you."

As they walked down the road Jesse revealed to Mark the visit from the old man. He shared Peter's plans with him to create a freedom movement that would harass and resist Heinrich's every move.

"Jesse, you know he will come after you. He will torture and kill you if you are caught."

"I understand all of that. If, and when he does, my people will see that I am willing to die for what I believe in."

"Let me come with you Jesse."

"No Mark. I have other plans for you. Your skills are needed here and people trust you. They are willing to give you information. Peter will remain for the time being, and I am asking both of you to work together. If I am not here, Heinrich's men will focus on where they think I am, and you will have time to become organized."

"Why now Jesse?"

"The old man..."

"I don't understand."

"Mark, he asked me if I truly believed in what I was teaching. When I said I did, he informed me that I am his son and the savior of the world."

"And you believe him?"

"I don't know about the savior part, but someone has to stop Heinrich. After what he has done to my village, and my family, I

211

have to try. That is what is being asked of me. Mark, I know I am to die trying, but I am willing to do so, if it helps stop this madness."

Slowly they continued to walk up and down the street. Neither spoke until they were close to the house where Maria and Elizabeth stayed, Finally Mark said, "I am with you."

They parted ways. Mark went into the house that he used as a hospital and Jesse continued down the street to where his mother and sister stayed. His heart clenched in fear not knowing what to expect

He knocked on the door and was surprised to see Elizabeth open it. He pulled her into his arms and hugged her tightly. "Thank God you are alive. How is our mother?"

Elizabeth pulled away from him. "Not well Jesse. I think she has given up. She sits in her chair staring straight ahead and she refuses to talk. I am worried about her. Maybe seeing you will cheer her up."

She took his hand and led him into the living room.

CHAPTER THIRTY TWO

When Jesse looked at his mother, he was shocked. Her bruises had faded with time, but there was no life in her eyes. She sat in a chair, exactly like Mark and Elizabeth had told him and stared out the window, her hands twisting and untwisting a piece of white cloth.

Fighting to get control of his emotions, he stood in the doorway and watched her for several minutes. She gave no indication that she knew he was there. Finally, he approached her, knelt down beside her chair and took her busy hands into his. "Mother, it's me, Jesse. I have come to see how you are doing."

She turned her head slowly toward him. When he saw the pain on her face, it was almost more than he could bear. A wave of guilt washed over him. *This is my fault. None of this would have happened if it were not for me.*

Elizabeth came into the room, put her hand on his shoulder and stood beside him, "Mark told me your plans. Must you leave?"

"Elizabeth, even though I don't want to, I have to go. You know, as well as I do, they will come back looking for me. I don't like to see her like this, have there been any signs of any improvement?"

"Not really. She sits like that most of the day, and then goes to bed. It is all we can do to get her to eat. At night I hear her weeping. I feel so helpless, Jesse. I wish there was something I could do for her."

Maria lifted her head and looked at him. "Where are you going Jesse?"

Jesse was surprised by the strength in her voice.

"Mother, I came to tell you that I am leaving. I can't stay here much longer. When I leave the village will be safe. As long as Heinrich thinks I am nearby, he will keep looking for me, and more people will die."

"That's not true Jesse," Elizabeth said, "It's not about you; he is set on destroying anybody who refuses to follow him."

"No, that is where you are wrong Elizabeth. Heinrich is making this personal. He is against the Believers, because I am the one leading them. I am quite sure, if it was anybody else, he wouldn't be so adamant in his pursuit. This has been going on for as long as I can remember. If I die, then all of the work I have done so far will be for nothing."

"Do you think running away is the answer? He will find you wherever you go. By not standing up against him he has branded you a coward. There is nothing wrong with that. We all know that's not the case."

Jesse got to his feet and began to pace back and forth. He knew Elizabeth was right. Turning to face her he replied, "We have sacrificed so much in God's name – our home, our brothers, sister and our father. You were raped, mother was raped and tortured. A whole village was massacred because Heinrich wanted to show me how powerful he is. If I go away and he knows I am gone these people" he said, sweeping his

214

hand around the room "will have a chance to live. If I stay, he will send his Brown Shirts again and again. Can't you see that?"

Before Elizabeth could answer, Maria spoke up, "he's right Elizabeth. This isn't about Jesse running away like a coward; this is about him continuing to lead the Believers. He is the only person Heinrich is afraid of. He has known, since they were children, that Jesse is the stronger of the two."

"Then I am going with you," Elizabeth declared.

"No, I need you here. When you talk with Peter, he will help you understand. I don't have time to explain all of the details today. Mother, I must leave now. I have asked Mark and Elizabeth to take care of you until my return."

"I am going with you," Maria stated, wincing as she pulled herself out of the chair.

"No, you aren't strong enough yet. You have been through too much. You must take time to heal your body heal, as well as your spirit. Elizabeth needs your help here."

Maria looked at Jesse firmly declaring. "I am your mother; you are a part of me. I have known since before you were born that your life has a purpose, and that one day you would leave to fulfill that purpose. I was there at the beginning of your journey, and I will be there at the end."

"Mother, listen to Jesse, you are needed here," Elizabeth interjected.

"I am going and neither of you will stop me. Give me time to get my things together. I don't have much to take, just what the villagers were able to donate. Elizabeth, go pack my things. Jesse, go outside and talk to Mark until I am ready. We will leave as soon as evening comes."

Elizabeth went into the bedroom, and then returned handing Jesse a few coins. "This is all I have, but this should be enough for you and Mother to get by for a while. Personally, I think it will be better for you to be seen leaving town during the day. Where will you go Jesse, do you have any ideas?" Elizabeth asked"

"I am not sure but you will hear from me. It's better if you don't know

An hour later, Jesse went back into the house to talk to his mother and try once again to dissuade from coming with him. He was surprised to see her fully dressed with a small valise waiting at the door. Her eyes were clear and her cheeks were a healthy rosy color. Gone were all the signs of the despondent woman he talked to only an hour before.

"Mother," he said" I have been thinking about this, and I don't think it's a good idea for you to come with me. I think you will be better off staying here."

"Why, if I may ask, do you think that?" Maria questioned.

"I don't think you are strong enough yet. You have been through a terrible ordeal. I mean, after what they did to you, losing the baby and all. We have a long dangerous journey ahead of us."

'So what you are saying is that I should stay here, moan with grief while you are gone and don't know what is happening to you. I should sit here every day and wonder if you are dead or alive and constantly thinking what those brutes did to me. Is that what you want?"

"I didn't say that. I mean you should stay here and help Elizabeth and Mark."

"So what if the Brown Shirts find out I am still alive?"

"I don't understand. What you are trying to tell me. They will come looking for me, why would they come after you?" Then, tapping himself on the forehead with two fingers, he said "Oh now I understand why you must go with me. Why didn't I think about this? If they find you they will torture you until you tell them where I am."

Maria stood up, put on her coat which hung over the back of the chair picked up her small valise and walked toward the door.

Jesse could see how determined she was, He attempted to dissuade her one more time.

"Mother, you know as well as I that Heinrich will not rest until I am dead. I don't want you there if, and when that happens. I have much work to do, and I fear, not a long time to do it. Heinrich must be stopped."

"Jesse," she replied, putting a hand on each side of his face, "I have known since you were born that you have a special purpose. Your father would want me to be with you. Why won't you let me help you?"

"What about Elizabeth? She needs you too."

"She and I spoke earlier about this. She also feels I should be by your side. She said I would have more value being with you than hanging around here and getting in her way. Come, let's not waste any more time and get going."

She flicked out the light, quietly opened the door and peered outside. Seeing no one about she motioned to Jesse, "Come, it is safe."

With a resigned shrug of his shoulders Jesse left first, and then Maria quietly closed the door and followed him. Together they slipped out into the night and made their way out of town.

Elizabeth and Mark stood at the window, watching as they left. "What is going to become of the two of them?" she asked looking up at Mark with tears in her eyes. "Will I ever see them again?"

"Come Elizabeth," he said gently, "we have much to do before Jesse returns."

* * *

Several days later, a car filled with officers dressed in Brown Shirts pulled up in front of Mark's house. "We came to see Jesse. Get him."

"He isn't here. He left earlier in the week with his mother. I don't know where they have gone." Mark replied.

The leader of the Brown Shirts started to laugh. "Heinrich was right. Jesse is running like a scared rabbit, just as he predicted. He will be pleased to hear that."

Although Mark wanted to retaliate, he said nothing. The men laughed and joked as they drove away. Once again, Heinrich had misjudged Jesse.

CHAPTER THIRTY THREE

Jesse and Maria travelled by night. During the second evening of their journey Timothy caught up to them. Maria gasped when he stepped out of the trees and approached them. Jesse immediately recognized his friend.

"Timothy, where did you come from? What are you doing here?" he asked. Maria gripped his arm in fear.

"It isn't safe for you and your mother to travel alone when you don't know the countryside. I am going with you. You do realize Heinrich knows you are alive and is searching for you. I know people in the nearby villages who are Believers and I know for a fact, they are willing to hide you during the day, in order for the two of you to travel safely through this area." Timothy whispered. Both men were aware voices could carry a long way on a quiet night.

"Do they understand if they are found out they will be killed? I can't bear the thought of more people dying because of me." Jesse whispered back.

"They are willing to take the risk. It is their choice to make, not yours." Timothy replied.

Maria stood back and listened to their conversation. She touched Jesse's arm. "Listen to what he is saying Jesse. Timothy has a good idea, and we need to trust somebody. If, as Timothy says, they are your followers, then they stand with you against

Heinrich. You can't take that away from them. Each person has to be allowed to do his or her part, no matter how small it may be."

"As usual you are right mother," Jesse replied, "Timothy, go ahead of us and make what arrangements you feel are necessary for us.

Timothy slipped away as quietly as he had come. Jesse and Maria, now on guard, continued to walk down the road. Just before sunrise Jesse noticed a man who appeared to be drunk standing at the side of the road. He staggered and talked as though someone were walking beside him.

Maria was frightened. "Jesse what shall we do? He has seen us, and it looks like he is coming our way."

"The best thing we can do is cross over to the other side of the road before we have to pass him. I'm sure he means us no harm. It is still dark enough that he won't be able see our faces. Even if he does, he probably won't remember them."

But as they approached the man, he also crossed to the other side of the road. There was no way Jesse and Maria were going to be able to avoid him.

"Who are you?" he slurred. "I don't remember seeing you around here before."

Jesse and Maria stopped. "Merely two travellers," Jesse replied. He didn't want a confrontation. The man stood in front of them and weaved back and forth.

"I have been waiting for you," he whispered. "Look down."

The man made the secret sign of the Believers <u>< > =</u> in the dust of the road and Jesse made the sign of the cross on top.

"Wait a few minutes, and then follow me," the stranger said. He staggered to the side of the road and Jesse heard him urinating. Then he disappeared into the trees.

Jesse looked around. Seeing nobody, he took Maria's arm and guided her off the road into the trees where the man waited for them. "Come," he said, "My farm is at the top of the hill. I have food and a clean bed waiting for you."

Maria was exhausted. She stumbled several times going up the hill, and hoped Jesse wouldn't notice. She didn't want him to see how weak and tired she was.

As they neared the house the farmer said "My name is Joe and my wife's name is Eva. Timothy asked us to give you a place to rest this evening."

"Thank you," Jesse replied. "As you can see my mother is tired. A good night's sleep will do her good."

The farmer's wife waited for them. She fed them a breakfast of porridge, bread and milk. When Maria was done eating, she was led to a small bedroom at the back of the house where a tin tub filled with warm water waited for her.

"Allow me to take your clothes, and I will wash them for you" the woman said shyly to Maria. "I put a clean nightgown beside the tub for you."

Maria was grateful for the kindness. She bathed quickly, crawled into the bed, and instantly fell asleep. Her body ached from walking and sleeping in odd places and this bed, even though lumpy, felt like heaven.

Jesse stayed awake for several hours talking with the farmer and his wife. He told them what happened to his mother and sister and the other occupants of his village. The husband and wife were shocked to hear his story. Suddenly the wife realized who sat with them.

"Is it you Jesse, our blessed leader? We weren't told it was you coming, only that a man and woman needed our help. What would you have us do for you?"

"You have already risked more than necessary. Share word of our God's love and forgiveness. Tell others what took place in my village and to my family. Heinrich must be stopped. Tell nobody I was here. Be very careful about whom you trust, and pray this madness will end soon."

After their discussion, Jesse went to the barn and climbed into the loft. Wrapping himself in the warm quilt Eva had given him he fell into a deep sleep. When evening approached, she fed them supper and packed a bundle of food for them to take. At dusk, Joe led them back across his field emerging farther down the road from where they had entered the trees

"Thank you" Jesse said "You have done us a great honor by protecting us on our journey. I pray you will be safe."

Maria and Jesse travelled south and east across the country for seven more days and often received help along the way. Sometimes it was ride in the back of a wagon, other times a gift of food and still others, a bed to sleep in and a hot meal.

On the ninth day they arrived in the town of Canna. Peter waited for them as they neared the entrance the town. "I am going to take you to my parents' house. Maria will have a safe place to rest and regain her strength, and we can use it as a base for our travels. It is located a short distance away from the town. We shouldn't have to worry about being seen."

For once Maria didn't argue with Jesse when she was told of the plan. She had reached a point where she was too exhausted to continue.

CHAPTER THIRTY FOUR

While Maria rested and regained her strength, Jesse, and several of his loyal followers, travelled to the nearby towns speaking of God's love. They asked thought provoking questions meant to encourage people to question Heinrich's leadership. Jesse could not, in good conscience, ask them to kill and revolt, but he could make them stop and think.. Too many lives had been sacrificed already.

His message never changed. "God has given you the gift of freedom of choice. How you use that gift is up to you. You alone are responsible for the outcome. Each one of you must do what you think is best for you and your family. Heinrich wants you to believe everything he says, and is forcing you to do what he wants. Is this what you want? I offer you hope that one day Heinrich will be defeated, and there will be no need to fear that you talk to, or need to be careful about what you say. Hope is God's way of telling us this too shall end."

The Believers were encouraged by Jessie's message. They were afraid. To openly oppose Heinrich's decrees was dangerous. No one was sure about who they could trust any more.

Jesse's message was spread by word of mouth. Everywhere he went the crowds grew larger. His message was simple – follow the path that is right for you. After he spoke to a crowd small groups of resistance grew.

After a month of travel Jesse returned to see his mother. There he rested away from the public eye and held private meetings with his men. He spent a great deal of time alone, meditating on what he should do next.

Within a short period of time, Jesse began to hear stories that the Brown Shirts were looking for him. In the beginning they went from village to village asking questions. The less information they found out the more physical they became. They grew into a drunk and disorderly lot leaving a path of destruction behind them – women and girls were openly raped in the streets, men tortured, businesses broken into and destroyed.

Jesse watched their advance with growing concern. Finally he said to his mother, "we must leave quickly. I received word this morning the Brown Shirts will arrive in Canna sometime tomorrow. Somebody is sure to tell them we have been seen at Peter's home, and they will come looking for us. His family stands a better chance if we aren't found here.

I am making arrangements for us to be taken to Hielberg, which is about a hundred miles away. As soon as Peter's family is safe, he will join us.

I am worried about you mother. It isn't safe to leave you here, and I'm not sure if you are strong enough to travel yet."

"Don't worry about me Jesse. I am fully recovered from my injuries and our journey here. I will be ready to leave when you are."

"Good. I will speak to Peter about finalizing arrangements for us to leave. First, we must plant a story that I ran away when I heard the Brown Shirts were coming, and headed east. In the meantime we will go in a different direction. I'm sure the

Believers will be able to convince them we left several days ago."

Early the next morning an old farm truck carrying two market sized pigs stopped briefly in front of Peter's home. An old man and old woman moved quietly out of the shadows and climbed into the back of the truck.

Four hours later, Jesse and Maria were safely in Hielberg. The farm truck drove to the market place, and the old man and old woman got out. As the truck pulled away, a young man approached them.

"Grandma, Grandpa, you are here. How wonderful it is to have you come and visit. Come with me, Father will be surprised. He didn't expect you to arrive for several more days."

CHAPTER THIRTY FIVE

Jesse and Maria were led to the Boar's Head Inn located in the poorer part of the city. The young man opened the door and ushered them inside the tavern. The room reeked of stale beer and old tobacco smoke. Old scarred wooden tables and benches lined both sides of the walls, and a few tables were scattered down the middle of the room.

Several benches along the wall were occupied. Two men were playing chess in a corner. A young girl leaned over the bar and talked to the bar tender. An older, a partially bald man stood behind the bar, wiping a glass with a dirty dish rag.

Maria was frightened and moved closer to Jesse. "Don't be afraid," he whispered to her. "These are good people." Jesse put his hand in the middle of Maria's back and urged her walk ahead of him.

"Father guess who has come to visit us? Grandma and Grandpa Tony have arrived early," the young man announced, "Lucky for me I found them wandering around the market place."

The old man looked up and rushed out from behind the bar. Picking Maria up off her feet, he swung her around and kissed her on the cheek, "Mama." Then he threw his arms around Jesse. "Papa, it has been too long since we last saw you. Mother why didn't you let me know the two of you would be arriving early? I am so glad you have finally come to visit us. Come, sit down, you must be tired and hungry from your long journey."

He led them to a table close to the bar and with a flourish wiped it off. "Mariska," he shouted "bring them a glass of beer to quench their thirst, and then go to the kitchen and find them something to eat."

Turning to Jesse and Maria he said, "Marika helps me during the days Helena isn't here. I only let her work once a week during the day – she can't seem to keep the orders straight." Looking at Jesse he winked. "If I could find someone better, I would let her go."

As she headed into the kitchen Marika turned and smiled at Jesse. He smiled back, his heart filled with joy to see her. Peter hadn't told him she would be here waiting for him.

They ate hungrily. When they finished Jesse said "Marika, would you please take my mother to her room. I can see she is tired from our long journey."

Maria followed the young girl up a flight of stairs, then down the hall, and paused at door number six. "It should be quieter for you here. At night the tavern gets very loud and you will still be able to hear some of the noise, but not all." Marika said.

She unlocked the door and Maria followed her in. The room was shabby, but clean. Marika closed the door and turned to Maria, "I know who you are. You will be safe here. Peter has asked me to look after you. Keep your door locked at all times. Try to get some rest, and I will be back later."

"Where will Jesse be?" Maria asked.

"In the room across the hall."

After Marika left, Maria locked the door, and lay down on top of the bed waiting for Jesse to come upstairs. Within minutes, she was asleep. She didn't hear Jesse and Marika go into his room.

As soon as the door closed behind them, Jesse put his arms around her and pulled her close. "I have missed you so much. How did you get here?"

"Peter brought me. Come, sit," she said patting the side of the bed. "He told me what happened in your village, and to your family. Jesse I am so sorry."

Jesse sat down beside her and she wrapped her arms around him. Her simple touch destroyed his outer façade, and he began to sob. For the first time since the tragedy, he was finally able to acknowledge his feelings. Marika pulled him back onto the bed and comforted him the only way she knew how.

Several hours later Maria was awakened by a noise in the hallway. When she opened her door to investigate she saw Jesse's door open and Marika step out. Her hair was messed up and she wore the look of a woman who had been well loved.

She quietly closed her door and smiled. "So that's how it is," she said to the empty room, "I am glad Jesse has found someone to love. Life is too short to always be alone."

She waited for a few minutes, crossed the hallway then knocked quietly on Jesse's door. "Did you forget something my love?" he said as he opened the door. When he saw who was standing there his face turned red and he stammered "Mother I..."

Maria entered the room and closed the door behind her. The bed was rumpled and Jesse was tongue tied. "Is that girl Marika a close friend of yours?"

"How do you know she was with me?"

"I heard a noise in the hallway, and when looked out I saw her coming out of your room. Who is she and where did she come from? What is she to you?"

Jesse got a funny look on his face, "I guess you could call her more than a close friend. Actually she is my wife."

Now it was Maria's turn to look stunned. "Your wife? How long have you two been married?"

"Only for a short time. I planned to tell you and father when I came home, but with everything that happened I couldn't."

"Where did you meet her?"

"When I was in the city. I wanted you to know her story before I brought her to meet you. She came to me wondering if my God could forgive her. At age eleven her father sold her to pay off his gambling debts and the man who bought her forced her into prostitution. I was going to send for her after you and father got used to the idea. Thank God she wasn't there or she would be dead too."

Before he could say any more Maria interrupted, "Stop right there. I don't need to know any more. Do you love her?"

"Yes."

"Does she love you?"

"Yes."

"Are you happy Jesse?"

"Happier than I have ever been. She is my island in the storm,

232

my sanctuary."

"Then that's all that matters." She walked over and hugged her son, and kissed him on the cheek. "The reason I came to see you is to see what your plans are for supper? I am hungry. After that you can explain to me what we are doing here."

CHAPTER THIRTY SIX

Entering Heinrich's office Sig Rotter said "we missed him again. We followed him as far as Canna, but by the time we got there, he disappeared."

Heinrich was furious. "You stupid idiot," he screamed, "Your one job is to find Jesse and bring him here, to me. I will tell you why you can't catch him – he knows when your men were are coming. How did he know that? By the actions of your men and the incompetent man you sent to do the job, that's how. You are their leader, and I hold you responsible for their failure.

It's unacceptable that they wasted their time getting drunk and fucking anything that wears a skirt. They left a path of destruction behind them. If you can't do your job any better than this, I will brand you as a traitor, and have you shot. Jesse has informers too, and they knew exactly where you were." Then, with cold menacing eyes, he looked at Rotter, "the next time you fail me, you will be a dead man. Get out of my sight, you make me sick."

Heinrich turned his back on Rotter. As he heard the door open he turned around and said, "Put a price on his head – thirty silver kroners to anybody who turns him in."

After Rotter had left Heinrich muttered, *every moment that man doesn't capture Jesse he makes me look like a fool.*

Picking up a heavy glass ashtray, he heaved it through the window. There was glass everywhere. Then he opened the door and bellowed into the hallway, "someone get in here and clean up this mess."

Sig Rotter was furious as he walked out of the building. *Just who does he think he is? Nobody talks to me like that, and gets away with it. Your turn is coming Heinrich. One of these days you will be begging me for your life.*

Rotter went to his office and dictated a memo to his officers located in the south-eastern part of the country. Each unit was to appoint two people whose sole purpose was to locate Jesse within the next seventy-two hours, and report back to him. They could apply whatever force was necessary.

He harangued them about the conduct of their men. There was entirely too much drunkenness within their units. He reminded them of their duty which was to root out Jesse's Believers and cleanse the area of their presence. In future, all were to be sent to the indoctrination camps. Cattle cars would be made available, as well as new guidelines for a selection process. Only the healthiest would be used for labor, the rest were to be exterminated - like the vermin they were.

Next he dictated a memo to Adolph Getzlinger, head of the committee for the indoctrination camps. Operation 'Extinguish" was now in effect. He was to follow the instructions exactly as given in the documents he was enclosing. All Believers were now to be considered traitors against the state, and to be dealt with accordingly. Heinrich, who fully supported his plans, was the last to receive a copy of the memo.

Operation "Extinguish" was Rotter's idea. Move the believers to camps out in the country and provide them with limited food and water. Heinrich could use the strongest for the work camps; the rest would be left to die. To conserve food and water, the oldest and youngest were to be killed immediately, and the healthiest women and girls were to be put into brothels as sex slaves for the enlisted men and officers. .

Within a day, Rotter received a phone call. "Jesse is still in Canna, I am awaiting orders on how to proceed."

Rotter responded immediately. "Move men into the area as quietly as possible. Surround the town, and, in two days we will close the net on him. Set up guards on all the roads leading in and out of town. Nobody is to enter or leave until they have been checked. Jesse is to be captured alive and delivered to Heinrich."

Rotter was furious when he found out he missed Jesse by half a day. Rumor was that Jesse was seen heading east out of the city and Rotter had no choice, but to send men in that direction. He was determined to deliver Jesse to Heinrich - no matter how long it took or what he had to do.

CHAPTER THIRTY SEVEN

Once again, word passed from one person to another that Jesse was in Hielberg. People travelled from far and wide to hear him speak. When the town couldn't accommodate the hundreds of travelers, they pitched tents in a large nearby field. Each day Jesse went to them. When he wasn't speaking, he walked among them and listened to their stories and offered words of comfort.

On the third day, he motioned Timothy to his side, "can you get the men together? I have no doubt that Heinrich will soon hear where we are, and I must know what is actually going on. Some of the stories I am being told are horrendous. Meet with me at the Boar's Inn tomorrow evening. Maria, Marika, and I will leave early the next morning. Can you arrange transportation from here to Bern for us?"

"Do you think it is safe to go there? Surely you will be caught." Timothy replied.

"What better place to hide than in Heinrich's backyard. He will never look for us there because his efforts will be concentrated on trying to find us along the road."

"I will get back to you on this later. Perhaps it would be better if you left tomorrow morning?"

"I think we are safe enough for now. If the Brown shirts find us there are many who will protect us."

When he went back to the Inn he called Maria and Marika to

him, "we are leaving the day after tomorrow, early in the morning. Timothy is arranging for a ride to take us to Bern."

Jesse left to meet with his men and Marika started to cry. "I am so afraid for him. I am worried that he will be captured and tortured. He is the only good thing that has ever come into my life," she said to Maria.

In that instant Maria knew that everything Marika was afraid of would come to pass. She took Marika to her room and spoke to her gently. "Come child, I have something to tell you. I don't think my words will comfort you, but, at least you will understand why he is so driven."

Maria shared with her daughter-in-law the circumstances of Jesse conception and birth. She told her about the massacre in the village, and how her family was killed. She related the story of Jesse's visit from the old man and the knowledge which was passed to him. Marika sat listening, without saying a word.

"Marika, Jesse is a special man born to a specific purpose. He is fully aware of the fact he is going to have a life that meets a violent end. He doesn't let this bother him, but gets up every day and carries out his mission. I never thought that Jesse would marry, but I am pleased he chose you. I couldn't think of a better person to be by his side, but you must learn to be strong for his sake."

"Did he tell you how we met, what I was?"

"Yes, but it doesn't matter. You are his refuge, his strength, the one person who can give him what he needs. Cherish your time together. Love him with all of your heart. Shower him with love every day, and build enough memories to last you a lifetime."

"Jesse wants me to come with you when we leave," Marika said. "He wants me to look out for you when he is not around."

"I would like that very much," Maria replied. "Together we can support each other through the difficult times ahead."

CHAPTER THIRTY EIGHT

Just before supper, the following evening, the Boars Inn began to fill with men. Some were local, most were strangers. A large contingency of loud boisterous Brown Shirts also appeared.

Some of the men ate quietly then slowly drifted away. Others, when they finished their meal, went upstairs to return to their rooms. Still others went out the front door, around to the back and up the back stairs. Marika was working in the bar and Maria was in her room.

One by one the men, who were part of the resistance, gathered in Jesse's room. Keeping their voices low, they discussed plans for the continued harassment and resistance against Heinrich. Each man knew he was risking his life and Jesse's if they were caught. The uncommon number of Brown Shirts downstairs in the tavern had them all on edge.

Jesse spoke to them, thanked them for their support, and encouraged their non-violent activities while bolstering their confidence. Suddenly they heard gunfire and screams coming from the town. Marika began pounding on the door.

When Timothy opened it she said "you must leave. The Brown Shirts are taking over the town. There are dozens of them. They are everywhere."

Jacque Divers, one of the local residents slipped out the door. "I will go into the tavern to see if I can find out what is happening."

Within five minutes he was back, a shocked look on his face. "They are going door to door forcing the Believers out into the streets. Anyone who resists is being shot. They will be here soon, we must leave."

Marika saw Jacque move unobtrusively up the stairs and followed him. "Quickly" she said, "There is an attic, climb up there and lay quietly." Several of the men, including Jesse and Timothy followed her.

She removed an access panel to the roof and a rope ladder tumbled down. The men scrambled up the ladder and the last one pulled it up behind them. Marika replaced the panel and slipped out of the door.

Others, concerned for their families, tried to leave through the back door. Their screams were heard as each was shot and killed. Jesse wondered if they had been betrayed and by whom. It seemed as though the Brown Shirts knew Jesse and the resistance were meeting that evening.

Those from out of town made their way back into the tavern, sat in groups of two or three and pretended they had been sitting there all evening.

Maria, upon hearing the commotion, opened her door and came into the hallway. Marika shoved her back into her room. "Disguise who you are," she whispered said, and then went back down the stairs to the tavern.

Seconds later, a large contingent of Brown Shirts burst through the tavern door. "Where is

he?" the leader demanded. He stopped, carefully looked over the men seated at the tables and then turned to Marika.

"Who are you looking for?" she asked, trying to appear as provocative as possible. "Maybe it is me?" she simpered, bringing her body closer to his.

He reached over and squeezed one of her breasts. She gasped in pain. "Not now, but you will do when I come back. I will have need for a woman by then." Marika shuddered at his words.

"Search the Inn, and bring everyone down here," the leader bellowed. One of the young guards came in the door, saluted and whispered something to him. "My man tells me Jesse must still be here - that he hasn't left. If he is, we will find him."

. "This man, Jesse, you are looking for isn't here. We haven't seen him." Marika declared

.The leader of the Brown Shirts slapped her across the face. "I know you are lying, and when we find him, I will make him watch as my men and I take turns with you in front of him. That," he said slapping her again, "will teach you to lie to me."

Marika could hear the men banging on doors, rousing the guests in their rooms. Soon they began filing into the tavern with terror written over their faces. Some were bleeding. She breathed a sigh of relief when she saw Maria come down the stairs. She was dressed like an old peasant lady with a kerchief over her hair, limping as though she were in great pain.

She rushed over to her, took her arm and led her to a chair. "Grandmother, sit here." She shouted as if Maria was hard of hearing. Maria limped over to the chair and sat down.

A short time later two of the Brown Shirts came down the stairs. "He is not here. We have searched every room."

"He must be, the guards outside didn't see him leave. Search

245

again."

Marika could hear them upstairs. Finally, one came back and reported, "He is not here. Somehow he slipped past us and got away. The window in room Six was open. He could have easily jumped from there, and hid in the shadows when he heard the gunfire in the streets."

The leader shouted, "Search the outbuildings and the alleys. He hasn't had time to get very far."

He grabbed Marika, roughly kissed her and fondled her breast. "Wait for me. I will be back." As he walked away she wiped her hand across her mouth, and her eyes filled with panic.

It seemed like a lifetime before the Brown Shirts left the tavern. The leader didn't come back for Marika, for which she was grateful.

"You must stay in my room tonight in case that brute returns," Maria told her, "but I don't think he will, He will be too busy, trying to explain to his superiors how Jesse got away again."

Jesse and Timothy stayed in the attic all of the next day. One by one the resistance leaders who hid with them left, and Jesse prayed they got away safely. They had no way of knowing what was taking place in the streets.

The next morning the Brown Shirts let the people who had been standing outside overnight go back to their homes. They shuffled back to their houses cold, hungry and exhausted, leaving the bodies of the Believers lying in the street.

Jeeps arrived and the Brown Shirts left the town. Some were proud of what they did and openly boasted about the number of

Believes they had killed. Others were quiet, unable to cope with the brutality they left behind.

Marika went into the empty room and called out, "Jesse, you can come down now. They are gone."

"We must leave tonight" he told her. "There is an old barn two miles out of town. Timothy will be waiting there for us. Take Maria there and I will come as quickly as I can. The men there will protect you. You will be safe with them."

Jesse went down to the kitchen and conferred with the owner of the Inn. He was not as tall as Jesse, but round through the middle. They disappeared into the back, and when Jesse returned he looked totally different. He was dressed in black with a pillow under his shirt. They used shoe polish to turn his hair and eyebrows black. The clothes hung on him, and he had a patch over one eye.

Without looking back, he boldly stepped out of the Inn and staggered down the street. When he was sure that nobody was paying attention to him, he disappeared into an alley between two buildings.

When it began to get dark, Maria and Marika left the Inn. They too looked different. Maria wore a tattered brown coat and leaned heavily on a cane. Marika was dressed as a young boy, her long hair tucked into a cap. Slowly they made their way towards the outskirts of town. They hadn't gone far when a Brown Shirt stepped out of the shadows.

"Where are you going at this time of night?" He demanded.

"I am walking my grandmother home." Mariska replied, "She is old, and we worry that she may fall in the dark. She is afraid to walk alone."

The Brown Shirt studied them for a minute and then said "off with you. Go quickly. It is too dangerous for you to be out here at night. There are many unsavory characters hanging around." The two of them followed the road out of town. They walked for nearly an hour when a group of uniformed soldiers stopped them.

"Where are you going out so late at night?" their leader asked. Some of them were drunk and taunted the two women. One grabbed for Marika's cap, and before she could stop him, her long hair fell to her shoulders.

He grabbed her by the hair, "look at what we have here, a girl pretending to be a boy."

"What about the other one?'

He grabbed Maria by the arm and yanked the kerchief off her head. "Not as young as the first, but not as old as she appears. This one is a little old for my liking, but in the dark they are all the same."

Incensed Maria grabbed her cane and hit the man who held her. "No one is going to do that to me again." she screamed at him. Another soldier grabbed her from behind, wrapped his arms around her and forced her into the bushes.

"Leave me alone," she screamed at him. "Do you have no respect?" She fought him as hard as she could, but she wasn't strong enough to fight him off.

Another came up to Marika and tried to kiss her. She turned her head from one side to the other trying to avoid him. Behind her, a man's husky voice said "I'm going to be the first with this one."

"Please no," She begged. "Please don't do this to me."

"We should flip a coin to see who is first. I am sure whoever wins will be the first man she has known."

Marika watched as two of them dragged Maria into the bush. All the time she begged the men "Please don't do this."

Suddenly Maria heard a voice she recognized. "Jesse?"

"Yes, come quickly. Cry out as though you are being hurt."

Maria didn't have to pretend. She continued to whimper, "Please don't hurt me."

Marika and two of the soldiers appeared at her side, but Maria was so frightened that she couldn't understand what Jesse was trying to tell her. He took her hand and led her through the trees into a clearing where a truck was waiting. The three of them crawled into the back, and a tarp was thrown over them

"Forgive me Mother, those men are with me. We had to make it look and sound real, so that if there were any Brown Shirts hanging around they would think we were one of them. I didn't mean to frighten you."

Two of Jesse's soldiers walked out of the trees back onto the road and adjusted their pants. "Now that was worth it," one commented to the other. "Even the old lady had a lot to offer, although she put up quite a fight. I will have scratch marks on my back for days. I could use a drink after that. I am sure the others will want the same, after they have taken taking their turns."

In the back of the truck Jesse had one arm around Marika as she lay with her head on his chest, sobbing. The other he placed around Maria's shoulders and drew her close to him. She still shook and whimpered from the encounter. As the truck travelled through the dark night he held them both tight in his arms.

CHAPTER THIRTY NINE

After the massacre and destruction at Nurnberg, Mark moved the survivors to the village of Johli, located on a direct route to the border of a neighboring country and freedom. The Brown Shirts patrolled the border with orders to shoot anyone caught trying to sneak across.

Many, who thought they had nothing more to lose, risked their lives to escape Heinrich's tyrannical rule. Several of those shot while trying to escape, were brought back to Mark to care for. Conditions were harsh under Heinrich's rule and for many, especially the Believers, escaping was the only means of surviving.

Mark was the only doctor for miles around. He and Elizabeth worked in cramped quarters and were constantly short of room and medical supplies.

One day Gustave Olesson, a wealthy merchant in the village invited Mark to come to his office. "I am leaving," he said, "and taking my family away from here. My business here is failing and if we stay, I fear for the safety of my wife and daughters. I have business interests in the south that I can rely on, and where the Brown Shirts are less active."

Handing Mark a set of keys he added, "I have a small warehouse on the edge of town which I thought you could use as a hospital. There is no use in letting it deteriorate while I am away. You are free to use it until I return."

Mark was surprised. Gustave was considered a miser, a man who never went out of his way for anybody unless there was a profit to be made. "Thank you," Mark replied, "But I don't understand."

Gustave replied in a gruff voice. "Most people think I am a hard hearted and cruel man, and in many ways, they are right. Day after day I have watched you dedicate yourself to helping the people of this area, making do with what space you have. You need a place to set up a proper hospital far more than I need another empty building."

Then, in a surprising move, he took his pen out of his pocket, drew the sign of the Believers

≤ ≥= on a piece of paper and handed it to Mark. "I am one of you, and this is the least I can do to support Jesse and his cause."

Retrieving the paper from Mark's hand, he lit a match and burned it. "Nobody must ever know. I have family members deeply involved in Heinrich's organization."

Mark's eyes filled with tears. "Thank you Gustave. You have no idea how much this means to us."

The two men shook hands. As Mark turned to leave, Gustave added, "Be sure to pay attention to the cellar shelves. They are a good place for storage."

From there, Mark walked to the warehouse, unlocked the door and went inside. It smelled musty and needed a good cleaning, but was more than adequate for his needs. He located a light switch and opened the door to the cellar. The stairs were steep. At the bottom he found a room lined with shelves along three sides. The single light bulb in the middle didn't provide much light, but Mark could see well enough to inspect each shelf. He tried to understand why Gustave had made a special point of mentioning this to him.

Then he noticed that the set of shelves at the far end of the room appeared narrower and more forward from the rest. With his curiosity aroused, he walked over to align the shelves with the other, and noticed something seemed to be out of place behind them. Giving the shelves a tug, they swung open to reveal a small room hidden behind.

This must be what Gustave wanted me to find. There is a hidden room. I wonder what he used it for and why he had he built it?

Running his hand along the inside wall, he found a light switch that turned on a dim light. The room was roughly eight feet by eight feet, big enough to hide one or two people, if necessary. In the middle there was a table, two chairs, and two cots along the side walls.

Turning off the light, he pushed the shelves into place, then left to find Elizabeth. "Come with me," he said to her, "I have something I want to show you."

As they walked to the warehouse he explained what Gustave had done and why. He held back the fact that Gustave was also one of the Believers.

Elizabeth was excited when she entered the warehouse. "Oh Mark, this is exactly what we need. We can easily convert it into a hospital. It won't be perfect, but it will be far better than what we have now. I can ask the ladies from the village to help me clean and get it ready."

"That's not all Elizabeth; I want to show you something." He took her hand and led her down the cellar stairs. She watched as he moved the shelf out of the way to reveal the hidden room. "If we had to, we could hide somebody in here or anything else we may wish to keep secret. If the Brown Shirts come down here they would have to inspect every shelf to notice the difference."

Within two weeks the women of the village, under Elizabeth's supervision, turned the warehouse into a hospital. They whitewashed the walls and scrubbed the wooden floor until it shone. They used ropes and old bedsheets to hang between the beds to provide a degree of privacy. The front office was turned into Mark's examining room. Some of the villagers donated tables and chairs, others old bed frames, mattresses and bedding.

Elizabeth was pleased when they finished. It was crude, but more than adequate to serve their needs. There was a small kitchen at the back, and some of the women decided they would take turns using it to prepare meals for the patients. A bathroom with a single toilet was located behind the kitchen.

Because of its purpose, and the fact there would be people always coming and going, the hospital quickly became an information center. Trusted people left messages for Jesse, and coded messages for the Believers. Others passed along information on the activities of the Brown shirts. Still others told stories of people starving to death in the indoctrination camps, and of the mass killings and deportations taking place in the towns and villages. All of this information was passed onto the resistance.

On one of their frequent raids on the Brown Shirts, the resistance stole several radios. Mark was given one which he hid in the secret room, and used it to pass along any pertinent information he received.

CHAPTER FORTY

Late one evening Mark was sitting by the side of a frightened young girl about to deliver her first child. He was concerned because she wasn't much more than a child herself. Earlier Elizabeth had checked each of the other fifteen patients, and gone down to the cellar. This was the night she contacted the resistance with what information they received over the last few days. Most of it was routine information, but once a week she checked in to let them know they were still safe.

Mark examined the young girl again. Her contractions were getting harder and closer together. *If Elizabeth doesn't come back soon, I am going to have to go and get her. This child is nearly ready, and I am going to need her help.*

Suddenly the front door of the hospital burst open, and dozens of Brown Shirts, with guns in hand stormed in. Each moved to a predetermined position around the room.

"Who is in charge here?" a man bellowed as he strutted in the door. He was a short heavy set man, with his gun belt riding beneath his abdomen. He had a dark mustache and piercing blue eyes which seemed to be looking in all directions at once.

Mark stood up, "I am" he replied. "What do you want?"

"I am Commander Igor Pauley. Where is it?"

"Where is what?" Mark answered, "As you can see this is a hospital, and you are disturbing my patients. I don't know what you are looking for?"

"We have been tracking an illegal radio transmission in this area for several weeks. We know it's coming from here. Turn the radio over to me immediately, and nobody will get hurt."

"I don't know what you are talking about. There is no radio here."

The commander strutted over to Mark and punched him in the abdomen. "We know you have a radio here, it was transmitting even as we drove up."

Mark tried not to panic. *What is Elizabeth doing? I hope she can hear the commotion and hide. I have no way of warning her.*

Just then the young girl screamed in pain, "I can't take this much longer. Please make it stop."

"I need to go to her." Mark said, turning to move to her side, "she needs my help. This is her first baby."

"Stay where you are," he barked, then to one of his officers he added, "Get those patients out of those beds, and force them to stand at attention at the foot end. I will ask each one of them to tell me where the radio is. The rest of you tear this place apart until you find it."

The young girl screamed again, "somebody please help me."

The Commander pointed his pistol at Mark, "move and I will shoot you."

Mark looked on helplessly as his patients were routed out of their beds; some so weak they could barely stand. He looked over at Joseph Schultz who was refusing to get up. "Leave him. He is an old man and dying from cancer. He is too weak to get out of bed."

Helplessly Mark watched as the Commander nodded, and one of the Brown Shirts shot the old man in the head. "Let that be a lesson to the rest of you. Now do as you were told."

Once all of the patients were standing at the foot of their bed the Commander began pacing back and forth in front of the line of people. He stopped in front of several, yelling into their faces, "Where is the radio?"

Each one replied "There is no radio here. If there is, I don't know anything about it."

One young man, recovering from a gunshot wound in the stomach, vomited blood all over the Commander's shoes and pants.

"Shoot him." A shot rang out and the young man's body slumped to the floor.

"That is what is going to happen to the rest of you if you don't start telling me the truth right now." Turning to the next man in line, "you will be next if you don't tell me what I want to know. Where is the radio?"

Behind him Mark heard Elizabeth's voice. "What is going on here? What are you doing to these poor people? They should be in their beds."

Mark turned to see her coming up from the cellar; her arms filled with blankets and clean linen. A wave of relief washed over him.

Just then the young girl screamed again, "it is coming. I can feel the head. Please somebody, come and help me."

Elizabeth dropped the blankets on a counter top and rushed

to the girl's side. She stared at the Commander, as if to say I dare you to shoot me.

The officer leading the search sent one of his men down into the cellar. After a few minutes he came back shaking his head. "There is nothing here. We have searched this building thoroughly, and we can't find the radio."

"Are you satisfied now," Elizabeth demanded, "or are you going to let this woman and her child die. Even a bastard like you wouldn't go that far."

The Commander turned his gun on Elizabeth, and said to Mark, "Go catch the brat so she shuts up." Then, looking at his men he said "let's go."

The men moved toward the door. Shifting his pistol toward Mark, he said "I know there is a radio here, and I will find it." Keeping his pistol trained on Mark, he backed out the door. "We will meet again."

Elizabeth ran to the door and locked it. Mark turned his attention to the sobbing young woman just in time to watch, as a little girl slid into the world crying.

While Mark attended to the girl and her baby Elizabeth turned her attention to the frightened patients and helped them back to bed. Not a word passed between them. She placed a sheet over Joseph's face. Tugging the blanket from the foot of the old man's bed, she covered the young man who lay dead on the floor.

Hours later, when everyone was settled, and the blood was washed from the floor, Mark pulled her close to him, "I was afraid for you."

"I heard the noise downstairs. I sent a hurried transmission that the Brown Shirts were in the hospital, and then closed the shelves tight. It is a good thing we store most of our supplies down there. That gave me the perfect excuse to come back up. I wasn't going to leave you here alone.

Mark, you know they will be back, and they will keep looking," she added, "but we can't let that frighten us. I can't stand by and do nothing. If I do, then the people of my village will have died for nothing.

CHAPTER FORTY ONE

What Heinrich didn't fully understand was that in all corners of his country discontent was growing. The Brown Shirts were out of control and roamed the countryside ravishing the people. Those suspected of being a Believer were beaten on the street, some to their death. Businesses were ransacked and destroyed. Women and girls were forced into alleys and raped. Reports of massacres were received from other villages.

Many of the people in the outer areas, Believers or not, began to oppose Heinrich's methods. The very foundations of their lives were stripped away. More edicts were issued; groups of more than five were forbidden to meet publicly, churches remained closed, and neighbor turned against neighbor. People became afraid to express their views in case they were overheard and reported to the Brown Shirts.

Systematically the farms were stripped of their crops. The food and animals were hauled away to help feed the vast army Heinrich assembled. If the land owner dared to protest, he and his family were killed, and their homes burned.

In the hardest hit areas the people starved and their anger continued to fester. They grumbled amongst themselves, "Heinrich is dining on rich foods and wine, and our children are dying of hunger and sickness."

In many places suspected Believers were rounded up like cattle. Hundreds were forced to move into ghettos and locked behind high fences. Others were forced into cattle cars, and transported to the indoctrination camps. Many of the older men, women and young children died on route from lack of water and food, and overcrowded conditions.

As the skills of the Freedom Fighters grew, other rebel groups joined them. They became better equipped and more organized. Together they inflicted serious damage on Heinrich's forces, but still he refused to take them seriously.

"Soon they will tire of their silly games" he declared. "I have nothing to be afraid of. I am the head of state and of the church and I am invincible."

In the meantime Heinrich reveled in his power. Wherever he went there were huge adulating crowds of people saluting him and calling out his name. Women pushed their babies into his arms to be kissed. Every second baby boy born was named after him.

Thousands, even tens of thousands attended the huge rallies he sponsored. Whenever he rode in his open air jeep, people cheered and tried to touch him. He held the power of life and death in his hands. One word from him altered people's lives forever.

When he heard the first reports of the resistance efforts he publicly scoffed. He often stood on the stage publicly denouncing their efforts. "I am invincible. Let them try. They are like ants waiting to be squashed under my foot. Watch and you shall see what becomes of their efforts."

In his private chambers, Rotter and his Army commanders were alarmed at his attitude. His officers repeatedly informed him of the growing restlessness and open rebellion, begging him to take them seriously. Equipment was disappearing: guns and thousands of rounds of ammunition were being stolen. Radios, tools, and explosives failed to arrive at their destinations. They tried to make him understand that serious forces were at work against him.

He laughed at their efforts, "you will s nothing will come of this. These so called freedom fighters are wasting their time."

"Sir," his secretary said one day," we are receiving word of incidents in all parts of the country, trains switched to the wrong tracks, tires slashed, arms and ammunition stolen from the armories. Today I received a memo from Sig Rotter, wanting to know what he should do. He asked me to bring this to your fullest attention."

Heinrich laughed at him. "Why are you bothering me with this? I have told you a hundred times it is nothing serious to worry about. These are scattered idealists; nobody dares stand up to me."

Repeatedly Heinrich's officers tried to keep him apprised of the many incidents. Unchallenged the resistance grew stronger, bolder and better organized. Still he refused to consider the idea that there were people who opposed him and his actions.

All of this changed the day Rotter came to him. "Sir, I have received word that Commander Rudolph and his troops were attacked this morning. He and his aides died when their jeep was blown up. Our men fought back bravely and managed to kill some of the attackers, but most got away. My men are searching for them as we speak.

Heinrich turned to him "Commander Rudolph? Who is responsible for this outrage?"

265

. "The men we killed all wore the yellow star of the Believers. We believe there is an organized resistance movement in that southern area."

"How could this happen?" he raged at his officers. "Why didn't you tell me how serious this threat had become? Call my officers to meet with me immediately."

"Sir, we have been trying to tell you for months about a growing, country wide resistance movement. At first it was small minor things, but because of your inability to act, they have become better organized. Just yesterday a train filled with soldiers was derailed, twenty-seven were killed, and ninety were injured. Our main supply line to the north is cut off until we can get the mess cleaned up."

"Do you have any idea who is behind this, besides Jesse? I know he is the one responsible. On one hand he preaches about love and forgiveness, but on the other he is out to destroy me."

"We know the resistance movement started with the Believers, but has escalated beyond that. Ordinary citizens are joining the resistance; some are calling for a revolution to depose you."

"I will make a statement, one that shows I mean business, and will make people afraid to rise against me. I will not tolerate any further civil disobedience. Is that clear?"

"Sir, as yet we don't have a situation we can use as an example."

"Then we will manufacture something," Heinrich replied, coldly.

Calmly Rotter looked at him. "Do you think this is wise? All we will be doing is inciting the resistance to further action."

"Don't stand there and argue with me," Heinrich screamed at him. "Why didn't you, of all people, tell me how serious this so called resistance movement had become? That is your job isn't it?"

"Yes sir." Although Rotter tried many times to make Heinrich aware of the situation, he wasn't about to argue the point now.

"Again you have failed me, but I am going to give you one more chance to redeem yourself. Here is what I want you to do."

Heinrich revealed his idea of a manufactured incident blamed on the Believers and publicly showing what happens to those who rise against him.

"Leave it to me," Rotter replied. "Whatever it is, it has to be big enough that the rebels will think twice. What we do must is make a statement that serves not only as a warning, but as a new policy from now on."

Rotter went to work. He instructed some of his guards to arrest any person who looked like a Believer. Within days a public trial was held, and ten men were declared guilty of conspiring against the government and sentenced to be hung.

Before the week was out, on the front page of every newspaper, there was a gruesome picture of ten dead men hanging from a gallows. The headlines read 'Resistance Leaders Hung' The story went on to read that these men had been tried and sentenced to death for blowing up the tracks, and derailing an army train which killed three hundred soldiers and wounded hundreds more..

Heinrich issued a statement which was included with the

article "My deepest sympathies to the families of my army officers killed in the derailment. Their sacrifice has been avenged. Now it has become necessary to stamp out any interference that endangers the lives of our military and civilians From now on any man, woman, or child caught perpetrating any act of defiance will be dealt with harshly."

Instead of having the desired effect, the campaign against Heinrich increased. It didn't take long to become public knowledge that the men who had been hung were innocent, and that the train derailment had killed twenty-seven, not three-hundred as reported.

Heinrich publicly hung a medal of honor around Sig Rotter's neck, congratulating him for the swift apprehension of the men responsible for the killings.

CHAPTER FORTY TWO

Exuberantly Heinrich walked away from the large outdoor stage where he had spoken for the last hour. The crowd in the background was still chanting his name "Heinrich, Heinrich," as he walked briskly to the waiting cavalcade of jeeps. As usual, Sig Rotter waited for him as he left the stage.

"See how they love me," he boasted. "Heinrich, they call out over and over. They run up to my jeep and try to touch me."

"You need to be more careful who you let get close to you. There are many who would like nothing more than to see you dead."

"Now you are talking foolishness Rotter. This shows you how much they care for me as their Leader. Who would want to see me dead? You tell me."

"The resistance for one."

"We have nothing to fear from them. They are like little boys trying to get attention by making noise that's all."

"Heinrich, you need to understand that they are serious and their movement is growing. While you scoff at them entire secret networks are being built. At first the groups were formed by the Believes but now we think many of the discontented citizens are joining them. The longer you do nothing, the greater the problem will become."

The two men stopped beside Heinrich's open air jeep. "Who

do you think is behind this so called resistance?"

"Jesse's men." Rotter replied.

"Then we have absolutely nothing to be afraid of. The sooner we put a stop to Jesse, the sooner this foolishness will end."

Rotter put his hand on Hienrich's arm to stop him. Irritated Heinrich shook it off. "You must listen to me. This problem isn't going to go away; it is only going to get bigger."

Heinrich turned to his driver and said "it's time to go." Then turning back to Rotter he added, "You worry too much. You wait and see this will amount to nothing."

Rotter got into the next jeep. *You stupid stupid man, whatever happens today you have coming.*

* * *

Heinrich felt the pain in his shoulder before he heard the sound of the rifle. As he collapsed onto the floor of the moving vehicle, a second bullet struck his driver in the back of the head. The jeep swerved to the left, careening into the crowd before coming to rest against a store front. People all around him screamed.

Immediately Brown Shirts converged on the jeep. Hanging onto the back of the seat in front of him Heinrich pulled himself to his feet and stood up, with a glazed look in his eyes. Blood was streaming down the front of his uniform.

Sig Rotter, who was in the jeep immediately behind Heinrich's helped his men drag the wounded man to his car. The crowd on the street stood in shocked silence. One Brown Shirt attended to the driver, ignoring the civilians lying on the ground.

The legs of a child poked out from under the back of the jeep.

"To the hospital," Rotter screamed at his driver.

"Sir, are you okay" he asked bending over Heinrich. Opening Heinrich's jacket and taking a handkerchief from his pocket, he began to apply pressure to the wound.

"Faster," he yelled at his driver. Already the handkerchief was soaked with blood.

The driver screeched around a corner throwing Rotter off balance, then stopped in front of the Bern hospital. He ran inside. "Heinrich has been shot" he bellowed.

Instantly people came running from all directions. Two grabbed a stretcher and ran outside. One lifted Heinrich's legs, the other his head and shoulders and unceremoniously, transferred Heinrich onto it.

Immediately taking charge of the situation, Rotter yelled at his men, "surround the building," "Nobody goes in or out until I say so."

A furious Rotter yanked the heavy glass door open and strode inside. *How could he have missed at that distance? It was a wide open shot, now there is going to be hell to pay. If Heinrich was paranoid before, he will be worse now. It will be a long time before we get this opportunity again. Damn!*

He marched down a hallway and approached a guard, standing outside treatment room four. "Is he in there? Is there any word yet on how serious his wound is?"

"Nothing yet sir but I was told to let you in as soon as you arrived."

271

When Rotter went through the door Heinrich was pale and shaken, but sat on the side of a cot, his left arm in a sling. He could see Heinrich was furious.

"Sir," he said.

"I want you to catch whoever did this immediately. I want him hung, and his body left to rot, so others can see what I do to traitors. I demand you find some answers. Go on the radio and announce that anybody who has information about the attack has twenty-four hours to turn the traitor in. After that, I will execute ten people every hour until I find out who is responsible.

I know who is behind this plot. It is Jesse and his worthless trouble making band of Believers. You do whatever is necessary to bring him to me. Do you understand?"

"Yes sir," Rotter was pleased. This was going better than he thought it would. *I assumed he would blame the resistance, but blaming Jesse is even better. It will be easy to feed Heinrich's anger and successfully divert any suspicion away from me. This was too easy; it's just too bad we failed.*

Saluting Heinrich Rotter turned and walked out of the hospital. He pulled one of his men aside. "Get hold of Otto Gramler and have him meet me under the South Bergen river bridge at five o'clock."

CHAPTER FORTY THREE

At five o'clock that same afternoon Sig Rotter drove a down a side road that branched off from the highway which crossed the south Bergen River Bridge. He parked his car where it couldn't be seen, then made his way carefully through the tall weeds and deep grass down the embankment to the river where Otto Gramler waited for him

When they were face to face, Rotter shrieked at the man, "What happened? How could you miss? It was the perfect location; all you had to do was shoot straight. He was the perfect target."

"What can I say?" Gramler said, attempting to defend himself, "Just as I pulled the trigger Heinrich moved to the right."

"Did anybody see you?"

"No. Next time I won't miss," Gramler replied bravely. He saw that Rotter was extremely upset. Now his only wish was to get away from the man in front of him.

"There isn't going to be a next time for you." Rotter said, as he pulled a gun from his pocket. Before Gramler could utter a protest, Rotter shot him between the eyes. He dragged Gramler's body under the bridge where he was sure it wouldn't be seen from the road, and then tossed the gun into the middle of the swift flowing river. Frantically scrambling on his hands and knees, he climbed the embankment, got into his car and drove away.

As soon as he was back in his office he called his two most trusted men to him. "Otto Gramler is dead under the south Bergen River Bridge. I want you to change him from his uniform into peasant clothing, and make sure there is a yellow cross on the front of his shirt so that everyone can see. Wait several hours, then take the dogs and discover him hiding out. Your story is that he tried to attack you, and you shot him. Create a scene so anyone travelling on the bridge gets the idea that something important is taking place.

When you have finished come back here. Then I will contact Heinrich, and tell him we caught the man who tried to shoot him. Unfortunately he fought back and was killed."

When his men returned, and he was sure that his plan was successful Rotter phoned Heinrich at his home. "We caught him sir. We found him hiding under a bridge. With a little persuasion he admitted that he shot at you. Unfortunately he tried to attack one of the guards and was killed. We are sure he was one of Jesse's Believers. He wore a yellow cross on the front of his shirt and a crude map of the parade route was found in his pocket."

He listened to Heinrich for a few moments, and then replied, "I will have a full report on your desk in the morning. As we speak I have men on route to arrest his family and friends. First they will be taken to Duvenvald prison, and then they will disappear into one of the camps. I am sure one of them will know who his accomplices were."

When he hung up Rotter smiled smugly, *that takes care of that. There will be a next time Heinrich, and I will not fail. Soon I will be the leader of this country.*

CHAPTER FORTY FOUR

The assassination attempt and its possibility of success proved Heinrich wasn't as invulnerable as everyone thought.

Some of the students attending the University of Bern, who initially backed Heinrich's government and movements, were beginning to have second thoughts. Small groups of students met secretly as unrest built among them. Their initial beliefs that Heinrich would be good for the economy and spur employment gave way to disbelief as they saw their friends and family members arrested.

One group of students made and passed out handbills, another group drew graffiti depicting Heinrich on the walls of prominent buildings. Notices of Heinrich's decrees were torn down as quickly as the Brown Shirts posted them.

Slowly the movement began to grow. The smaller groups joined forces and marches were held on Bern streets. The unions began calling for the workers to participate in rotating strikes. Bern University became the hot bed of an anti-Heinrich movement.

The voices became louder and more demanding. As the students marched bi-partisan, and representatives of other organized resistance groups infiltrated the groups giving them a sense of direction and continuity.

In order to make their point, the students planned a rally on July fifth. Leaflets were distributed throughout the city encouraging mass strikes for that day, and offered the workers an opportunity to join the rally.

By noon five-thousand people gathered in front of government house where Heinrich's office was located. The crowd chanted, waved placards and urged Heinrich to hold an election. As these crowds surged forward, other revolutionary groups captured the mayor's office, and the radio station. When squads of Brown Shirts tried to stop them, the resistance fought back, forcing the Brown Shirts to pull back and regroup.

For two days the revolutionary groups advanced, overrunning and taking command of the police force, and other prominent buildings. Heinrich, trapped in his office, was in a panic and in a rage. *I haven't been able to leave this office for two days. I hope Rotter and his Brown Shirts manage to keep the rebels out. If they find me here, I don't know what they will do. I am the head of this country and the church, how dare they treat me this way?*

During the evening of the second day, when the streets appeared quieter, Heinrich sent a message with one of his aides to the Brown Shirts who guarded the building. "Tell them to find Rotter and bring him here as soon as possible."

Several hours later, Rotter, dressed in civilian clothes, appeared at Heinrich's office door. "You sent for me? Are you aware I could have been killed trying to get here?"

Heinrich turned to him, "I want this ended now. I refuse to negotiate with traitors. I want a show of force to put an end to this nonsense. No matter what you have to do I want this over. You have twenty-four hours and no more. Show those rebels who they are dealing with and that I will not tolerate their disrespect one minute longer. If you have to, use the army."

276

On the morning of the third day, the ominous sound of tanks was heard on the city streets. Every road leading from the University to the city center was blocked. Squads of army troops accompanied the tanks, and snipers appeared on the roofs of the buildings. The marchers were trapped.

One at a time, the snipers opened fire, randomly shooting into the crowds below. The marchers panicked and tried to run away. The moans and screams of the dying filled the air -dead bodies littered the street. Some tried desperately to find a way around the tanks, but they too were killed.

Some of the marchers were armed, and fought back as best they could, but they were no match for the better equipped army. Slowly the tanks moved forward, and forced the marchers into a smaller and smaller area in the center of the square. The army walked ahead, shooting or beating any person who tried to stand up to them. The noise, the confusion, and the rising count of dead and wounded bodies were something the city never experienced before.

As the army advanced, the people tried desperately to defend themselves by throwing rocks, swinging broken boards, using anything that could be used as a weapon. In a matter of minutes the insurrection was over. The marchers had no choice but to surrender or be killed.

In a final act of defiance, they sat down where they had previously stood. They watched in silence and horror, as dozens of army trucks lined up at the end of the street and began to force the marchers inside. Those who refused to stand up and board a truck willingly were killed on the spot. The marchers were herded onto the trucks like cattle and driven away.

A few of the protestors tried to run away, but were quickly

gunned down by snipers on the closest roof tops. A few managed to get passed the army that patrolled the streets, and carry word that the students being butchered in cold blood.

The trucks drove to a gully about five miles out of town. The protestors, forced out at gun point walked into a living hell. Bodies of those who tried to run away soon littered the ground. The protesters were forced to march to the gully and line up along the edge.

Some dropped to their knees and begged for their lives. Some prayed, lovers kissed and still others stared at the carnage in front of them. Four men with machine guns lined up behind them and fired. One by one the students fell on top of the other bodies.

When the shooting stopped there was a deathly silence, even the birds had fled. Truck after truck disgorged its human contents, and turned around to go back to the city. Later they returned, once again filled with people. This went on for hours.

As the bodies fell on top of those already dead the gully filled. Those who were not killed outright were silenced by the guns of men who patrolled the bank. The earth ran red.

In the small hours of the morning the last truck filled with Brown Shirts drove away. Moans and voices calling for help filled the air.

Several of the wounded protestors managed to escape and make their way back to the city to get help. Other citizens took it upon themselves to follow the trucks out of town. When the last of the Brown shirts drove away, a crowd descended on the gully.

Armed with flashlights and lanterns they dug through the

dead, desperately trying to rescue the still living and injured. Most of them covered in blood were in a state of shock. Others were heard cursing at what had taken place. As the sun came up, fifty people were rescued. An estimated two thousand marchers had gone to their death. The exact count was never known.

As soon as the tanks and army pulled back from the town center, people rushed into the streets to help those lying there. Most were dead and their bodies were taken away to a makeshift morgue at the nearby hospital where their families could find and identify them. The smell of death and gun smoke hung like a pall over the city.

The next morning Heinrich called a meeting of his officers. He gloated over the success of his strategy which stopped the march. He congratulated them in public and announced on the radio that any further acts of resistance would be halted in a similar fashion.

Heinrich had made a tactical error. Whatever he hoped to accomplish with his display of force had the opposite effect. People, who previously were impartial or indifferent, realized for the first time what their leadership was. All Heinrich had accomplished was to strengthen the resolve of the resistance to destroy him.

PART THREE

THE FINAL SOLUTION

CHAPTER FORTY FIVE

Jesse was in Bern holding a meeting with a small group of followers when a young man burst through the door. His eyes were wild; he gasped for breath and tried to speak between sobs.

Jesse went to him and put his arms around the trembling boy, "Take deep breaths and tell me what's wrong."

"They are killing them," he managed to get out. "They are taking them by the truck load and shooting them."

Jesse put both hands on the boy's shoulders, "look at me, tell me what is happening," he asked. A feeling of deja vu filled him with trepidation.

"The protesters from the University – the tanks – the soldiers – nobody can get away. There are dead people everywhere."

Jesse spoke over the boy's head to Hans Enright, one of his staunchest followers. "Go. See if what he is telling us is true."

Hans left immediately. Jesse led the young man to a chair. 'Tell me what you know."

Hans returned a short time later, his eyes red from crying. "It's true Jesse. There are dead, dying and wounded laying the streets. The army brought in tanks, trapped the students, and mercilessly shot them down. It is horrible.

Those who surrendered are being loaded into the back of trucks and driven away. I heard a rumor they are being taken to the gully north of the city, lined up and shot.

How can this be," he continued, "I know some of the students were unhappy with Heinrich, but did it have to come to this? Why? What is the matter with that man? These students are our future. Is he mad?"

More and more of Jesse's followers arrived, all in a state of shock and all telling the identical story. As Jesse listened to them, he became inconsolable. He stared out the window and waited to hear back from Peter. Jesse had sent him out to the gully to find out what was really happening, and if the stories were true.

When Peter returned, he took Jesse aside. "It is too horrible to talk about. I stood in the trees and watched as they marched a truckload of students to the edge; lined them up, then gunned them down. Some begged for their lives, while others accepted their fate."

Jesse grabbed his jacket from the back of a chair, and headed out the door.

"Come back Jesse. It isn't safe for you to go there. What if someone sees you?"

"Peter don't try and stop me. I must see for myself, not even Heinrich is that stupid."

Peter and Timothy went with him. Jesse practically ran all the way. He said nothing. When they arrived at the gully, the army was gone.

"I will go with you," Peter said.

Jesse stared at him. "I am going alone. Wait for me until I

return."

Peter started to protest, and then seeing the look on Jesse's he said, "We will wait here for you. Be careful."

Jesse walked to the gully alone, his mind on a village far away. He wasn't prepared for what he came upon. Bodies were piled into the gully - arms and legs entangled. People stood at the side of the gully and cried while others searched among the bodies for their loved ones. The stench was unbelievable, thousands of flies hung over the area and wild animals were squabbled over body parts. It was like a scene out of his worst nightmare.

How could this have happened? I have to go to Heinrich and ask him to stop this insanity. Is all of this death because of me?

. When he returned to Timothy and Peter, he was as pale as a ghost. They watched him stop and retch several times on his way back.

"Should we go to him Peter?" Timothy asked.

"No, leave him. He needs time to process what he has seen. This isn't the first time he has been witness to Heinrich's atrocities, and I fear it won't be the last either."

"How does he do it? Why does he keep on going? I would have given up a long time ago."

"I'm not sure. It is his calling, I think. He feels that he must do everything in his power to stop Heinrich. I fear that if he stops now he will go insane."

By the time Jesse reached them, the look on his face said it all. The three of them turned and walked back to town.

Finally, he turned to Peter. "I have to try and put a stop this "

"How Jesse? I'm not even sure that if Heinrich were to die tomorrow, this would stop. I'm sure there are others who would step in and possibly be worse."

"I am going to talk to him. If I have to, I will beg. He has to stop this madness."

"Are you crazy? The minute you get close to him his guards will take you prisoner."

"I don't think that will happen. I am sure he will let me walk away for the simple reason that he always has to win. Victory for him will be a public execution. If he captured me because I walked into his office that would rob him of his chance to say he finally over powered me."

"I see where you are going with this, but I urge you not to put yourself in that position. If you are wrong, then what?"

"I don't know," Jesse replied.

The very next morning Jesse, in a borrowed black suit and hat, walked into the government building where Heinrich's office was located. He looked like a wealthy businessman on an important errand. He walked past the guards at the front door, up the stairs and stopped in front of Heinrich's secretary. *I am surprised; this is easier than I thought it would be. I was sure after the attempt on Heinrich's life there would be better security than this. I have proven anyone could walk in here.*

Stepping to the front of the desk he announced, "I wish to speak to Heinrich."

Without looking up the secretary replied, "he is busy. Make

an appointment."

"He will see me," Jesse calmly announced.

The secretary looked up and his face blanched. Quickly he picked up his pen and wrote the secret sign $\leq \geq =$ on a piece of paper. "What are you doing here Jesse? Are you crazy walking in here like this? Do you know what he will do to you?"

"I am fully aware of what he would like to do, but nothing will happen. Now take me to him."

Visibly shaking the young man came out from behind his desk, and knocked on the office door behind him.

"Come in," Heinrich's voice came through the door, "what do you want now?"

The young man went into Heinrich's office and closed the door behind him. Seconds later he returned. "He will see you."

When Jesse entered the office Heinrich stood stiffly beside his desk hastily buttoning up the front of his uniform. "To what do I owe this honor Jesse?" he inquired sarcastically.

Jesse stood there and looked Heinrich up and down, with distain written all over his face. "It's good to see you too Heinrich."

He walked over to one of the wooden chairs placed in front of the desk and sat down. Nonchalantly he crossed one leg over the other. He seemed unconcerned about the situation he was in. "Sit down," he commanded Heinrich, "We need to talk."

Heinrich moved to the back of his desk, casually pulled out his chair, and sat down. "You know that all I have to do is pick up the phone and this will be over." he said.

"Go ahead," Jesse replied calmly, "you could, but you won't."

Rather than pick up the phone Heinrich stared back at Jesse. "As always you are so sure of yourself. I give you credit, you have a lot of balls to walk in here like this. What do you want?"

"I went to the gully yesterday. The time has come for you to put a stop to all this killing. It serves no purpose."

Heinrich shrugged. "I had nothing to do with that, the Army is responsible. I don't deliberately give orders to kill people. The instructions I gave were to find you, and subdue the resistance from the Believers."

"Heinrich, you and I both know that very few of those killed were Believers - they were students expressing their opinion. Next week they would have been protesting something different. Did you issue an order to the Army not to kill the students?

"No, why should I?"

"Then you are as responsible as they are. What do you want from me? I am not hurting you. All I am doing is talking to people, giving them boundaries they can live within, and serve God at the same time. Why do you feel so threatened by what I say?"

Heinrich stood up, his face getting redder. "What you preach has nothing to do with it. I am the head of this country and I am the head of the church. You need to acknowledge me as such. Thousands listen to me every day. I am respected."

"You are feared," Jesse retorted. "Your officers lie to you.

288

Those ten men that were hung were innocent of any crime. I have asked around, and only one of them was a Believer. The other nine were fathers, husbands, businessmen, who had done nothing to harm you.

Through the thick door the Secretary could hear them shouting at each other. Officers walking in the hallway stopped and wondered who Heinrich was arguing with. He assured them all was well. "You know he gets a little excited sometimes," he commented to them.

Inside the office, Heinrich and Jesse stared at each other across the desk. "I am asking you to stop this madness," Jesse pleaded. "Stop killing innocent people. Stop sending them to the camps because they believe in something different than you. Let the citizens live without having to look over their shoulders, always wondering if someone is going to turn them in, because they dared to express an opinion."

"I will on one condition." Heinrich replied, "You will stand beside me and publicly acknowledge I am the head of the church, that my doctrine is correct, and that you were wrong to oppose it."

Jesse stood up. "You know I can't do that."

Heinrich moved out from behind his desk, his fists clenched. "Then anything that happens from now on is on your head. When you give me your obedience, I will stop, and not before."

Jesse looked at him sadly, "neither one of us is going to survive this conflict. I will be remembered for showing others a better way to live – one of peace, harmony and love. When people remember you, they will curse the day you were born."

Jesse walked to the door and opened it. Turning to face Heinrich he said "I will pray for you."

Heinrich began screaming at him. "Don't you dare walk out of here? I'm not finished with you yet. You get back here you snivelling coward."

Closing the door behind him, Jesse calmly walked down the hallway. He could still hear Heinrich ranting in his office. He walked down the stairs, passed the guards, and out the front door. Taking a deep breath he pulled the brim of his hat down and hurried down the street before anyone recognized him. Peter and Timothy were waiting for him at the entrance of the closest alley.

"How did it go Jesse?"

"Just as I expected, he won't listen to me, but I had to try. There is only one way this is going to end and I hope God gives me the strength and courage to do what I have been called to do. I hope I haven't made things worse."

CHAPTER FORTY SIX

Fear began eating at Heinrich from the inside out. *How dare somebody try to kill me? I am the supreme leader of this country. Resistance attacks, riots, – it will take more than that to get rid of me. Don't they realize I have put my all into doing what is best, why would they turn against me?*

I know this is all because of Jesse. What a fool I was to let him walk out of here that day, now he is not afraid of me. What if he becomes more powerful than me? What is going to happen to me if he gets control?

The wound in Heinrich's shoulder healed quickly. Other than a puckered scar, there was no permanent damage. Yet, to Heinrich, he was in unbearable pain. So much so the pain kept him awake at night.

His doctor gave him a strong sleeping medication to counteract the pain and help him sleep, but this left him groggy in the mornings, unable to function. Then the doctor gave him medication to take in the morning that would keep him awake and alert during the day

It wasn't long before the drugs began to take their toll. He became convinced that somebody was stalking him, and that Jesse was poisoning his food. His public speeches turned into rambling discourses which made no sense.

He frequently called meetings with his commanding officers and Rotter, and then incoherently rambled for hours. They became more and more concerned.

After one such meeting, three of the officers took Rotter aside. "You must do something. You are closest to him, he will listen to you. Talk to his doctor, get him off the medication. If the public or resistance finds out he has become a raving lunatic they will quickly use this to their advantage. Already there are rumors he has died or fled the country. We can't allow this to happen. The people need to know Heinrich is still in control.

"What do you want me to do?" Rotter asked. "You see how he is. Even if I did approach him, I don't think he is capable of understanding me."

"We are counting on you to find a way. If not, and soon, all will be lost. We have wives and families to think of. If the Believers or other opposing forces gain control, we won't stay around long enough to be captured, and our families tortured."

The discussion went on for hours. On the surface Rotter appeared reluctant to go along with their scheme, but in his mind was formulating a plan. *I will talk to Heinrich as they asked, and then step in and take over Heinrich's position. I will issue orders in Heinrich's name and, when I am in complete control, arrange for an overdose of the sleeping medication. Once Heinrich is dead, I will name myself his successor.*

"I will do what you ask," he said to the commanders," but if anybody asks, you must deny this meeting took place. No one must ever know. If Heinrich ever finds out, he will have us all executed for treason."

The commanders agreed and left shortly after that. Once he was alone, Rotter gloated. *Stupid fools! They have played right into my hands.*

In a twist of fate, Heinrich summoned Rotter to his office the next morning. When Rotter entered he was surprised to find him more rational than he had been for weeks.

"Sir," he said saluting and standing at attention. "You asked for me?"

Heinrich sat behind his desk, but it was plain to see he wasn't well. His eyes were red and his nose was running. "I did. What has been going on around here? Jesse is still roaming around the countryside. The industrialists are complaining about the poor quality of worker they have been getting. My commanders, when I met with them yesterday, had nothing of interest to report. As a group they are useless, but they still want lots of things- more guns, and more ammunition. They aren't even using what they have, why do they need more? I have a mind to replace all of them, including you. Not only that a small group of our party supporters are threatening to withdraw their support."

"What can I do to help Sir?"

"I gave you one order, to get rid of Jesse and his Believers, and you have failed miserably." Heinrich took a handkerchief from his pocket and blew his nose noisily. "Are you aware that I have several men in mind that will gladly do what you have failed to accomplish?"

Rotter had to think fast. Heinrich had upbraided him before, but this was the first time he had threatened to actually replace him. "You are right," he replied "I offer no excuses. I will work harder from now on. I will put every resource available into capturing Jesse."

"I am giving you one more chance. Get back to me today with a plan. Get rid of those Believers once and for all, and I don't care how you do it. Is that understood? Now get out of here and get to work."

"Sir," Rotter saluted and left. *I had better take him seriously. He's not as out of it as we all think. We are underestimating him.*

Rotter was shaken by how rational Heinrich seemed, but when he went back later that evening with a new plan, Heinrich was once again incoherent.

CHAPTER FORTY SEVEN

Rotter didn't waste any time putting his plans into action. By noon the next day, the commanders received orders in Heinrich's name. They breathed a sigh of relief. Rotter had done as they asked and taken over as they suggested. Once again, they had orders to follow without responsibility for the outcome. Now, if questioned, they could simply say, "I was only following orders."

Over the next few days, the tone of the directives began to change. The first order to the commanders was to compile four lists and forward them to Rotter within a week. The first list asked for the names of any known believers or followers of Jesse. The second, asked for the names of who may have connections with the resistance or other opposing forces. The third, was the names of undesirables – the old, inform, crippled, homosexuals, gypsies and mentally ill. The last was a list of the outspoken supporters of Heinrich. They were instructed to approach the names on the last list and ask for their support when the time came.

Within a few days a new more sinister directive was received by the commanders. They were shocked, but had no options except to follow. Some thought they had traded one mad man for another but kept quiet. To speak out now would endanger them and their families.

The time has come to remove the scourge to our land of Jesse and his believers. On October Thirty-first, at seven in the evening, we will begin to remove all undesirable elements

from our society. We will no longer be divided by religious zealots and opposition. Those who are left will be true followers of Heinrich's doctrines.

1. All believers and followers of Jesse and other undesirables will be removed from their homes, taken to a guarded central location to await transport to the indoctrination camps.
2. Any person suspected to have links to the resistance and/or other opposition forces is to be executed immediately.
3. Believers found not wearing the yellow cross, or anyone caught harboring a Believer fugitive, shall be executed.
4. Property of Believers awaiting transport shall be confiscated immediately. All valuable contents are to be packed and readied for shipment.
5. All money confiscated from those who are transported shall be turned over to the commanders to be used at their discretion.
6. A reward of 3000 Kroners is offered for information leading to the capture of Jesse.
7. Enlist the loyal followers of Heinrich to assist you in this process.

This edict shall be in force from 7:00 p.m. October 31 until 7:00 a.m. November 3. At that time, trains will be dispatched to move the Believers to the camps. Itemized lists of all goods confiscated will be forwarded to me that same day, and then packaged and sent to Bern by November 6th.

Once Rotter received word of acknowledgement from all of the commanders he laughed. *Heinrich will be blamed and I will be a very rich man. As long as Heinrich remains insensible I am the leader. Why, it may even be that Heinrich becomes so despondent that he takes his own life.*

CHAPTER FORTY EIGHT

All Hallows Eve, celebrated on October thirty- first each year, was a night of fun and revelry in the villages. The people gathered in the village square around a huge bonfire, children ran around playing, food and drinks were shared. Later in the evening music was played and everybody danced. At midnight there was a display of fireworks to mark the end of the celebration. The next day, on All Souls day, the villagers paid their respects to the dead by visiting the cemetery and praying.

This All Hallows Eve the wind was chilly but the huge bonfire provided warmth as people arrived. They seemed a little more subdued than usual, but that soon changed as the beer began to flow and the square took on a party atmosphere.

Later one of the villagers described what took place as "all hell breaking loose." Suddenly spotlights lit up the square. There was shouting and explosions as Brown Shirts rushed toward the fire, with guns in hand. The people in the square became very quiet. Mothers pulled their children closer to them. The men prepared to fight, if necessary.

Randolph Lien, the Commander of the nearby village approached the fire. His voce dripped with sarcasm. "Ladies and gentlemen, I am sorry to disrupt your celebrations this evening. Follow my instructions carefully, and then we will leave and let you continue your little party."

Pulling a list from his pocket he added, "As I call out your names, you and your family members, will move to my left and wait there. If your name is not called, you are free to resume your festivities."

Once the first few names were called out, the villagers realized it was only the Believers who were being singled out.

A man's voice called out, "finally we can get rid of this scum."

The people, whose names were called, moved in an orderly fashion. They were in shock. Each wondered what was going to become of them.

One woman, who moved to the commander's left, approached him. "My baby is sick. I must take her home and get the medicine the doctor gave me."

"Get back in line, or you won't have a baby to worry about"

Clutching her baby to her chest, she moved back to stand with her husband and children.

When he was finished the Commander asked, "anybody else wish to join us?' There was silence. "I thought not."

To the guards he hollered, "Take them away."

The Believers, surrounded by armed Brown Shirts had no choice but to begin moving away from the fire.

"Where are you taking them?" a man's voice shouted out.

"None of your business. These people daily defy Heinrich by following the teachings of Jesse and they will be dealt with accordingly. You can go back to your party now."

Slowly the Brown Shirts backed away, leaving as silently as

they had come. The villagers who still remained by the fire slowly returned to their homes.

The Believers were marched to the railway station. There wasn't enough room inside for them to fit, so the last to arrive were forced to remain outside on the platform. A heavy presence of guards surrounded the building.

For two days the group huddled together frequently hearing shots and screams from the village. Toilets overflowed, and the stench of fear and unwashed bodies permeated the air.

Their numbers began to swell as more and more people were forced to join them. First to arrive were the old and sick who had stayed in their homes, instead of attending the bonfire. Some could barely walk, others were too ill to be out of their beds. The women on the platform did what they could, but without food and water and exposure to the elements, some would die.

Those, who arrived later, told stories that any family suspected of having a connection to the resistance, was shot on sight. They tried to understand why their homes were being ransacked and only the items of value were taken, and the rest thrown out into the streets.

Rumors abounded about being shipped to the camps, and the children cried because they were thirsty and hungry. The men plotted how to get away to get help, yet all they could do was wait to find out their fate.

Because their Rotter's orders were not specific each commander followed them in his own way. Some were carried out in a civilized manner, in other towns and villages the dead littered the streets.

On the fourth day the trains began to arrive as scheduled. The Believers were forced into cattle cars and packed so tightly they couldn't move. Those who tried to run away or refused to get in were shot. Some of the trains unloaded their human cargo at the smaller work camps, but the majority were taken to the Jawal River camp and left to die.

On the return trip, the empty cattle cars were filled with the valuables procured from the villages. These goods were then taken to the city of Bern, and unloaded into empty warehouses Sig Rotter had confiscated from the owners.

CHAPTER FORTY NINE

The villagers of Bengenoa were sleeping peacefully in the pre-dawn hours of a Sunday morning. The sun was just beginning to peak over the horizon, and it was going to be another beautiful day. Sundays were a day of rest in the village, spending time with family, and mingling after church.

From out of nowhere the stillness was shattered by the sounds of trucks on the main street. Men shouted, dogs barked, and gun shots echoed in the air.

Abram Rousseau, the mayor, looked out the window and tried to pull on his pants at the same time. To him, it looked like a whole army of Brown Shirts had taken over his village.

"Who is it father?" Joey, his oldest son, asked, "What do they want?"

"Brown shirts, dozens of them. Slip out the back door, make your way to the forest and find the resistance. Tell them we need their help."

Quickly, Joey dressed and let himself out the back door. Within minutes Abram heard gunfire and a scream, and he knew, without a doubt, that he had sent his son to his death. He turned to go to the back door, but saw his wife and three daughters cowering in the doorway behind him.

"Go quickly and get dressed," he told them. "Stay close together. We don't know what they want yet."

Someone pounded on the front door interrupting him.

"Abram?" his wife questioned.

"It will be okay love. Go get dressed, then stay with the girls in the back bedroom."

The pounding on the door continued.

Taking a deep breath, he walked to the door and opened it. "What do you want? I was sleeping, tired from doing a hard day's work yesterday."

The local Commander walked in and looked around. "This place is no better than a hovel. I don't know how you people can live like this." Three guards walked in behind him and stood off to the side, their hands on their guns.

To one of them he said, "Go see who else is here."

Minutes later the guard came back into the room, herding the women in front of him. Abram could see they were terrified.

"Put them over there and keep an eye on them." he ordered. He turned to Abram, "Are you the mayor of this village?"

"Yes," he replied cautiously. "Why?"

"Then you must know everything that goes on here in the village and surrounding area?'

"No, not everything."

"Is it true that this village does a great deal of business with the resistance?"

"I don't know what you are talking about. We are simple

304

people who mind our own business." A sinking feeling was developing in the pit of his stomach.

"Is it true that there is a resistance base nearby?"
"I don't know? Even if I did, I wouldn't tell you."

"Yes, you do know, and you are going to tell us where the resistance camp is located." Walking over to Abram's oldest daughter, a girl of about thirteen years, the commander put his hand under her chin. "Tell me, little one, does your father know where the resistance camp is?"

She started to cry.

"Leave her alone," Abram cried out. "She is a child, she knows nothing."

One of the guards came behind Abram, and hit him across the back. He fell to his knees.

The commander stayed where he was, toying with the girl's hair. Leering at her he said, "Did you know I like little girls, especially virgins. What is your name?"

"Miriam," she answered edging closer to her mother, but he put a hand on her shoulder to stop her.

"Miriam? That is pretty name. Take off your clothes"

"Leave her alone," Abram hollered, "she is an innocent, a child. What would she know of the resistance?"

The commander walked over to Abram. "Tell me what I want to know now. If you don't, I will save her for myself and make you watch. The others I will give to the men outside. They are always willing to take part in the sport I have in mind."

305

"I don't know where the camp is. Once in a while, one or two members of the resistance pass through, but I don't know where they are going or where they are coming from. It is best not to ask too many questions."

Suddenly the commander's demeanor changed. Shouting at his men he ordered, "Take them outside. I have had enough of this stone walling. Go wake up the rest of the village and move them out into the street. Put the women and children in the church and line the men up outside. If we cannot go to the resistance, we will make them come to us, and somebody go shut those stupid dogs up."

Each of the dozen homes in the village was emptied, the women and children herded inside the church, the men and older boys lined up along the side. Surprisingly there was little weeping or wailing as the families were separated. Once all of the women, girls and small children were inside the church, the doors were locked.

The commander paced back and forth in front of the men and boys, "tell me where the resistance is located and I will spare your village."

Nobody said a word. All stared back at him defiantly.

"Go ahead," he said to one of the guards, and several men appeared with flaming torches.

"Stop," Abram shouted out, "are you crazy?" You can't do this."

With one wave of the commander's hand, the men lit the dry grass around the church and watched as it began to climb the wooden walls. Within minutes the men heard banging on the church door. The women inside screamed "let us out."

The commander watched as the flames crawled higher, and then turned and said to the guards "shoot them." One by one shots rang out and the men fell.

The screaming and shouting from inside the church slowly died out as the fire claimed the building.

The commander looked around. There was nothing more for him to do. He ordered his men back into the trucks, and they drove away from the village. The commander did not look back.

Behind him, black smoke filled the air and all was silent.

Within an hour, after seeing the smoke in the sky, a squad of armed resistance fighters made their way silently into the village. They saw the dead men lying in the grass, and the smoldering ruins of the church. Some checked the homes of the village, but no one was left alive. A quick inspection of the smoldering ruins told the story. A crush of blackened bodies was piled up at the door.

"They are all dead," a young man sobbed, "those bastards killed them all. They will pay for this."

Grimly they set about burying the dead. When the task was done, they left the village as quietly as they entered.

Hours later a dirty, sooty, dispirited group of resistance members arrived back at their camp. Each one of them was determined to make Heinrich and the Brown Shirts pay for what they had done. The compound was quiet. Men sat around the fires drinking coffee and grieving as many had friends and family killed in the village. One by one they drifted off to bed. In the silence some could be heard weeping.

In the meantime the leaders met and quietly discussed ways to retaliate. Finally one of them spoke up, "we must wait. They will expect us to lash out in anger but we will do nothing. Then, when the time is right we will make sure they hear us. We cannot bring those poor people back but we can find a way to make their sacrifice stand for something."

Over the next several weeks resistance group leaders developed a plan. They needed to be coordinated in order to hit Heinrich where it would hurt the most – the indoctrination camps.

After his campaign against the Believers was carried out Rotter expected he would have full control of the commanders and their Brown Shirts, but that was not the case.

Roaming bands of Brown Shirts ignored his orders, and took it upon them to act as judge and jury - all in Heinrich's name. Even the smallest crime was punished by death. Nobody was safe. Men and boys were forced to watch as their wives and mothers were raped. Any person who tried to stop them was killed.

Many citizens took to the roads, other hid in the hills to get away from the terror. Chaos reigned over the land. Atrocity after atrocity took place, the worst being the destruction of the village of Bengenoa.

As word of this atrocity got out, delegations of citizens came to see Heinrich, begging him to get control of the Brown Shirts. Party members threatened to withdraw their support if the situation wasn't handled quickly. Rotter did his best to pacify all those who came, but it soon became apparent the tide of public opinion was beginning to turn against them.

CHAPTER FIFTY

As the hunt for Jesse and the persecution of the Believers escalated, the question became where is Jesse? At any given time sightings of him were received from all across the country. He seemed to have disappeared, and yet be every place aat the same time.

Jesse went underground. He moved silently from place to place, meeting with small groups of people in their homes, in barns, or in clearings. He was closely guarded by members of the resistance. With the turn of events more and more people were reaching out to him.

As Jesse spoke to these groups, his message changed. "You must love your neighbor as you love yourself. Forgive those who have turned against you. Don't give up, remain strong. Even as I speak Heinrich and Rotter are destroying themselves from the inside. Their horrific deeds and actions will defeat them in the end. Those who believe will soon be charged with putting the country back together again. Continue to be patient, be kind and when the time comes practice forgiveness. Failure to do so will result in more of the same."

Some argued with him. "How can you, of all people, ask this of us? We can't trust our neighbor, and even our family members could betray us and report us to the Brown Shirts. Have you forgotten what happened to your own family? We should be killing every Brown Shirt we come upon, and their families, because of what they have done. You ask too much. We are in hiding, my family is hungry, and we live in constant fear of being betrayed. If this madness ever ends, how can you expect us to live as if nothing happened? Am I to forgive Heinrich, or walk up to one I know who sided with him and say "I forgive you?"

When Jesse looked around he could see the fear and anger on the faces of the others in the room. "You must make a choice. You can continue to be angry until you die, and allow this to poison your spirit, or for your own peace of mind you can forgive. Neither is easy.

Thousands are caught up in the same situation as you. Not all are against you, even though it may feel like that, they are afraid - just as you are. The same goes for many wearing the uniform of the Brown Shirts, not every person is a crazed killer. Some are good people caught up in a situation they disagree with. Like you, to disobey their orders is to put their family in danger.

I'm not saying you go up to each person and declare 'I forgive you' for the entire world to hear. You forgive for your own sake, so you can put the past behind you, and move into your future. To fail to do so keeps you stuck, and filled with hate and contempt as you are right now. To forgive is the first step in building trust, and as we rebuild our country, we must vow to never allow this to happen again.

I have lost more than I can bear – my parents, brothers, sisters, aunts, uncles, and friends. I too was angry. I wanted to kill those who destroyed my village, but to do that would make me no better than them.

I detest their actions, but I forgive their hearts. At some point they will remember, and have to live with the hurt and misery they inflicted. I have to believe in my God and his teachings, and I am asking you to do the same."

Another man shouted out, "You say this will end soon. How can you be sure? When will this happen?"

"I don't know for sure, but after my death people will turn against Heinrich and this will be over. Even as we speak, a shadow government of Believers, led by Otto Rohm, is ready to step into the void that Heinrich's death will bring."

"Otto Rohm? Is that the same one who was responsible for putting Heinrich into power? After that debacle how can you trust a man like that?"

"He has worked with us for many years. He came to me, asked for forgiveness, and now in exile he is a staunch dedicated follower. Certainly he can do no worse than what Heinrich has done. We have to put our faith in someone."

The men sat quietly and digested what Jesse told them.

Peter came and touched Jesse on the shoulder, "it's time to go. It is dangerous to stay for too long in one place."

Jesse nodded, and as the men began discussing among themselves what Jesse had said, they slipped silently left.

* * *

After they were safely away Peter turned to Jesse. "What is this talk about death? I have never heard you talk this way before. Why tonight? Why now?"

"It is necessary. The force of good is stronger than the force of evil. My execution by Heinrich will be the turning point in this crusade of his. By thinking he has won, he will lose everything."

311

"Why you Jesse? Why not one of us?"

"I have known since the beginning what was going to become of me. After my family was killed, the old man in the white robe told me what was to happen, and that I would be strong enough.

"Jesse…"

"No more Peter. Come we have work to do. Know that I am not afraid, and that I am prepared for the outcome. I don't want to leave you or Maria, and especially not Marika, but it is preordained. I must die so others can live and carry on my legacy,

When the time comes, I ask that you look after Maria and Marika. It is possible they will still be in danger, and I will rest easier knowing they are in your hands. I am entrusting you the two people I value most in this world. Will you do this for me?"

"Yes."

They continued walking through the night. Jesse walked confidently, knowing that all would be well, and Peter felt as though his world was crashing around him.

CHAPTER FIFTY ONE

Over the next few weeks the resistance remained unusually quiet and Rotter gloated at his achievement. *I had to show them who is the boss. I am tired of being on the losing side against the resistance, and as soon as they realized I would strike back, they gave up. But so far, I still don't know where Jesse is.*

What Rotter didn't realize was that he had finally pushed the resistance too far. The only choice he left them with was to strike back in a big way.

The largest indoctrination, or termination camp, was in the Jawal River valley. It was bordered by high hills on three sides, and was heavily guarded. As an extra measure of caution, the prisoners were forced to build a ten foot high barbed wire fence, above the camp.

At the entrance of the camp was a ten foot high steel fence with a large Welcome sign. Two guard posts, one on either side of the entrance, were built to guard the open perimeter of the valley.

The camp was a pitiful sight. Crude huts housed the prisoners. Thousands of starving, emaciated, hollow eyed people were packed into the small area. A thick, black, heavy cloud hung over the valley as the ovens consumed the dead and those deemed not worthy of living. If the wind blew in the wrong direction the guards complained that their eyes were burning. The acrid smell of death floated for miles.

Six miles from the camp a town was constructed to house the

guards, the officers and their families. Built along the railway tracks, it contained all of the amenities of home, and easy access to the nearby cities. There was a theatre, library, cafes, bars and shops. The guards were ferried back and forth to the camp by truck. A visitor wouldn't suspect that a few miles away people were dying for what they believed in.

The rail line was the life line of the town. A spur line had been built by the prisoners to the camp. Over the Jawal River canyon a wooden trestle bridge stood with guard posts on each end. If the bridge was destroyed the closest highway was ten miles from the newly erected town.

The first hint of trouble was a mighty blast that shook the town. An explosion and fire from the direction of the bridge lit up the night. Immediately truckloads of guards raced to the bridge where the resistance waited. By the time the fire fight was over, dozens of guards and several resistance fighters died.

At the same time, while the guards at the camp were distracted by the explosion, another group blew up the guard towers and cut holes in the steel fence. Members of the resistance ran into the camp shouting "get out, get out now. You are free. Come with me if you are able to fight." Those who could streamed towards the unmanned gate.

The last group attacked the base commander's office in the town and quickly gained control of the few guards who remained. Women and children were forced from their beds at gun point to stand in the town square.

After several hours they were lined up four across and marched out of town toward the highway. When they realized what was expected of them some begged for transportation, but were refused. When they insisted, a man from the resistance declared, "You are luckier than the people of Bengenoa. They were burned alive in their church; you still have a chance to live."

Once the area was secure, a convoy of trucks converged upon the camp and ferried the prisoners to the town. Those who were able were resettled into the homes of the guards where food and water was available. Some of the healthier new arrivals helped the resistance move the sick and injured to an area set aside as a hospital.

The few resources of the resistance were exhausted by the needs of the prisoners. An urgent appeal was sent out for food, clothing and medical assistance. Within hours the first train of many arrived and dropped off supplies, and moved the sick and most vulnerable to safety.

At the end of twenty four hours the indoctrination camp by the Jawal River was no more. When the last of the prisoners was evacuated, the buildings were set on fire, the ovens blown up and destroyed. Heinrich received a terse message from the resistance. "Jawal River indoctrination camp has been liberated. This is just the first."

Within hours, rumors and pictures began circulating about the liberation, and the deplorable conditions the prisoners were forced to live in. Many members of the general public and the Army, who discounted the existence of the camps, were now faced with the evidence which forced them to acknowledge the truth.

Jesse was elated when he heard the news. This action marked the beginning of the end for Heinrich.

CHAPTER FIFTY TWO

The desire for power and control was so great in Heinrich that his psyche demanded he put his demons aside and re-emerge into his world.

Slowly he became aware of what was going on around him – the orders he was sure he hadn't given, and the rumors of his insanity. He heard people talking around him as though he wasn't there, discussing things he knew nothing about. In one clear lucid moment, he realized that everything he worked for would be lost if he didn't regain control.

The next day, when the doctor came in to give him his morning pills, he refused. "My shoulder doesn't hurt today, and I slept well last night. I don't need anything this morning." These were lies, but he had to get off the medication and be able to think properly.

"Heinrich, you can't. You need this to keep the pain from overwhelming you again."

'No more pills today, now get out."

He continued refusing all forms of medication offered by the doctor. At first he thought he was living in hell, his body crying out for relief. He finally relented for a small dose at night so he could sleep. He kept up the pretense of being under influence, while taking in all that was spoken around him and who was doing the talking.

The doctor continually cautioned him, "You are putting your

body through too much. You are hurting yourself with your actions. If you aren't going to listen to me, I refuse to sit here and watch you commit suicide."

"Then leave," Heinrich shouted at him. "I don't need you. I have looked after myself all my life and I know what is best for me."

"Heinrich I beg you not to do this," he started to say.

But Heinrich screamed at him, Get out of my sight."

The doctor left shaking his head. In his opinion, Heinrich was determined not to take care of himself, yet he would be the one to suffer the consequences, when, and if, something happened.

Heinrich became increasingly more frustrated. Even though his mind and thinking skills were clear his orders were not taken seriously. Finally, one day in a fit of pique, he called a meeting of Rotter and his most influential commanders.

"I am once again taking charge. I will be the only one giving orders from now on If you are not sure about an order you receive, check with me. I don't like what has gone on during my illness. Because of your inability to see the bigger picture, you have destroyed what little faith the citizens had left in me.

As of right now, I am replacing each and every one of you. Your second in commands have all been notified that you will not be returning and they are to take over."

"You can't do that," they sputtered, all talking at the same time. "How will you manage without us? We have been true and loyal comrades. We have done everything you asked of us, and then some."

318

Without saying a word Heinrich opened the door to his office and nodded. Twenty armed guards walked into the room. Two walked over to each officer, one on either side, and stood there, waiting Heinrich's orders.

"Take them to Duvenwald prison and hold them until you hear from me." To Rotter he said, "I am not done with you yet."

Quickly the guards stripped the officers of their weapons and handcuffed their hands behind their backs. The commanders were in shock. Then, surrounded by guards, they were taken to trucks that waited at the back door.

Within hours, rumors began to circulate that all of Heinrich's top Commanders had been executed for treason, and their families moved to the indoctrination camps.

When Rotter heard what had transpired, he fled the city and stayed out of communication with Heinrich. He shook his head. *Heinrich in one fell swoop has put his Army in disarray and decimated its leadership. I wonder if he is aware enough to handle the fallout from these actions. Now is not the time to push him any further. I am sure he will find me when he needs me again.*

CHAPTER FIFTY THREE

Despite knowing the danger, the resistance leaders still decided to meet. They knew it was dangerous for them to all be in the same place at the same time, but they needed to coordinate their efforts if they were going continue to be successful. Help, in the form of money, men and weapons was beginning to filter into the country from outside sources.

Jesse sent Samuel ahead to make arrangements. The first thing Samuel noticed when he walked into the town was the number of Brown Shirts. He knew some were stationed in the town, but not so many, and he had no way of contacting the resistance to stop the meeting from proceeding.

Immediately he felt the tension in the air. Brown Shirts strutted up and down the streets and stopped people randomly. To Samuel it looked as though they were checking for identification papers. He watched as a young man argued with them. A Brown Shirt came up behind him, pulled his truncheon from his belt and hit him. When the young man fell to the ground two more Brown Shirts beat and kicked him. When they were done, they dragged him down the nearest alley. He shuddered to think what they had done to him once they were out of sight.

"What was that all about?" He asked a man who also stopped to watch.

"There are rumors that Jesse, the leader of the Believers, is coming here. Heinrich has issued orders for him to be captured alive and held as a prisoner."

"Here? Why would he come here?"

The man looked at him strangely, "Why not here? He goes to every other place."

Samuel realized that if he said any more, he might make the man suspicious. Changing the topic he asked, "I am passing through. Can you point me in the direction of a decent place to stay for a couple of days?"

"The Guest House is one of the best. They will serve you anything you ask for," he replied winking at Samuel. "They cater to all tastes, if you know what I mean."

"Then the Guest House it shall be," Samuel answered, winking back at the man before heading off in the direction the man pointed to. *It's not safe for Jesse to come here. There are too many Brown shirts around. Maybe, on second thought, they will never think to look for Jesse in a house of ill repute.*

He found the Inn and went directly into the tavern. It was dark, noisy and smoky. He sat down at the nearest empty table and ordered a beer. Over the next several hours, he watched the comings and goings of those in the tavern. The serving girls would bring the men a drink, money would change hands, and then the man would leave and go up the back stairs. Minutes later the girl would follow. Later the man returned with a smug satisfied looks on his face.

It didn't take long for him to discern who the owner was. After they returned, each girl went to the same woman, and money once again changed hands.

He had no sooner decided to see about getting a room for Jesse and him, when a stranger sat down beside him. He held up two fingers to the serving girl.

"I know who you are," the man said quietly, "you are Samuel, a follower of Jesse."

Samuels's stomach gave a lurch. Immediately he checked to see how close he was to the door if he had to get away quickly.

"What makes you think that?" he replied cautiously.

Just then the serving girl slammed two glasses of beer on the table nearly spilling one. The stranger paid her.

"Watch my hand," The stranger whispered. Then in the spilled beer he made the sign of the Believers $\leq \geq=$. Samuel didn't know whether to believe him or not.

"I am one of the resistance leaders Jesse is coming to meet tonight," the man whispered

Still Samuel said nothing. He still hadn't decided if he could trust this man.

"I have arranged for two rooms for tonight, one for you and one for me. Find Jesse or get word to him that he must not be seen coming into town. At eight o'clock I will leave the fire escape door open for him. Our rooms are on the second floor one on either side of the exit door.

Samuel looked at him. "How do I know I can trust you? What if this is a ruse, and once Jesse is here, you will turn him over to the Brown Shirts?"

The stranger coolly looked at him. "You can't. Give Jesse the following message, 'Olaf owns the big brown bear' and he will come with you. Sit here, finish your beer, and then go find

Jesse. As for me, I plan to enjoy the entertainment offered by the establishment."

Leaving his half full glass of beer on the table, the man walked over to the youngest serving girl, and whispered something into her ear. She laughed at him; wrapped her arms around his waist, and led him up the stairs.

Samuel finished his drink in two swallows and casually walked out the door. He staggered down the street appearing to be drunk, all the while checking over his shoulder to make sure nobody was following him. When he was convinced, he ducked into an alley and left town.

Jesse anxiously waited for him in a farmer's barn two miles east of the town. He whistled as he approached, giving the signal they agreed upon.

Patting Samuel on the shoulder he said, "It's good to see you back. Does it look safe enough to go in?"

"I'm not sure. There are many Brown Shirts in town, far more than we expected, and it is rumored they are expecting you to show up. They are stopping people at random, and checking their identification papers. I don't think we should go."

Then looking at Jesse Samuel asked, "Does the phrase, "Olaf owns the big brown bear" mean anything to you. A man sat down with me at my table, and told me to tell you this phrase. He seemed to think I should know you."

"Describe the man who said this to you."

Samuel described the stranger in as much detail as he could, and the fact he had written the secret sign of the Believers in the spilled beer on the table. "He said to tell you to be very careful about being seen, and to come up the fire escape. He will leave the door open, and you should come around eight o'clock. I still don't know Jesse. After he left me, he went upstairs with one of the serving girls. That struck me as odd."

"Was she short, with long red hair?'

"Why yes. Do you know her?"

"That is Trudy, his youngest sister. She works there as a serving girl, but not as a prostitute. She helps gather information for us, and passes along messages. The Brown Shirts always talk too much when they are drinking, or when they are bedding one of the girls. The owner is also one of us."

Samuel and Jesse waited until the supper hour before making their way into town. Both dressed in stained coveralls and straw hats and easily blended in with the workers returning home from the fields. When they got to town, they slipped into the alley behind the Inn, to see if they were followed. There they waited in the shadows until it was time to go in.

At eight o'clock, Samuel went up the steps of the fire escape to make sure the door was unlocked. He checked the hallway to be sure it was empty, before he motioned Jesse that it was safe to enter.

It was quiet, much too early for the rooms to be filled with the serving girls and their guests. Samuel knocked softly on the door overlooking the alley. It opened, and both went in.

There were five people in the room. No introductions were made. Jesse told him earlier, the fewer names a person knew, the less chance of betraying others if you were caught or tortured.

Samuel remained by the door listening for noises in the

hallway. He didn't pay much attention to the orders Jesse gave the resistance leaders or to the quiet discussions that followed.

As the evening wore on, he became more aware of the different sounds of the Inn. The walls were thin and every sound carried - cries of satisfaction, swearing, and the occasional scream when someone was hit

.   At first, he thought he was imagining the sound of fingernails scraping across the door.   Then he heard a woman's voice say, "Why Sargent, I think you have had far too much to drink. Let me help you to your bed." The man's answer was undistinguishable.

"I don't know why you brought so many of your friends with you tonight" the female voice continued, "it will be all my girls can do to accommodate each and every one of them. There are just too many." Then he heard the Sargent mumble something again.

"You go in and get yourself ready for me," she replied, "I'll be back in a minute. I want to tell my girls that I don't want to disturbed for any reason."

Then through the door Samuel heard the female voice say softly "Brown Shirts – dozens of them outside."

Samuel crossed the room quickly. "Turn out the light, I need to look outside." he said to the men in the room. "Something isn't right."

The light was extinguished, and Samuel moved a corner of the curtains aside and peered through the dirty window. He saw men gathered in the alley, clustered around the back door and fire escape. Acting on instinct, the men formed a circle around Jesse to protect him.

Jesse whispered to them. "You have each been given a part of the plan. Don't worry about what you hear, or what happens to me. It is meant to be. Your role is to help those who can't help themselves, and soon you will be needed more than ever. I have sent a message to Otto Rohm and he knows what to do, and when to put his part of our plan into action. Go with God and be safe."

Unknown to most of the resistance leaders Rohm had been one of his earliest and most dependable followers. They often discussed with him what the country would need after Heinrich was defeated.

Rohm, and several of his advisors, were forced to leave the country when Heinrich won the election and formed a shadow government. Realizing the mistake he had made helping Heinrich he asked Jesse for forgiveness and offered to help. He crossed the border several times to meet with Jesse. When the time was right, his government would return, seize command, and try to put the country back together again.

Quickly the men gathered their papers, stuffing them into the fronts of their shirts and rolled up the maps. Olaf stepped out into the hallway, and lurched and bellowed as though he was drunk.

"Trudy, where did you go? I paid for the whole night. Bring me some more beer, and get your pretty little ass back here."

Soon they could hear him in the tavern below. "Where did she go? I paid for a whole night and I am going to get what I paid for. You come with me," he said, grabbing one of the other girls, around the waist, "you will do instead. If she comes back, I can handle both of you for one night."

All was quiet for a time and then Samuel heard him again in the hallway. "What's your name honey?"

"Esther," she answered.

"Esther," he repeated, "that's a nice name. My room is at the end of the hallway on the left side. Be a good girl and don't make me have to chase you like I did the other one. When I get my hands on her she'll be sorry."

. There was a noise at the door, and the sound of a key in the lock. Olaf and Esther entered. Instantly Olaf was sober. "This is Esther. She is one of us, and the owner of this fine establishment. She is going to help Jesse get away."

Esther's gaze passed over the men. "The Brown Shirts found out the resistance leaders were meeting, but they don't know Jesse is here. You have to get out of here now. The room next door has an access to the roof through a trap door in the ceiling. Once you get to the roof the buildings are close enough that you can escape."

Trudy left the door unlocked, and on my instructions, the serving girls are passing out free beer. Go now, before it is too late."

Three of the men left, one after the other. Olaf, Jesse and Samuel were the only three left in the room.

Esther, with tears in her eyes, dropped to her knees in front of Jesse Taking his hand she pleaded, "Forgive me Jesse. I have been a sinner."

He reached down, pulled her to her feet, and kissed her on the cheek. "God will forgive you. You have put your life in danger for your beliefs. Spread the word Esther, God forgives and loves us no matter how much we have sinned."

The voices in the tavern became louder. They could hear someone in the tavern taking command and giving orders.

"You must get out of here before they come." Esther said. She opened the door and peaked into the hallway. "It is clear, go now. Olaf, undress and get into the bed."

While saying, this she removed her dress and rumpled her hair. In an instant she looked like a woman who had just climbed out of bed.

Jesse and Samuel slipped across the hallway - and none too soon. They heard footsteps marching up the stairs, and then the door of Esther's room forced open.

Esther and Olaf were in the bed, him lying on top of her. When the door opened, they both appeared stunned. "Get out," she said.

Olaf rolled off her and Esther sat up covering her bare breasts with the sheet. "It's hard enough to make a living around here without you brutes forcing your way in, and interrupting his pleasure."

"Did you see any strangers in the hallway? We are looking for five men who will be together."

Olaf, still pretending to be very drunk, grabbed at Esther and tried to pull her back down on the bed. She slapped his hands away. "As you can see I have been busy. I don't know what I was thinking when I accepted his payment for a complete night. At the rate he is going I won't be able to walk in the morning."

"If you see or hear anything unusual, report it to me immediately." The Brown Shirt said, and then added, "If this guy doesn't please you, I will be glad to take his place, if you know what I mean."

The other men standing in the hallway snickered and made rude comments. As he closed the door he heard the bed creak and Elizabeth say, "I hope we don't get interrupted this time."

Jesse made his way to the roof top. The others long since dispersed, were on their way back to where they came from. Samuel could hear the Brown Shirts ordering people out of their rooms.

Then he heard the Sargent demand, "where is the man you brought up here earlier?"

A woman answered, "He was here when I excused myself to go to the bathroom." Then she began to screech, "Where did he go. He has taken off without paying me. Now, I am left without being paid for my services, as well as, all the beer he drank. Instead of making good money tonight, I am left with nothing." Then she let go a string of curses that would shock anyone who heard them.

Samuel heard enough He closed the trap door quietly, climbed to the roof top, and then motioned to Jesse that they should move. He looked around to get his bearings, and led Jesse from one roof top to the other until he felt it was safe to get down. Hiding in the shadows, they made their way out of town.

Hours later Olaf arrived at the barn, and entered, closed the door behind him. Samuel waited for him. Jesse is gone," he said, "He asked me to tell you he will meet you at the next stop, and that you know where that is. He was concerned about Esther, will she be safe enough here?"

:"She will be fine," Olaf replied. "It is quiet now, the Brown Shirts are leaving town."

"What about our people?"

"All are safe."

The two men shook hands and briefly hugged each other. Opening the barn door, they stepped out into the dark of the night, each walking in a separate direction.

CHAPTER FIFTY FOUR

Of all of Jesse's followers, Eli was the most disgruntled. When he began following Jesse he hoped for prestige and recognition but instead found he was moving from one town to another, and being hunted like an animal.

He also had a habit of frequenting the bars whenever he was close to a town. He tried to justify his actions by calling it reconnaissance work, but when he had too much to drink, he complained how poorly Jesse was treating him.

One evening, while sitting by the fire with others from the group, he got carried away. Peter heard him and took him aside. "If you insist on speaking ill of Jesse, then you are going to have to leave our group. He trusts you and depends upon your loyalty for his safety. If you feel so strongly that you are being mistreated, you need to tell him. Nobody is forcing you to stay with us, and you are free to leave any time."

"Peter, I am sorry," Eli said, "I didn't mean what I said, I'm just having a hard day." The last thing he wanted was to be excluded from being in the middle of the action.

Peter must have said something to Jesse because, after several weeks, Eli found he was included more in the discussions and given more important tasks to do.

Rotter had spies in every town and village and Eli's rants hadn't gone unnoticed. In fact his bitterness unwittingly brought attention to himself. The Brown Shirts were quick to draw this to Rotter's attention.

"Good, encourage him to speak out," Rotter told them, "find out what information you can. It will be a pleasure to finally hand Jesse over to Heinrich. Have someone follow him day and night to see where he goes and who he talks to."

Within days Eli felt someone was following him. Whenever he went to join Jesse's group he took extra precautions. He didn't see anyone behind him when he looked but he couldn't shake the feeling. He stopped going to the bars, stopped talking about Jesse and withdrew into himself. As a precautionary measure, he rented a room in a boarding house in case Jesse was captured. He didn't want to be caught with him.

He wasn't prepared for the sound of heavy footsteps coming up the stairs, followed by a pounding on his door. "Eli Jacobs, we know you are in there. Open this door immediately."

Eli was afraid. He ran to the window and prepared to jump but hesitated when he remembered he was on the third floor. He saw the Brown Shirts had the house surrounded. If he jumped, either the fall would kill him, or one of the guards would shoot him.

The pounding on the door became louder and more insistent.

Oh God, what should I do? He heard the many stories of torture and seen the haunted eyes and broken bodies of people released from Duvenwald prison. More than once he heard their screams late in the night.

There was a loud crash, and the old door jamb crumbled from the excessive force. His room filled with men with guns in their

334

hands, all of them pointed at him.

"Eli Jacobs?"

"Yes," he replied, shaking with fear.

"You are to come with me." Two men roughly grabbed him, one on each arm.

"No, I'm not going anywhere," he replied, trying to pull his arms out of their strong grips.

Something hit him in the middle of his back and knocked the breath out of him. He fell forward and landed on his hands and knees. The two men forced him to his feet, tightened their grip and dragged him out the door, down the hallway and down the stairs. He felt his knee twist on the way down. Once outside he was shoved into the back seat of a black Mercedes car.

As the car raced through the streets, he grew more and more afraid. *What is going on here? Who are these men? What do they want and what is going to happen to me.* Eli was afraid of pain, and the thought of being beaten scared him to death.

The car stopped in front of Duvenwald prison. "Get out," a raspy voice demanded. One of the Brown Shirts, who had been riding in the front seat, got out and opened the back door.

Eli was pushed out and immediately looked for a way to escape, but there was none. With so many men with guns pointed at him and a sore knee, he wouldn't get very far.

He was forced through the black, ornately carved, wooden doors of the prison and down a long dimly lit hallway. The small procession stopped in front of a door.

"Wait here," Eli was commanded.

He stood waiting as the Brown Shirt knocked twice on the door, and then let himself in. Eli heard voices, and then the door opened again. Someone gave him a shove from behind and he stumbled into the room, barely keeping himself from falling. Instantly his knee began to throb.

"Eli Jacobs, you always did like to make an entrance." Another voice said, and then added, "Leave him with me."

Eli recognized the voice right away. It was Dieter Schmidt, a friend from his past. "Dieter, is it you?" he asked. "It has been a long time."

The tension slowly began to ease from his body. Dieter was the son of a neighbor when he was a child.

"In the flesh Eli, I heard you were in town, and I wish to renew our acquaintance. Come, sit down," he said, motioning to a chair, "have a drink with me. We can talk about old times."

Dieter walked over to the side board along one wall and poured two glasses of Cognac. Handing one to Eli he asked, "Tell me how you have been my old friend?"

They chatted back and forth for a few minutes, recalling some of their childhood pranks and then Dieter's questions became more pointed. "I hear you know Jesse the Believer. Is that true?"

"Yes, I have heard of him. Why do you ask?"

"I heard he was a good friend of yours, is that true?'

"I have met him a time or two," Eli replied cautiously. He wanted to see where these questions were leading before he committed himself.

Dieter got up from his chair and walked to the front of the desk. Casually he sat on one corner. "I have also been told that you travel with him."

Eli tried to bluff. "Now who would tell you a thing like that? They are lying. Jesse is a religious zealot, why would I be with him? You must remember how I felt about things like that."

Dieter stood up from the desk, walked over to Eli, and slapped him across the face.

Eli said nothing. He didn't know what to do. The man in front of him was a stranger, no longer the youth he once called a friend.

"Now answer me truthfully. Do you know where he is?" Dieter demanded.

"No, he is always moving around. I'm not always told of where he is going and when."

Dieter slapped him again. "You lie. I will ask you one more time. Do you know where Jesse is?"

"No! Even if I did, I wouldn't tell you." Eli sputtered.

A fist caught him in the face. He heard or felt his nose break, he wasn't sure. He tasted the blood filling his mouth. The glass of cognac he was drinking lay on the concrete floor.

Dieter walked to his office door opened it, and gave an order to the two guards who waited outside. "Take him to the interrogation room. You know what to do when you get there."

Two pairs of hands grabbed him again, dragged him out the

door, and down another hallway

"We will talk again later Eli." Dieter laughed, as he closed his office door behind him.

The two guards half dragged, half shoved him down a flight of stairs. One of them unlocked a door and pushed him inside. The pain from his twisted knee became excruciating.

They came in behind him, laughing and talking between themselves. Eli looked around the room – it smelled of fear. The walls and floor were spattered with blood, the smell of vomit and feces hung in the air. A single chair was placed in the middle of the room.

One of the guards stuck his rifle into Eli's back, and forced him to sit in the chair and then tied his arms and feet. Still laughing, they turned out the light and left him in the dark.

Eli didn't know how long he sat there, but it was long enough to hear the screams of a woman somewhere down the hall. He tried not to listen, but the shriek was like something he had never heard before. He couldn't find the words to describe it. He could only imagine what they were doing to her that caused such a sound. Then there was silence.

Eli was afraid of the dark and had been since he was a little boy, and Dieter knew that. The screams and the blackness of the room terrified him. The panic he so desperately tried to hold back overwhelmed him and he screamed, "Let me out of here."

The door opened, and one of the guards stepped in, and buttoning the fly on the front of his pants. "That was a nice sweet little piece of ass. My men and I enjoyed her very much. If you keep screaming like a woman, we are going to do the same thing to you. My men aren't fussy what they stick their cocks into." Then he left, closing the door behind him. Once again Eli was in total darkness.

He began to shiver uncontrollably. After what seemed like an eternity, the light came on and blinded him. Dieter and two men walked into the room.

"Did you enjoy sitting in the dark Eli? I remember how frightened you were as a child."

"You bastard," Eli spit out. "I did just fine. Untie me and let me go. You have no reason to hold me here against my will."

"Of course, you are right Eli, but here you are anyway. When you tell me where Jesse is, I will let you go. I have given you more than enough time to think about what you are going to say. Are you ready to tell me now where we can find Jesse?"

"No," Eli responded.

Dieter nodded, and the two guards who had moved in behind Eli approached and began beating him over the head and shoulders with rubber truncheons. The guards beat him until Eli called out "stop, I will tell you what I do know." Dieter nodded again and the men quit.

"Where is he?"

"I am not sure where he is today, but if you let me go I can find out."

Dieter punched him in the face. The guards untied his feet, dragged him out of the chair and shoved him against the wall. Dieter stood facing him, and then punched him in the groin. Eli crumpled to the ground in a fetal position moaning. The second guard forced him onto his back and kicked him in the same place again. Eli rolled around the floor in agony.

"Now will you tell me?" Dieter asked very calmly.

"I told you I'm not sure. I can find him for you and then take you there."

The guard drew back his foot and kicked him in the ribs. He heard the bones break. "I will I promise. Please Dieter, don't let them hurt me anymore."

Dieter looked at him. "Yes Eli, I think you will keep your word. I have always been able to tell when you were lying." Then he told one of the guards "untie him his hands."

"You do this, and I will pay you handsomely – enough money to get you out of the country. If you fail to deliver Jesse to me within a week, I will bring you back here and show you no mercy. Somebody will be watching you all the time. If you try to run away, they will have orders to shoot. Now, get him cleaned up and take him back to his room."

Several hours later Eli stumbled through the broken door of his apartment. Staring at the calendar on the wall, he saw that only one day had passed, but it felt like a lifetime. He had suffered twenty-four hours of absolute terror.

He lay down on his bed and wept. *I can't go back there. If I do, the guards will kill me. I have given my all to Jesse's cause, but I'm not prepared to give him my life too.*

Three days later he contacted Dieter at his office. "I know where Jesse will be on Tuesday of next week."

"You will take me to him, then?"

"Yes. But Dieter you must understand I can't stay here, I will have to leave. The resistance will hunt me down and kill me. I will need a substantial amount of money and clearance through the border to get away safely."

"So, in the end, you will betray Jesse for money. Everybody has a price. Tell me how much yours is."

"I want the thirty silver kroners Heinrich is offering."

"Done," Dieter replied. "When Jesse is in our hands you will be paid." Then he chuckled, "you sold yourself too cheap Eli, I would have gladly paid three times that amount."

CHAPTER FIFTY FIVE

Within hours of Eli being hauled away by the Brown Shirts, the resistance heard about it and passed word to Jesse. In turn, he sent out a message that his men were to meet him at the cave within two days. Eli was also told to come.

Under the cover of darkness Jesse, Marika and Maria travelled to the burned-out village that used to be his home. Sending the women ahead to the cave, Jesse walked through the village. The smell of death and fire still lingered in the air. As he walked, he recalled the happy days of his childhood home; the eagerness he embraced becoming a minister, and the bitterness he felt at the betrayal of the elders.

He thought of the Brown Shirts and the death and destruction of the village then realized that this was all part of the pattern that had brought him to the place in his life - where he was at today. *I am aware what the future holds for me but it is too soon. I'm not ready for what is coming. I thought I would have more time. Left to me, I would take Maria and Marika and go away from here, to spare them the pain that is coming.*

His wanderings took him through the village to the graveyard, to the mound of dirt that held his family and the many others who played important roles in his life. Somebody, probably from a neighboring village, had placed a simple wooden cross on top of the mound.

Throwing himself spread eagle across the mound of dirt he begged, "Please don't ask me to do this. How can I leave my

343

wife, my mother and my country? There is much I have to do yet."

Tears streamed down his cheeks, spasms wracked his body, "My work is not close to being done yet. If I am gone Heinrich and all like him, will flourish."

Suddenly, he felt he wasn't alone, he rose and turned around. The man in white stood watching him.

Jesse stared at him "please don't ask this of me," he begged. "What will my death serve?"

"Jesse you have known from the beginning that your life will be short. This does not mean defeat for you, and victory for Heinrich, in fact, the opposite is true. Your death will signify the beginning of the end, and your name will live forever. The people will begin to rally and fight back. They will see Heinrich for what he really is."

"You don't understand? What is going to happen to my mother and Marika? Who is going to provide for them when I am gone? How will they live?"

The old man stood quietly as Jesse paced back and forth, alternating between words of anger and trying to find a compromise which would allow him to stay. Finally Jesse stopped in front of him. "Is there no other way?"

"No Jesse, this is how it must be. This is the purpose for which you were put on this earth."

"I am afraid," Jesse replied, "not of my death, but of what Heinrich is going to do to me. I don't know if I am strong enough."

"You will not be alone. I will always be by your side. When you fall I will pick you up. When you cry out in pain, I will comfort you, and when you need courage and strength I will give you all that you need. I will be with Maria and Marika as they mourn, urging them to continue what you have started. Your death will become an instrument of change for the world, and your name will be spoken with reverence."

Jesse looked at the old man sadly, "so it shall be." He drew his shoulders back, stood tall and a look of calmness and serenity came over his face.

The old man gathered Jesse into his arms and held him close. "Your work here will not be done; it's just that you shall be guiding it from a different place."

When the old man released him, Jesse turned, and with a firm and steady step, he left the graveyard and headed for the cave in the hills. There was much he had to do yet before Heinrich came for him.

CHAPTER FIFTY SIX

Marika, worried because Jesse was gone for so long, stood at the cave entrance waiting for him to return. When she saw him coming up the path she ran to him and threw her arms around him.

"I was getting worried about you. Where did you go? Why have you been gone so long?"

Kissing her on the forehead he replied "I am fine my love. I was wandering in the village then I went to the graveyard to visit my family and friends. Somebody put a wooden cross on the top of the mound." Then he inquired, "Has Peter arrived yet?"

"Yes, sometime ago. He asked for you."

"The rest should arrive soon. I want you and Maria to make a large kettle of soup. They will be hungry when they get here. Go tell Peter I am here, and ask him to come to me. I have much to say to him."

When Peter found Jesse, he was relaxing on a large rock outside the entrance of the cave. At first Peter thought he was asleep, but then he noticed his mouth moving ever so slightly. He realized Jesse was praying.

"You sent for me Jesse?" he asked.

"Yes. We don't have much time, and I have much to tell you." Taking a deep breath, Jesse replied, "This is the last time we will have an opportunity to talk like this."

"What do you mean? Are you going someplace?"

"You might say that. Eli has betrayed me. The Brown Shirts will capture me and take me in front of Heinrich. He will have me killed to prove his point and be rid of me once and for all."

Peter grabbed Jesse's arm, and tried to pull him off the rock. Panic and disbelief were written over his face. "We must leave here immediately, and find a place for you to hide. How do you know this has happened? Who told you? Are you just going to stand by and let Heinrich get away with this?"

"Sit down here Peter and I will tell you."

Jesse explained about the visit of the old man in the graveyard.

"I have accepted this is my fate Peter, and you must too. Take Maria and Marika to live with Elizabeth and Mark. They will hide them and make sure they are safe until this is over. After that, please find them a small house to live in and take care of them for me."

Peter was angry, "I am not going to stand by and let this happen. We will form an army – every day there are men coming from all over to join our movement. If Heinrich wants a war we will give him one. Within days we can be ready."

"No," Jesse replied, "I don't want that to happen. Too many have died because of me already."

"Are you crazy Jesse? Then what are we supposed to do, stand by and let Heinrich do whatever he wants, even if it means you are killed? Ten of thousands have died, believing in you. What will they have died for? If the others find out that you knew you were going to die and did nothing to prevent it, what will they think?"

"Don't you understand what I am trying to tell you Peter? I have to do it this way. Do I not preach love and forgiveness? If I raise an army against Heinrich, thousands more will die, and in the end, we will be no better than he is. Heinrich will think he has won, but it will be a hollow victory. My death will be the catalyst for change, and he will be defeated. Even his own soldiers will turn against him."

Then Jesse said sadly to Peter, "Before this is over, even you will deny that you know me."

"Never, I promised to walk by your side no matter what happens. I would put my life on the line for you."

"You will, but I have more important things for you to do. You must take over from me, and spread the word of our God throughout the world. You are to be the person who will unite my followers after my death – they will follow you because they trust you."

Peter looked at Jesse and replied angrily. "I will not allow you to do this. I am going to form an army and we will fight Heinrich. I will begin today to make arrangements to get you out of the country."

Jesse sighed. It hurt to see his best friend in such a state. "Peter please I know how much I am hurting you, but you have to understand. If I am to fulfill the purpose I was born for, it has to be this way."

"Dead is dead Jesse. I don't see how your death is going to make a difference. We need you here, with us."

"Peter, I don't want this any more than you do, but you must

349

trust me. I am passing the responsibility of my ministry on to you. Come, my friend, tonight we will forget what we have talked about, and eat together one last time."

When the last of the men arrived they sat down and ate together. After they were finished Jesse stood up and spoke to them. "I have been betrayed. I ask you not to wage a war against Heinrich if I am killed. Follow Peter, and continue to spread my message." The men listened in disbelief. When Jesse was finished talking they broke into small groups each trying to figure how to prevent Heinrich from getting Jesse.

Taking Marika by the hand he said, "Come walk with me." He led her outside to a flat clearing out of sight of the cave.

"Jesse what is going on? I don't understand what you are doing. Why are all of your men here, and why have you designated Peter as their leader?"

"Marika, my love, Eli has betrayed me and soon I will be in Heinrich's hands. I doubt very much if he will allow me to live."

"Jesse, no," she cried out, throwing her arms around him. "We must leave the country tonight. We can protect you."

"Marika," Jesse replied, holding her tight against his chest, "I can't do that. This is my destiny. To run away now would give truth to Heinrich's claim that I am a coward."

"We both know he will kill you Jesse. If for no other reason, Heinrich will kill you because he can. You are his only opposition; if you are dead there is no one to stop him. Please don't do this. I need you here with me."

"It only appears that way. With my death the people, not only my followers will see how truly evil he is. My death will become a rallying call for all that is good. Heinrich will be defeated."

She began to cry. Jesse held her until she stopped, and then laying his jacket on the ground pulled her down with him. They made love slowly and tenderly, each aware this was probably the last time.

"From tonight we will have a son, and through him I will always be with you. You will call him Jessie. He will continue my work and become a great man. He will become the hope of the world."

He held her tightly as she slept with her head resting on his chest. For this short period of time he was not afraid. As dawn began to break, he woke her up and made love to her again. In that moment, their son was conceived.

"I need you to be brave," he whispered to her, "and don't lose faith. No matter what happens don't let me see you cry. If I do, I may lose my courage because I don't want to leave you. That thought hurts me more than you will ever know. Promise me that."

He helped Marika to her feet and wrapped his jacket around her. "We must go back. I have much to prepare for."

Putting a hand on each side of his face, she stood on her toes, and kissed him. "I will always love you Jesse."

In silence they made their way back to the cave. They walked slowly with his arm around her shoulders, and her arm around his waist.

Maria was waiting for them when they returned. "Marika, go inside. If you don't mind I wish to spend a few moments alone with my son."

"Mother," Jesse said, when they were alone, "I want you to take Marika and go live with Elizabeth and Mark. You will be safe there. I have already instructed Peter to make the necessary arrangements. Marika doesn't know yet, but we will have a son. I wish him to grow up in peace, in a world filled with love."

Maria put her hand on her son's cheek. "I promise I will look after her and the child as though they were my own."

For a few seconds Jesse allowed his brave façade to slip. Maria saw the fear in his eyes. "Mother, I don't know if I can do this. I am afraid."

"I know you are my son, we are too. We have both known that you were born for a special purpose. We must trust in God and follow his will. Whatever the outcome, it will be as it is meant to be." Maria hugged him. "You must go to your men now, they are wondering where you are."

Taking Jesse by the hand, she led him to the cave entrance. "Go now, my son and fulfill your purpose."

Jesse headed further into the cave. Maria walked over to where Marika waited took her in her arms and held her close.

CHAPTER FIFTY SEVEN

With a heavy heart Jesse prepared his men for what was to come by giving those instructions about what to when he was captured. This isn't what they expected when they were called to meet with him.   After he finished, most of them they walked away with tears in their eyes.

"Keep a calm and level head. Don't fight for me but encourage my followers to set an example. To go to war against Heinrich is to be defeated, but to continue to stand against him as we have been will be more effective. Compare our beliefs of love and forgiveness to Heinrich's brutality, and then let each person decide who he/she wants to follow.

Because of my death Heinrich will be defeated. The church will turn against him, his military forces will be weakened by large numbers of deserters and his power will crumble. Go with God, and know that this is not the last time you shall see me. We will meet again."

As most of the dispirited men left Jesse kissed each on the cheek and blessed them. "Go with God" he told each one. When most were gone, Jesse said to those remaining, "Come, it is time."

They barely started down the hill when there was shouting. Brown Shirts with guns appeared all around them. Several of Jesse's men charged the group, trying to open a path for Jesse to escape but the Brown Shirts knocked them to the ground with the butts of their rifles.

One of the men grabbed Marika, and held a pistol to her head. Peter grabbed Maria and put her behind him.

"Stop," Jesse called out. "Let her go and I will go with you voluntarily. You came for me, not for her."

The Brown Shirt holding Marika looked to Sig Rotter and waited for instructions. "Let her go," he commanded.

The guard shoved Marika, and she landed at Jesse's feet.

"Bring the traitor here." Rotter commanded, and a guard pushed Eli forward. "Is this the man known as Jesse?' Rotter asked.

Eli did not reply. Instead he stared at his feet.

"Answer me. I will ask you again, is this man known as Jesse?"

Still Eli remained silent.

"One last time! If you don't answer my question, I will have you returned to your prison cell and you know what that means. Is this the man known as Jesse?"

Jesse looked at Eli and calmly said, "Answer the man. I forgive you for what you have done."

Eli looked at Jesse, tears streamed down his face, "I am sorry." Then turning to Rotter he replied, "Yes, this is the man."

"This is how it is meant to be," Jesse said sadly.

Rotter walked over to Jesse and slapped him across the face. "We meet again Jesse. Heinrich will be very pleased." He grabbed Jesse by the shoulder and dug his fingers into the bone, forcing him away from the group. He snarled, "You are coming with me."

Jesse didn't protest nor did he try to run away. Even when he stumbled and fell on the uneven ground he didn't ask for help. Finally the group of men reached the road where a large black car was waiting for them.

Jesse stopped. Looking at Rotter he said "I will get in only when you let the women go and I see they are safe with my friends. You must also assure me that the minute we leave your men will not turn on them like animals."

"Heinrich has no use for them but I can do whatever I wish. I don't have to make you any promises. You are not the one giving orders here, I am."

"Then I will not get in," Jesse said. "You will either have to shoot me or let me go. I don't think Heinrich will be too happy if you spoil what he has planned for me. Now let the women go."

Suddenly a guard appeared behind Jesse and slammed his head with the butt of his rifle. Jesse fell to the ground unconscious.

"Tie his hands and feet and put him in the car. Leave the others; they will be our witnesses that we captured Jesse and took him alive from here."

"What about the women?"

"Leave them be. They are of no use to us now. You," he said to one of the guards, "go tell the men to let them go. We have what we came for."

Rotter had completely forgotten about Eli. As soon as his

attention had turned to Jesse, Eli slipped away and hid in the rocks.   From his vantage point he watched as Jesse was manhandled roughly into the car. Looking around, he saw Peter help Maria and Marika back to the cave.

Overcome with grief, he stumbled down the hill. *What have I done* he mumbled over and over.

CHAPTER FIFTY EIGHT

When Jesse regained consciousness, he was in the back seat of a car sitting between two Brown Shirts. His hands were tied behind his back, and his feet bound together.

"Oh, I see you are awake finally. It's about time, we are nearly there," one of the men said to him.

When Jesse tried to open his eyes, his vision was blurry and he felt nauseated. Even the slightest movement increased the pain in his head. "Where are you taking me?" he mumbled.

"To Heinrich, where else? He has been looking forward to this day for a long time. He has a special place set aside at Duvenwald prison just for you, a place where nobody will hear your screams or hear you beg for your life."

"That's a waste of his time. No matter what he does to me, I will not change my mind."

"Maybe this will help change your mind." The guard drew back his fist and punched Jesse in the stomach as hard as he could. Jesse doubled over and gasped for breath.

"Or maybe this," the other guard said, grabbing his hair, pulling his head back and punching him in the face. Pain seared through Jesse like a knife. He wanted to scream, but managed not to.

"Leave him alone," Rotter said from the front seat. "Heinrich is going to be very unhappy if he can't talk when we get there. You will get your chance soon enough."

"What have you done with the women that were with me? If you hurt them..." Jesse gasped.

"The last time I saw them they were stumbling up the hill, bawling their eyes out. We left them behind just like you wanted; they were of no value to us, nothing but a pair of camp whores."

Jesse sighed with relief, grateful that Rotter hadn't realized that they were his wife and mother. If what he was being told was true Peter will have already moved them to safety.

No longer afraid, Jesse was quiet during the remainder of the journey. "Thy will be done," he prayed. "I put my life in your hands."

Rotter continued to gloat. "Do you know how much your life was worth to Eli? Thirty silver kroners. Not much, considering we would have paid much more. If Eli had held out for more, we would have given him whatever he wanted."

Jesse stared out the windshield as the car passed through the gates of Duvenwald prison and stopped in front of a large wooden door. "Untie his feet," Rotter said.

When his feet were untied Jesse was pushed from the car, and landed on his knees. The two guards dragged him to his feet and marched him through the front door.

"Put him in a cell until Heinrich arrives. I am sure he is anxious to get here as soon as possible."

Once inside the building, the guards forced Jesse down a

flight of stair and then down a long hallway with barred doors, lining each side. He heard whispers as he passed. "It's Jesse. They have captured Jesse." The smell of fear and misery overwhelmed him.

The guard stopped in front of one of the doors, unlocked it, untied Jesse's hands and pushed him into the cell with such force that he fell on his face. He heard the door lock behind him.

Jesse lay there, trying to catch his breath. The cell was dark as night. As his eyes became accustomed to the dark he saw a small opening in the door. Enough light came through that he was able to determine that the only piece of furniture was a cot. There wasn't even a pail to use, if he had to relieve himself.

Painfully he got to his feet and tried to look out the opening in the door, but could see very little. He stumbled over to the cot, and lay down with his arm over his eyes. *All I can do now is wait to see what Heinrich has planned for me.*

* * *

After what seemed like hours, Jesse heard footsteps come down the hallway and then the lock turn in his door. He took a deep breath. When the door opened, the bright light hurt his eyes. He was surprised to see Sig Rotter and a guard framed in the doorway.

"Heinrich has arrived and is more than a little anxious to speak with you," Rotter sneered.

Getting unsteadily to his feet Jesse replied, "I am ready, there is no use keeping the man waiting."

"Take him to interrogation room one," Rotter said to the guard. "Once he is there, he will get rid of his smart assed attitude."

The guard entered the cell and poked Jesse in the back with his revolver. As they walked down the hallway, Jesse once again heard whispers as he passed the other cells.

"Be strong, we are praying for you," some of the voices whispered.

He was taken to another room, and when he entered, Heinrich was sitting behind a desk waiting for him. The guard shoved Jesse to a wooden chair in front of the desk and tied him to it. He did not resist.

Rotter stood over him gloating, "He isn't so brave when he's alone."

"Leave us," Heinrich told Rotter. "Post a guard outside the door, and don't let anyone in. Jesse and I are going to have a long talk."

Then, turning to Jesse he added, "You look a little worse for wear. Would you like something to drink?' Opening the desk drawer he pulled out a half full bottle of cognac and two glasses.

Jesse didn't reply. He sat there and stared at Heinrich.

In his most soothing voice Heinrich said, "You know why you are here. You can save yourself a lot of pain if you do what I want. There is still time to save yourself. It's not too much to ask when you stop and think about it."

"You know I can't do that Heinrich."

"Why not Jesse? What's the big deal? All you have to do is declare to the public that I am head of the church, as well, as head of the state and that you were wrong. You will admit that what you did was in contravention to my authority. After that I will let you go, you will be a free man."

Jesse looked at him, "Heinrich, stop kidding yourself, we both understand what this is about. Even when we were kids you had to prove that you were better than I was. The question is why? What did I ever do to cause you to hate me so much?"

Heinrich moved from behind his desk and paced the floor. "You had it easy. You had a family, everybody liked you. I was treated like a gutter rat. You looked down your nose at me, all of you."

"That's all in your imagination."

Heinrich walked over to Jesse and put his face to his - foreheads almost touching "Why didn't you fight back. Not once did you lift your hand to protect yourself. You didn't show me any respect then, and even now you are still disrespectful to me. I control this country and I control the church. You owe it to me to do as I say."

"I owe you nothing," Jesse replied. "You are a thug and a murderer. People don't respect you; they despise you and everything you stand for. It is written this is how I shall die, but for you, it is merely the beginning of the end. We both know that if I gave into your demands, you can't afford to let me live."

Heinrich took a step back and slapped Jesse so hard across the face that the chair toppled over, and Jesse landed on his shoulder.

Heinrich went to the door, opened it and yelled at the guard, "get in here and stand this chair up."

The guard pulled the chair back up, but first he managed to drop it twice. Jesse winced as his shoulder bore the brunt of each fall. After the guard did as he was told he left. Heinrich looked at Jesse, "are you ready to change your mind?"

"No. My God is the only one I am prepared to pay homage to."

Heinrich was angry. He opened the door and bellowed "get Rotter back here and then teach him what he needs to say."

Two guards ran into the room, untied Jesse and forced him to his feet. They literally dragged him to another room, tied him to a chair and systematically began to beat him. Soon Sig Rotter joined them, and instead of his fists, he whipped Jesse with an iron rod. The only time Jesse cried out was when Rotter hit him across the arm with so much force that he felt the bone break.

"Stop, that's enough for now," Rotter finally said. "We will leave him for a while and let him choose. He can do as Heinrich requests, or endure more of this."

Rotter and one guard left, but the other hung back. "Please Jesse; tell him what he wants to hear. If you don't, he will kill you. There is no shame if it gets you out of here alive."

Although it hurt to talk Jesse replied, "He is going to kill me no matter what. He can't let me live now."

The guard looked at the door to make sure no others were near and whispered, "I am one of you. Please Jesse, don't do this. We need you. Without your guidance there is no way we can defeat Heinrich."

Jesse looked at him, "I am grateful for your advice, but this is how it must be. I'm not afraid, and I don't want you to be

362

either. Go, before they miss you."

Then Jesse was left alone, blood dripped from his head and mouth onto his torn shirt. He passed out from the pain.

A splash of cold water brought him around. He could barely open his swollen eyes. Heinrich stood in front of him, and slapped a truncheon against his hand.

"I see you are awake. A crowd is growing outside the prison, waiting to hear from you. Now is your chance to tell them that you were wrong, and have changed your mind about me."

"Never," Jesse struggled to reply through his bruised lips.

Heinrich's face turned red, his eyes bulged from their sockets. He beat Jesse with the truncheon, and screamed at him like a mad man with spittle dripping off his chin. Then, as suddenly as he started, he stopped.

"Jesse," he pleaded, "This is your own fault. You are making me do this. Are you willing to die for what you believe in? Is your faith that strong?"

Jesse looked at him and calmly answered. "Yes. Do what you must do, and get it over with. I won't allow you to blame me for what is happening here. This is a choice you made and now you are responsible for the consequences. Things didn't have to go this far."

Heinrich opened the door and shouted at the guards in the hallway. "Take him outside to be executed. That is the only way to get rid of him." Then turning to Jesse he growled "your own beliefs have condemned you."

Two guards entered the room. One untied Jesse and the other

forced him to his feet.

"Get him out of my sight." Heinrich ordered them, "I can't stand to look at him anymore."

When he was untied from the chair, Jesse took a deep breath, and, in spite of the pain, stood as tall as he could and walked out the door. One guard walked in front and the other, who was the Believer, walked behind with tears in his eyes.

CHAPTER FIFTY NINE

. When word of Jesse's capture began to circulate the Believers gathered outside the prison and kept a silent vigil all night. The large crowd gasped when Jesse, followed by two other prisoners, was brought through the front doors of the prison. He was naked, his face covered in blood. His right arm hung uselessly to one side, and he dragged his left leg behind him. Stumbling over the uneven ground Jesse fell to his knees. The guards watched impassively as he struggled to get back onto his feet.

"Somebody help him," Maria screamed from the crowd.

Jesse looked toward her and silently mouthed the words, "no, I can do it."

After several tries he was able to get his balance and get back on his feet. He sweated profusely, and pain etched his face. The crowed was silent as they watched him struggle across the open area toward a wooden a platform built overnight in front of a brick wall.

Maria held her breath. Something extraordinary began to happen. The closer Jesse got to the platform, the larger an aura of peace grew around him. He knew he was going to die, and wasn't afraid. Not a sound was heard as Jesse walked to his death with dignity and in peace.

The three prisoners were led up the steps, and then lined up against the wall. Jesse was placed in the middle, with one prisoner on each side of him. A guard grabbed Jesse and tied his arms to a hook which hung above his head. Then he spread Jesse's legs and tied them each to a stake. Jesse didn't make a sound, but a look of anguish crossed his face as his damaged limbs were forced into position. He struggled to remain conscious.

Heinrich, standing in the back of an open air jeep, emerged through the prison doors and was driven to the wall. Commanding his driver to stop in front of Jesse, he stared at him. Defiantly Jesse stared back at him.

"This is your last chance Jesse. If you acknowledge that I alone am the head of the church and the state. I will let you live. You will renounce all other teachings and go into exile."

"I will not" declared Jesse. Then, looking at the crowd, he continued, "You see for yourself what this man is capable of. You have heard the rumors. You have seen the friends and families of your fellow Believers being rounded up and shipped away. Is this the kind of man you want to follow? The Holy book tells us there is only one true God; believe in him, as I have taught you."

"Shut him up." Heinrich screamed.

A guard standing on the side of the platform walked in front of Jesse and drove the butt of his rifle into his stomach. Jesse didn't make a sound.

"Kill the others, and then get rid of the bodies." Heinrich commanded. Two shots rang out and both prisoners fell. Four men ran to the platform and hauled the bodies away.

Struggling to catch his breath from the overwhelming pain,

Jesse looked into Heinrich's eyes and said, "I am not afraid of you. I know that soon you will be defeated. This is the beginning of the end, and may my God have mercy on your soul."

Heinrich screamed in frustration, reached into his holster, pulled out his gun and shot Jesse in the knee. "I will give you one more chance. Will you admit the God you claim to believe in is false, and that I am head of the church?"

"No" Jesse replied calmly.

Heinrich shot him in the other knee. No longer able to hold himself upright Jesse sagged, and the ropes cut into his wrists.

Twice more Heinrich challenged him. Jesse lifted his head as best he could and spoke to the people. "Do you want to know the reason for the violence and discord we have lived through the past few years? I am the one person Heinrich is afraid of, the one man who has refused to bend to his will. Even as children, I refused to give into his demands. You have suffered much because of me and when I am dead, he will lose his will to survive. My God and my beliefs will defeat him, and all who follow him. Do not be afraid. Do whatever you need to do to bring this dictator to justice. Today Heinrich sows the seeds of his destruction. He can and will be defeated."

"Shut up," Heinrich screamed, then raising his pistol once again Jesse in each shoulder. "I will show you." he continued to scream at Jesse. Once again raising his pistol and shot him twice in the abdomen. The blood dripped from Jesses wounds onto the platform.

It took a long time for Jesse to die. His eyes focused on Maria and Marika .As his life ebbed away he mouthed the words, "Marika, I love you."

She tried to run to him, but Maria and Peter held her back. "I love you Jesse," she called out.

Just before his eyes closed for the final time, the crowd heard him utter the words "Thy will be done," and then he died. The sky grew dark, lightening flashed, and a large clap of thunder rolled over the crowd. The crowd stood there disbelieving what happened. Maria and Marika, with their arms wrapped around each other cried. Peter stood guard over them, his face blank.

Heinrich was terrified. He had never seen anything like this. "Get me out of here this minute" he screamed at his driver.

But before he could leave, Maria pushed her way through the crowd and spoke to him. "He is my son. I wish to bury him."

"No, let him hang there until he rots. To bury him is to give his followers a place to go to turn him into a martyr." Then drawing himself to his full height, he declared, "Leave him where he is."

Maria ran to her son, kneeled in front of him, wrapped her arms around his bloody body and cried. The crowd was silent. The unthinkable had taken place in front of them. Instead of being the grand leader that Heinrich pretended to be the people saw him for what he was, a pitiful, jealous wreck of a man. By standing true to his calling and denying Heinrich his victory, Jesse gave them an example to follow.

Nobody seemed to know what to do, or what to make of Heinrich's hate for Jesse. As Jesse predicted Heinrich had sown the seeds of his own destruction. Now it was merely a matter of time.

As Heinrich was being driven away from the prison, the feeling of triumph he expected didn't happen, and for the first time in his life he was afraid. Too late he understood that he had gone too far and that his jealousy of Jesse got the best of him.

I should have sent Jesse away to the worst of the camps, and let him die a slow death. I have made a terrible mistake. I have given the Believers an even greater reason to hate me. Now they will call Jesse's death an injustice and rally behind him. In death he will be more powerful than he was alive.

The driver looked over his shoulder. Heinrich was huddled in a corner of the back seat carrying on a conversation with someone only he could hear. He shook his head. "This man is truly mad," he declared.

After Heinrich left, Peter led Marika and Maria away. The Believers, beginning to recover from the shock and brutality of the morning mulled around and formed small groups. A cry began, and the people chanted, "We will avenge Jesse's death."

CHAPTER SIXTY

Early the next morning Heinrich was awakened by a loud banging on his bedroom door. His head ached and his eyes burned; an empty whiskey bottle lay on the floor beside the bed.

"Who is it, and what do you want?" he growled. "I left word I didn't want to be disturbed."

"Sir, I must speak with you. I have an urgent message."

"Then get in here you fool, don't stand out there bellowing. Do you want the whole world to hear?"

Heinrich got out of bed, and was tying his robe when the young soldier stepped into the room and saluted.

"Well what is this urgent message? Spit it out so I can go back to bed."

It reads "the body of Jesse the Believer has disappeared." The guards report that sometime between two and three this morning his body was taken. They didn't see or hear anybody."

"Here give me that."

Heinrich snatched the message from the soldier's hands and read it for himself. Then swearing, he crumpled it into a ball and threw it across the room. "Get my driver and a squad of men ready to leave within the hour. How can this be? Even dead, that man cannot leave me alone."

Several hours later Heinrich and his men drove up to the

front gates of Duvenvald prison. Before he was out of the car he began barking orders. "Search the area. Ask every person you see if they know what took place. Force them to wait for me outside the prison gates. I know those damn Believers stole Jesse's body, but I just don't know how they managed to get away with it."

Heinrich was furious. He marched into the prison, and slammed the large door behind him. "Bring me the guards who were supposed to make sure this didn't happen."

Within minutes, two terrified young men stood in front of Heinrich. He paced the floor and screamed at them, "How could you allow this to happen? You stupid idiots, do you know what you have done?"

"Sir, we neither saw nor heard anything. It was quiet. There was nobody about."

"Where were you during this time?"

One guard looked at the other and then replied, "It was cold last night, and we went inside for a cup of coffee, so we could warm up."

"You were inside drinking coffee, while someone was stealing Jesse's body?"

Looking at the guard who had brought the two men to Heinrich, he said, "Take them out and shoot them. Make an example of them."

Before the young men could protest, the guard took out his gun and shot them both in the back of the head.

"Not here stupid, I told you to take them outside first. Now clean up this mess and take their bodies outside, so others see what happens when you fail in your duty."

People once again began to gather in front of the prison. Somehow word got out that Jesse's body had disappeared. Some gathered in mourning, others because the Brown Shirts instructed them to go and wait.

Hearing the murmurs of the gathering crowd, Heinrich went outside and stood before them. "I want to know who took Jesse down and where he is."

There was silence. The crowd stared back at him in defiance.

"Tell me who did this," he ranted. "Who dared go against me?"

Once again there was no response.

He reached over to the nearest prison guard, grabbed his gun from the holster and began firing into the crowd. A woman screamed. Again and again he fired until the gun was empty, and then he reloaded it. Bodies littered the ground in front of him

Turning to the guard he said, "Bring me thirty children."

Several guards went into the crowd yanking children away from their mothers. Some were babies, the oldest about ten.

"You have one hour. After that I will personally shoot a child every ten minutes until someone tells me what I want to know. Where is Jesse's body?"

An old man pushed his way through the crowd and stood in front of Heinrich. "We cannot tell you what we don't know. When we arrived this morning, his body was gone. Even his wife and mother don't know. You must believe me." The crowd murmured assent.

Heinrich shot him between the eyes. "Somebody here knows," he shouted to the crowd. "Do you want to see your children killed in the same way?" Handing the gun back to the guard, he added, "I will be back in one hour, and then you will shoot the first."

The guard protested, "Sir, I can't do that. They are children. They have done nothing to harm you."

Heinrich glared at him. "You will do your duty or you will be the first."

Heinrich turned and walked back into the prison courtyard. *How dare they defy me?* He paced back and forth muttering to himself and reviling Jesse.

Outside the crowd continued to stand in silence. The children huddled in a group by the blood stained wall, and the little ones cried for their mothers. Other guards stood by, threatening the mothers who tried to approach their children.

The guard moved from group to group asking questions. At ten minutes before the hour he ran into the prison.

"Sir," he said breathlessly, "it was The Believers who came and took Jesse's body. An old lady saw them through her window. They were dressed in black from head to toe, and their faces were hidden. They wrapped his body in a blanket and carried him away."

"Which way did they go? Did she see?"

"She thinks they went toward the hills."

"Gather the men and search for him. Bring that old lady to me, so I can hear with my own ears what she has to say. She could be lying."

"Sir what do I do about the children?"

"Shoot one, and let the rest go. First bring me the old lady."

Heinrich smirked with satisfaction. "I knew they would talk – cowards all of them. Nobody is as smart as I am."

Outside, the guard had to think fast. Everything he told Heinrich was a lie. He could not, and would not kill children. He walked toward the children and lined them up in a row. The women screamed. He stood in front of the children with his gun in his hand, and fired one shot deliberately over their heads. Then he turned and walked away.

The women rushed forward, took hold of their children and the crowd quickly melted away.

The other guards turned and went back into the prison, with relief written over their faces, each one glad they were not the one chosen to shoot the children. They kept what had taken place to themselves.

Instead of going back into the prison, the guard continued walking out of town. *What kind of God has no concern for human life? Heinrich is no God; he was a crazy man who will stop at nothing to get his own way.*

Once outside of the town limits, he removed his guard's shirt and his gun belt. Hiding them under a tree, he began the long walk home.

CHAPTER SIXTY ONE

When Jesse's body couldn't be located Heinrich sent out a directive to the Brown Shirts, "bring Jesse's top advisors to me unharmed." He knew that until Jesse's body was found and destroyed he wouldn't rest easy.

Peter sat on a park bench and tried to make sense of all that had transpired in the last several days. *I was aware of Heinrich's jealousy and hatred for Jesse, but will what Jesse prophesied come true? Was this really the beginning of the end? How was the country going to rebuild from the devastation Heinrich has brought about? Where do I go from here? I know I don't have the strength and courage Jesse possessed to carry on his work.* He was so wrapped up in his thoughts that he didn't notice the two Brown Shirts standing in front of him.

"Are you Peter, the man who was an advisor to Jesse? If so you are to come with us."

"No, I am not," Peter replied, and then he remembered Jesse telling him that he would deny their association. Immediately he felt ashamed.

A thousand things flitted across Peter's mind. He stood up and squared his shoulders. *I will* not *let Jesse down again.* "I was wrong," he said, "Jesse was my friend."

"You are to come with us," one of the men said.

They escorted him out of the park, one on each side, and then he was put into the back seat of an awaiting car. One man sat in the back with him, the other drove.

"Where are we going?" Peter asked. So far the men were been friendly enough, but he also knew that could change any minute. "Am I under arrest? If so, for what reason?"

"Heinrich wants to see you."

The driver stopped in front of police headquarters. With a man walking on either side of him he was escorted to Heinrich's office.

When Peter was brought into the room Heinrich looked up from his desk. His hair was a mess, and he hadn't shaved for several days. His uniform had food stains on the front, but it was his eyes that caught Peter's attention. They were red rimmed and appeared to bounce from one side to the other, not focusing on any one thing in particular. A cold shiver passed over Peter. *The man is crazy.*

Then Heinrich focused on him. "Where is Jesse's body?" he demanded.

This is not what Peter expected. "I have no idea what you are talking about?"

"I repeat, where is Jesse's body? What have you done with him?"

"I don't know," Peter replied. "I wasn't part of the plan, nor am I privy to that information. I don't know where he was taken or where he was buried. I left after you killed him and haven't been back."

Heinrich rose from his desk, walked over to Peter and slapped him across the face. Peter stared back at him.

"I don't know," Peter said, emphasizing his words. "I had no knowledge of a plan, but I commend whoever came up with it, and the fact they were able to steal him from under your nose."

Heinrich slapped him again. "You will tell me before you leave here," he screamed in Peter's face.

"I can't tell you what I don't know." Peter replied. His face stung from the blows and he could taste blood in his mouth.

Heinrich paced back and forth in front of Peter ranting and raving, little of what made sense. Every once in a while he slapped Peter again.

Finally Peter had enough. "Stop right now. I have had enough of this." he commanded.

Heinrich stopped in front of him, his hands on his hips.

"What does it matter whether you find Jesse's body, or not? It's too late to stop what you have already started. You will never be able to stop the momentum of Jesse's teachings. It's over Heinrich. In death Jesse has defeated you once again. His name will be remembered with love and his teachings will grow stronger. When people hear your name, they will spit on the ground. You will have the glory you seek, but it will be as the most despised man to have ever lived."

Heinrich's face turned a deep red. "Get out of my sight. Get out of here before I have you thrown into one of cells where you will rot until you die."

Peter didn't waste any time. He left the room, hurried down the hallway, and out the front door. Once outside he ran down the nearest alley and kept running, until he was sure he wasn't being followed.

379

How could I tell him what I don't know? His eye was swollen shut and his face hurt. Avoiding people, he made his way to a place where he knew he would be safe for the time being.

CHAPTER SIXTY TWO

Heinrich awoke with a start. He thought he felt a presence standing beside his bed watching him. When he opened his eyes, he didn't know if he was awake or dreaming. Jesse stood at the side of the bed in his bloody clothes – exactly the way Heinrich had last seen him.

"You are dead. I shot you myself," he stuttered, "I watched you bleed to death. Your blood is still splattered on the wall."

"You killed my body," Jesse replied, "but you cannot kill my spirit. My spirit lives in all who witnessed that day, and in those who believe in me. Heinrich, you should have quit when you were ahead. Now you have made a mistake that is going to cost you your life, and defeat your cause."

"How can that be?" Heinrich scoffed. "With you gone, the people have to acknowledge I am stronger than you. They have nobody left to follow, no one to look up to as a leader. I am going to track down every one of your men, and get rid of them too. By the time I am finished, you will be a distant memory."

"My followers have been instructed to continue spreading the word. If you capture one, another will step in and take his place."

"So what do you want with me? I know this isn't real and I am dreaming. Two guards are posted outside my door, and all I have to do is call for them."

"No, you are not dreaming. I am here – with you - in your bedroom. Three times you will know that I have appeared. I will appear to those who believe in me, and you are going to sink deeper into insanity. Your last moments will be filled with clarity, and you will see the pain and misery your brutality has wrought. Even in death you will never be forgiven."

"Get out of here," Heinrich sputtered; his face turning a deep red. "Guards, guards get in here right now."

The two guards ran into the room, with their guns drawn.

"Get him. Shoot him now," he screeched pointing to where Jesse stood. "Kill him."

"Sir?" one of the guards questioned, "shoot who? There is nobody here with you."

"Jesse is standing right there. Can't you see him?"

"Heinrich," Jesse said calmly, "they can't see me, only you can."

"Shoot him. He is standing at the end of my bed. Can't you see him?"

"No sir, there is no one there."

Heinrich reached over to grab Jesse, but he was gone. "He was here. I was talking to him." Curling into a fetal position he began crying, "He was here. I know I saw him. I was talking to him."

The second guard said. "Stay with him while I get the doctor. I think he is hallucinating. Did you see anything?"

The first guard shook his head, "no, there was nothing to
382

see."

The guard left, and within minutes the doctor, still in his night clothes, came puffing down the hallway, carrying his black leather bag.

"Wait outside," he said to the guards, "don't let anyone in here until I tell you differently. You can tell me what happened later."

Reaching into his bag, he pulled out a vial and syringe. Once the syringe was filled, he injected the contents into Heinrich's thigh.

It took several hours before Heinrich began to uncurl and lie in a normal position. All that time he was mumbling incoherently about Jesse being in his room.

The doctor kept Heinrich drugged for five days. Only he and Heinrich's immediate staff knew he had suffered a mental breakdown. Then gradually the doctor began to reduce the amount of sedation, and Heinrich became more coherent. By the end of seven days he was awake and acting as if nothing had happened.

Immediately he called a staff meeting in his bedroom. Still in his slippers and dressing gown he questioned them. "What has happened since I became ill?"

"There has been an increase of activity from the freedom fighters. They have blown up bridges hundreds of miles from here, but we are closing in on the leaders. It's only a matter of time until we catch them," his Secretary answered.

"I want the Believers destroyed," he screeched at them, "kill every last one of them. I don't care what you do. Send the women and children to the camps; shoot the men and boys on sight. I don't want any of them left."

"Heinrich, there are thousands out there. How are we to know who is who?"

Heinrich replied, "I want every person who believes in Jesse exterminated. Do you hear and understand what I am saying? If not, you will answer to me."

CHAPTER SIXTY THREE

The women directed toward the left were terrified. Everyone had heard the stories coming out of the camps about a selection process which determined if a person lived or died.

When the processing of this new group of Believers was complete, the guards marched the women into a large, gray concrete room lined with concrete benches and rows of hooks on the walls.

"Take off your clothes," a burly guard barked at them. "Hang them over there on the wall." One woman took off everything except her underwear. "All of it," he yelled again, smacking her across the face.

"I can't," she replied, "I have my period and will make a mess."

"Do it anyway." He struck her again, "another filthy believer. Tomorrow you can come back and clean up behind yourself."

Slowly the women obeyed. Those with small children undressed them first, neatly folded their clothes in piles, and placed their shoes on top. Then reluctantly did the same for themselves. Embarrassed to be naked in front of their children, they tried to cover their breasts and pubic area with their hands. Guards wandered among them squeezing their breasts and shoving their hands between their legs. The youngest and prettiest were forced away from the group and taken back outside.

When all of the women and children were naked he said, "Now you are going for a shower to wash the Believer filth off you. Run, I want to see your breasts bounce."

The women were forced outside, and at gun point, they ran down a long sidewalk into a smaller concrete room. Their naked breasts bounced just as the guard had ordered. They could hear the screams as more young women and girls were pulled aside. Those who couldn't run were beaten on the back with the heavy wooden sticks the guards carried.

The floor was cold. Those who entered first were forced against the wall at the back of the room. They screamed in fear of being suffocated because of the other bodies pressed against them. Many of the children cried and whimpered.

The last few at the end of the line refused to go in. Unnerved by the noise coming from the shower room, they begged to be allowed to stay out. The guards slammed the butts of their rifles into their heads and faces, driving them inside. When all of the women were in the room, one of the guards shut and locked the huge metal doors. They could hear the women screaming and begging for their lives through the concrete walls.

"Now let their God save them," one guard said to the other.

Then there was silence. The guards had learned to ignore the screams while they went about their duty. but this new strange silence unnerved them.

"Hurry up Heinz," one said, "The sooner we get this over with, the sooner we can share in the delights of the women we held back. We are going to have a good time once this is over. I like mine young and tight, and we have much to choose from this time."

The guard named Heinz climbed up the ladder on the side of the building, carrying two small gas canisters in his hand. He opened the trapdoor at the top and stood there as if transfixed.

"A light – it hurts my eyes," he cried out. Dropping the two canisters onto the roof he said, "I can't do this."

"Get the hell down from there and I will do it," another guard said, "that's what happens when you send a boy to do a man's job."

When he got on the roof, he punched Heinz in the face, and kicked him several times as he lay there. "Bloody coward," he said, and, without hesitation, opened the trap door and dropped the two canisters into the room below.

Climbing down the ladder, he said to no one in particular, "kill him when he comes down. Now my beauties you are going to find out what a real man feels like," he said turning to the frightened women, and rubbing his crotch in a crude manner. Still the silence endured

Inside the bunker, Jesse stood in the middle of the room bathed in a bright shining light. The women and children gathered around him, some praying, some kneeling, still others reaching out to touch him. Gathering the closest children into his arms he said, "Be not afraid for I am here with you."

The women stood in awe, as he managed to give each one a reassuring pat on the shoulder. Then, as the gas canisters dropped onto the concrete floor and their deadly fumes filled the room, he said "come, I am taking you to my Father's house."

The women forced to wait outside, huddled together, dreading what was to come.

Outside, the guards stood unbelieving. Where were the piercing screams they usually heard, and the pounding on the door? Where was the sound of people dying, fighting for their last breath? The silence became unbearable.

One guard turned and ran away. Soon others followed. Something unnatural was taking place, and they didn't want any part of it. Soon the burly guard stood alone. He wasn't exactly sure what happened, but he knew he couldn't leave any witnesses. He turned his gun on the women standing with him, and shot them. Then he went into the guard barracks and issued an ultimatum to the men, either they return to the chamber or be killed. Several refused, and he shot them on the spot. The rest followed him quietly.

The death workers from the camp arrived at the bunker. They picked up the bodies of the young women lying on the grass, loaded them into wheel barrows and carted them away. After being searched for gold and valuables, they would be incinerated.

Waiting until they were sure the gas was cleared from the bunker, one of the guards unlocked and opened the heavy doors. This was the part the death workers hated the most. It was a difficult job to pry the bodies apart, and then cart them off to the sorting area. The worst were the bodies of the children.

As the big door swung open, the workers were shocked to see that the room was empty. In the center of the room, etched into the floor was the mark of Jesse $\leq \geq=$.

At first the camp workers were terrified. They stood looking at each other, nobody moved. The burly guard pushed the men out of his way. "You good for nothing pieces of shit, get to work, or next time you will join them."

Forcing his way to the front, he stared at the empty room and the blackened mark on the floor. *How could this be? Three-hundred women and children were locked in this space. Where did they go?*

Suddenly the significance of the mark on the floor impaled his senses. It was the mark of the Believers.   Grabbing the man standing beside him he shouted, "Did you see him? Did one of you allow Jesse to escape?"

"No," one of the workers replied. "You were here all the time. None of us know how Jesse got in there, if he did. I thought he was dead."

The death workers were no longer frightened. They began whispering to each other. "Jesse was here. He saved the women and children."

The whispers spread first among the workers, and then to the camp. "Jesse still lives."

A frightened guard ran to the camp administrator's office and burst in without knocking. "They are gone. The bunker is empty." Taking a deep breath he added, "The mark of Jesse is etched into the floor."

Coming out from behind the desk the commander said, "You stupid man. How can they be gone? I watched the women go in there myself."

Hastily grabbing his hat from the coat tree and buttoning the front of his jacket, he stormed out of the room.   The guard ran behind him

The emaciated prisoners heard the commotion, and lined the fences. The commander was aware that thousands of eyes

389

followed him as he crossed the yard to the bunker. *This stupid guard will be sorry for playing me as a fool. I will make an example of him.*

Muttering he walked to the open door and then fell silent. The bunker was empty. The mark of Jesse was on the floor just as he had been told. He turned on his heel, and in a panic, ran back to his office.

Picking up the phone he dialled the number of Heinrich's office screaming hysterically, "Jesse lives."

The message was quickly relayed to Heinrich's home. His aide took the message and then rushed to the bedroom without knocking. "Sir, I have an important message for you from one of the camps. It cannot wait."

* **

Heinrich sat at a small table eating a bowl of potato soup accompanied by several slices of fresh white bread.. "How many times have I told you not to bother me when I am eating? You know how delicate my stomach is."

"I knew you would want this message from one of the outlying camps right away."

"Spit it out and then leave me alone. What can be more important than my lunch?"

"Sir the message says "Jesse lives."

Heinrich chocked on the tea he was drinking, "that is impossible. He is dead. I killed him myself." He was visibly shaken.

Suddenly he picked up the half full cup of tea and threw it at the aide. "Get out, get out of my sight. Find who is playing this sick joke and bring the fool to me."

The aide wasted no time getting out of the room. When Heinrich was in one of his rages the best place to be was out of sight.

Heinrich roamed around the room like a crazy man smashing everything he could get his hands on. Then he cowered in a corner and began to sob. *No. No, this is impossible. I can lose now. Jesse is dead, I know he is.*

CHAPTER SIXTY FOUR

What followed Jesse's death was a month of horror and madness, unlike the country had experienced before. Heinrich's edict, "Kill the Believers, eradicate the scum" turned friend against friend, family member against family member. Terror reigned over the country, People hid in their houses afraid to answer their door.

The Brown Shirts roamed the streets, looted the stores, and shot anybody who tried to stop them. Some, suspected of following Jesse, were dragged from their homes into the streets and killed. Women and girls were openly abused as others were forced to watch. Nobody knew how to stop what was taking place.

Heinrich decimated what was left of his army and had his top commanders killed. Rotter continued to stay away from the city, commanding his Brown Shirts from a hidden location.

Then, as suddenly as it started, the killing stopped. It was as though a giant voice had rumbled "that is enough."

Jesse's death and Heinrich's subsequent rampage against the Believers left Peter and the remainder of Jesse's closest follower with broken spirits. The resistance had been practically destroyed and the country was in ruins.

Peter moved the two women to the alley in the city and, in time, found them two tiny rooms not far from him. He was discouraged. Of all the promises he made to Jesse his only accomplishment so far was keeping Maria and Marika safe.

One evening he sought out Maria. Knocking softly on her door he said, "Maria, it is me, Peter."

Maria opened the door and invited him in. "Peter you look terrible. Is something wrong?"

Peter's eyes were red rimmed with dark shadows beneath them; his hair long and matted and his face gaunt. Closing the door, he took Maria's hands in his. "I failed him Maria. Jesse gave his life so we could continue his work, and it was for nothing."

Maria withdrew her hands, and led Peter to one of the two wooden chairs in the room. She turned the other so they could face each other.

"Talk to me Peter," she said. "Tell me what you are thinking."

Peter began to cry, "Maria, I miss him, and I don't know where to go from here. Heinrich is insane. Look at what he has done since Jesse's death. Thousands of people have died, neighbors have turned against each other, and people are starving. Jesse left me in charge of the Believers, and I was powerless to stop any of this."

Maria let him cry and ramble on for several minutes and then asked, "Peter, why do you think you are responsible for what Heinrich has done? Your specific duty was to protect the two of us, and you have done an admirable job. We are safe, and the inner core of Jesse's followers, although scattered, is still intact, and what is left of the resistance is hiding. Nearly all of Jesse's plans are still to be carried out. None of us could have predicted what Heinrich was going to do, and certainly none of us imagined him going completely mad. How can you feel responsible for all of that?"

Peter paused, wiped the tears from his eyes with his hand. "Maria, you are a very wise woman. Tell me what to do from here. How do we start over without Jesse to lead us?"

Maria looked at him, tears running down her cheeks, "I miss him too Peter, but Jesse knew all of this beforehand. Not only was he prepared to give his life, but he gave it willingly. If we stop now, then we have failed him. He would want us to keep going."

"You are right as usual," Peter exclaimed, "but the task of rebuilding feels overwhelming. Each time I think about what has to be done, I can't figure out where to start. Perhaps we should leave things the way they are, maybe it's for the best. I think we need to find someone who will do a better job than I have."

Searching his face Maria asked, "do you truly believe that Peter? If we follow that path then Jesse's life will truly have been wasted. Jesse knew what he was doing when he chose you."

"No, I don't believe that," Peter replied, "but I also don't know how to start."

The two of them sat in silence for a long time. Tears once again flowed down Peter's face. Maria watched as a variety of emotions moved over his face and through his body. Although she knew the answers to his questions, she thought it better if he figured it out for himself."

Wiping his hand across his face, he began to smile. "There is

395

only one thing to do Maria, start at the beginning again. Jesse's real battle against Heinrich began when the Elders were killed in front of the church. Jesse accepted his fate when he defied Heinrich that day, even if he didn't clearly know what it was."

"What are you thinking Peter?"

"Somehow we must get word to the men who are still part of Jesse's inner circle. I want them, to meet me at the cave."

Maria smiled. She watched the tension leave Peter's face, only to be replaced with a look of determination. "As usual you are right Peter the cave is the perfect place to start over."

"And then," he continued, "we must get word to the resistance to regroup and wait until they hear from me. We should set a date, say one week from today, to meet. That should give each of us time to travel without being conspicuous. Mark still has the radio, so he is the best person to spread the word. If not, he will know of ways to tell the others that I am calling a meeting."

He stood up and walked to the door. Before he left he pulled Maria into his arms, and hugged her tightly. "Thank you Maria, I can handle this now. You and Marika try to find a safe way to meet us at the cave."

Maria touched his cheek with her hand, "Peter, grief has a way of blinding us to what must be done. All you needed was someone to understand how you were feeling. Trust your instincts. You had the answers all the time, but your mind was too clouded for them to surface."

Shortly after Peter left, there was another soft knock on Maria's door. Marika entered the room, "I saw Peter leaving your room, is something wrong? He looked upset?"

"Nothing is wrong my child. We must make ready to travel back to the cave, and meet Peter there in one week. He wants to gather those of Jesse's closest followers who are still alive to see if we can come up with a plan to salvage Jesse's work."

"Are you well enough to travel?" Marika asked, "I know you spend most of your days in pain from what the Brown Shirts did to you."

"Don't worry about me. Nothing, not even a little pain will stop me from making this journey."

Marika paused for a moment. "Maria, you know, as well as I do, appearing in public with a yellow cross on our clothing is extremely dangerous. There is no telling what will happen if the Brown Shirts see us."

"Then we will take them off." Maria answered.

She went to the small closet in the room, and in frenzy began ripping the stars off her clothing, laughing as she did so.

Marika tried to stop her. "Maria, you mustn't do this. If you are caught..."

Maria turned to Marika. "Don't you see? We are the same as the other people. The only thing that makes us different is that we wear the cross on our clothing, that, and the fact we believe in God, and not Heinrich. Let the Brown Shirts find and punish us, I am tired of hiding and being afraid."

Then she collapsed on the floor sobbing. Marika went to her, gathered her into her arms, and rocked her back and forth as though she were a child. She understood. Maria cried for what she had lost – her husband, her children, her life and her son Jesse.

397

She held Maria until she stopped crying, helped her to her feet, led her to the bed and covered her with a thin blanket. "Rest Maria, I will stay with you. Tomorrow we will find Peter and make plans to take you home."

* * *

The two women left at noon the next day. On the outskirts of the town they joined a group of refugees fleeing the city. Maria spread her message. "Take off the yellow cross and do not be afraid. We are the same as the others; only the cross marks us as being different. If we take it off, nobody will know we are followers of Jesse. Stand up for who you are. Defy Heinrich. Follow Jesse's teaching and do not give up. Begin today to take back your freedom and your life."

One by one the refugees removed the stars from their clothing. As more joined the group, they were encouraged to do the same. Instead of anger and despair they walked with hope and purpose. In their own minds each had struck a blow against Heinrich.

CHAPTER SIXTY FIVE

Exactly one week later, those who remained as Jesse's trusted followers, began arriving at the cave. Maria and Marika, who had arrived the day before, greeted them with warm food and a fire. Peter stood guard outside the cave entrance. Their numbers were greatly reduced- Eli was not there, Remi and Jacob had been killed in the camps, and some had been unable to travel safely. Still there were enough to decide what they should do. The resistance waited for the results of the meeting.

They were a somber, demoralized group, each still acutely feeling the loss of Jesse, as a friend, and as a leader. Shame kept them from looking into the faces of Maria and Marika. Each blamed himself for not doing a better job of protecting him.

When Peter was satisfied all of the men had arrived, he went to the back of the cave and spoke to them. "I apologize to each of you. Jesse wanted me to step up into his place and continue with his work. Instead, I have been grief stricken, afraid and hiding in the city. I hoped, with Jesse dead that Heinrich would feel triumphant. None of us could have predicted the insanity that followed. One evening I went to Maria and spoke with her. She brought me to my senses, and that is why I have asked you to meet here today. If we can find a way, we must begin Jesse's work again. Jesse gave his life for what we believe in; the only difference is that he is no longer here, but his plans are still in place. All that is left for us to do is follow them to their conclusion, Heinrich still must be defeated

Jesse told us Heinrich would sow the seeds of his own destruction, and it has begun. Our countrymen are turning against him in droves. Leadership in the Army and Brown Shirts has been decimated. Rumor is that he has become completely unbalanced. Maria and Marika, on their journey here, bravely encouraged the Believers they met to remove the yellow crosses from their clothing, to stand up for themselves and defy Heinrich."

The men began to whisper among themselves. Finally one of them spoke, "where do we start Peter? How do we get reorganized when so much and so many have been lost?"

"Perhaps I can help with that," a quiet voice said from behind them.

Peter grabbed Maria and Marika shoving them behind him. The others rose to their feet ready to defend themselves.

"Who are you?" Peter demanded. "How did you get in here? Did you follow one of us?"

The man laughed, "Relax Peter, I'm not here to hurt you."

The sound of the laugh echoed in Peter's head, having heard it so many times before. "Jesse, is it you? How can this be? You are dead. We watched you die."

"It is him," Maria said, stepping out from behind Peter. The two women ran to him and threw their arms around him. Jesse kissed each of them on the forehead.

"Come," he said, "we have plans to make.

Moving closer to the fire where all could see him he sat down. Maria sat on one side, Marika on the other, near his feet.

His hand stroked her hair, and her eyes never left his face.

Peter came over, kneeled in front of Jesse, and burrowed his head into his lap. "Forgive me Jesse, I failed you miserably. I have been such a disappointment to all of us." He began to cry.

"Peter," Jesse replied, putting his hand on the back of Peter's head, "you have been like a brother to me. I could never be disappointed in you; my love runs too deep for that. You saved me when I gave up, now we need your courage to keep on going. Come," he spoke to the others "we need to find some answers to your questions."

The next few hours were spent discussing various ways to renew the faith of the Believers. In the end, each man was given the task to reach out to the Believers in their area, encourage them to remove the crosses from their clothing and stand up for themselves. They were also instructed to help the resistance regroup and keep fighting back.

One by one the men left. Jesse hugged each and kissed them on the cheek. "Well done," he said to each, "be strong and keep believing. Soon this will be over, and you will be needed as never before."

After the men were gone he went to Peter, "keep watch. I wish to speak to Marika in private."

First he hugged his mother. "Do not mourn for me. Marika is carrying my son. Through him I will always be with you." Tightening his arms around her and kissing her cheek he said," I love you."

Maria kissed him back. "I shall never forget you," and then she stepped out of Jesse's arms. Motioning to Marika, she said,

401

"He is your husband, go to him."

Taking Marika by the hand Jesse led her to the same spot they had last made love. Marika moved into his arms and they clung to each other. Both were crying. "Do you remember the last time we were here and we lay together? We conceived a son that night and you will name him after me. I wish I could lay with you one more time, but it is impossible. I love you Marika, more than you will ever know."

She stepped back out of his arms, and looked into his eyes. "Jesse what you have told me is impossible. I cannot have children. The men – they hurt me, I was too young."

"Believe me," he whispered, "it is the truth." Then, pulling her closer, he kissed her.

"Jesse, please stay here with us," she begged. "We can protect you. I can't bear the thought of you leaving me again."

"I cannot stay, I must go soon." He held Marika in his arms while she cried. Finally he said to her, "it is time for you to go back to Peter and Maria. You are not alone. Even though you will not be able to see me, I will always be at your side. When you cry I will be there to comfort you and now you will have our son to keep my memory alive. Go now." He held her tight and kissed her once more.

"I will always love you Jesse," she whispered.

She turned and slowly began making her way back to the entrance of the cave. She did not look back.

Peter and Maria were waiting for her. Marika saw them look past her to see if Jesse was behind her.

"He is gone," she said softly. Her hand went to her stomach. *There will be time later to tell them of Jesse's gift.*

CHAPTER SIXTY SIX

Since Jesse's death the mood in the city had changed. The last time Heinrich led a cavalcade through the streets the people threw stones and jeered at him. Others stood along the sides of the streets shaking their fists. Since then he had travelled from his home to his office under heavy guard. Fear of another visitation from Jesse kept him awake at night.

Civil disobedience started slowly. At first it was a few picketers brave enough to walk in front of his home and his office. Later small unorganized groups began to that gather, gradually growing in size. Up to that point the guards had been able to convince the crowds to disperse quietly.

One evening, a riot broke out in front of Heinrich's home. He huddled behind the locked door of his bedroom until it was over. Every window in his house was smashed and the guards had killed five armed men who rushed the front door. Hours later, after the riot was quelled, a contingent of guards, stood shoulder to shoulder around his house.

In the middle of the night Heinrich was spirited away to an empty office building next to his office. Most of the basement had been turned into a steel fortified bunker consisting of an office, a bedroom and an eating area. Water was piped in from the buildings main source and the sewer was connected to the main lines. There were no windows, and the room was sound proof. As long as he stayed within the walls Heinrich would be safe and comfortable until he was rescued.

Few people knew of this place because Heinrich had built it in secrecy, using slave labor. A small tunnel connected this building to his office in the neighboring building. The back entrance of the building was protected by a heavy wooden door, barred and locked from the inside. From outside the building appeared to be an empty, but on the inside it was a fortress.

Once he had been safely moved Heinrich paced back and forth. The room was as silent as a tomb and prevented him from hearing what was happening outside.

After several hours he couldn't stand the suspense any longer. He unbolted the steel door of his room and went in search of the guards.

"What is happening out there?" he demanded from the first guard he came upon.

"Sir" the guard saluted, "you shouldn't be out here. Your office has been ransacked, the contents thrown out on to the street and set on fire. The flags have been torn down and burned. The mood is ugly and getting uglier by the hour."

"Keep me posted," Heinrich barked. He returned to his safe room, but he left the door open. The area was too confining and quiet for his comfort.

The mob outside grew louder. The guards heard the upper windows of the house being systematically broken, and thought they heard voices coming from the upper floors. Something was being battered against the back door.

Four guards had been posted inside the building to protect Heinrich, two at the back door and two at the front. When they heard voices in the upper floors the two guarding the back left their post and joined the two at the front. They began talking among themselves.

"We should find a way out of here to protect ourselves if the crowd gets inside. There is little the four of us can do to protect Heinrich. He will be trapped downstairs, but he will be safe until reinforcement's arrive." one of the guards said.

Another replied, "I don't give a damn about what happens to Heinrich. Who is going to look after my wife and two children if something happens to me? I owe him nothing."

The youngest of the guards, barely nineteen, was trembling and muttering over and over "I don't want to die." The fourth guard stood by the front door listening to the unruly crowd outside.

They argued back and forth, ultimately deciding to turn Heinrich over to the crowd and make their escape. They could easily slip away because the crowd's attention would be focused on Heinrich, not them.

"We are all agreed then," one said. The other three nodded.

He went down the stairs into the basement. "Heinrich sir," he said, stopping in front of the open door, "the crowd has set the building on fire; we have to get you out of here."

Without stopping to think Heinrich grabbed his brief case and hurried out of the room and followed the guard up the stairs.

"Which way?" Heinrich asked, panic written all over his face and in his voice.

"Up the stairs, to the back door," the guard replied.

When Heinrich reached the top step two of the guards fell upon him, knocking him to the floor. One sat on his back while the other handcuffed his arms behind his back.

Heinrich was enraged." Take these off me immediately. How dare you treat me like this? As soon as I am free I will kill you, but first I will have your families butchered in front of you. You will watch your wives and daughters be mounted by every man present before they die. Let me go right now."

The oldest guard looked at Heinrich with disgust, "It's our families we are thinking of." Then turning to the trembling young guard he commanded, "Open the door. We are going to give the crowd what they want."

Heinrich fell to his knees. "Please don't do this, they will kill me. I will give you top positions in the Army – estates for your family, money - anything you ask for will be yours. Please I beg you, let me go."

"Get on your feet you sniveling coward. You deserve what is going to happen to you." He prodded Heinrich in the backside with his foot.

Then the four men, with Heinrich in the middle, walked through the open door. They paused on the top step and waited. The crowd grew silent as they became aware Heinrich was standing in front of them, and that four guards had their guns pointed at him.

Heinrich began to apologize. "I am sorry. Please I beg of you, give me a chance to make things right. I didn't mean any of this to happen. I trusted my advisors too much. They led me down the wrong path. Give me a second chance, and I will make this up to you, I promise."

"Liar," someone called out from the front of the crowd.

"Kill him like he did my brother," another called out.

The crowd began taunting Heinrich. Some threw rocks that hit him, but none moved forward.

Suddenly a commotion began at the back of the crowd, and rippled forward. The crowd separated to form an opening.

At first Heinrich couldn't see who was walking toward him, but as the figure drew closer he realized it was Jesse.

He stood there, his mouth gaping open. "You are dead. I killed you myself. I watched you die," he whimpered. Then, turning to the crowd, he shouted, "This man is an imposter, a fake. We all know Jesse is dead."

"And we know who killed him" a voice shouted out.

"It is me," Jesse said. "I was dead, but I have come back. You saw me in your bedroom. Your guards saw my mark on the killing floor at the indoctrination camp, and now the people will know I have returned."

To one of the guards he said, "Remove those handcuffs and put your guns away. He isn't going anywhere."

Once the handcuffs were removed, Heinrich dropped to his knees in front of Jesse. "You win Jesse. You are stronger than I. Please I beg you, don't let them have me. I am sorry for what I have done. I will reverse the edicts immediately, reopen the churches and close the indoctrination camps. You name what you want and I will do whatever you ask if you let me live."

The crowd began shouting again. Jesse held his hands over his head and waited for them to become silent. Then he began to speak.

"This cloud of terror we have been living under ends today.

This is not the time to relive the horrors of the past, but an opportunity to vow that we will never allow this to happen again.

You must find it in your hearts to forgive the neighbor who turned against you and the officials you put your trust in. They failed in their duty because, like you, they were afraid. You must also learn to forgive yourself for what you could have done to put an end to this madness, but didn't.

Like so many of you I lost people I loved – my father, my brothers and sisters and many of my closest friends. I watched your suffering, and I was killed for what I believed in."

Then, turning to Heinrich he said, "I cannot continue to carry the hatred I have for you in my heart. To do so will keep me in this place, and in this time. I don't pretend to understand why you did the things you did or how you chose to live. I will pray for you. God will be your final judge and may he have mercy on your soul."

As Jesse was speaking the air grew still and a bright light began to surround him. There was a loud clap of thunder and a bolt of lightning. When the crowd looked, Jesse was gone.

* * *

At first the crowd was stunned, and then the shouting began. Heinrich was still on his knees.

'Get Heinrich," a voice called out, "kill him before he gets away."

Heinrich reached over, grabbed a pistol out of the nearest guard's hands and scrabbled to the door on his hands and knees. Using the handle as a lever he pulled himself to his feet. *I can't let them get me. They will kill me and I can't let that happen. I*

410

am going to go down in history as the greatest leader this country has ever known. If they kill me, everything I have accomplished will be for nothing.

Yanking the heavy door open he stepped inside the quiet building, and then putting the pistol in his mouth pulled the trigger.

Sig Rotter had been informed earlier about what was taking place in front of Heinrich's building. As unobtrusively as possible he made his way through the crowd. When Heinrich disappeared through the door he made his way to the stairs and stood on the top step.

Turning to the crowd he began shouting. "Stop. Listen to me. I will make sure Heinrich is brought to justice. I will lead our country into more peaceful times. Yes, I was with him, but I was only following his orders. I didn't agree with him and his methods, and many times tried unsuccessfully to talk him out of what he wanted to do."

The crowd wasn't about to be fooled again. Most of them knew who he was and what he had done. Some had even suffered at the hands of his Brown Shirts.

Several of the men in front of the crowd rushed toward him and pulled him down from the steps. They dragged him into the crowd where men and women immediately began kicking and punching him. The frenzy continued until he was dead, and then his bloody body was laid on the top step for all to see. As this was going on, the four guards turned and ran away. Nobody paid any attention to them.

"Now to get Heinrich," somebody yelled.

Three men mounted the steps and walked toward the door. "We will bring him out," one of them shouted.

Cautiously they opened it and made their way inside. They knew Heinrich had a pistol, and could be hiding anywhere in the building.

They hadn't gone far when they came across Heinrich's body lying in a pool of blood. Half of his head had been blown away. One of the men walked over and kicked the lifeless body. "Looks like he took the coward's way out, and to think we were all afraid of him. " He kicked him again, even harder this time.

Two of the men lifted Heinrich from the floor, one at his head, and the other at his feet and dragged the body outside to the step and laid it beside Rotter's.

The crowd grew quiet again. One of the men stepped forward and said, "Go home. It's over."

Several men came out of the crowd each carrying a length of rope. They tied it around Heinrich's neck and dragged his lifeless body to the nearest lamp post and hung it there, for all to see. They used another length of rope to hang Rotter beside him.

When night came the street was empty. Flies buzzed around the two bodies. People had filed past for hours to bear witness that Heinrich was actually dead. Nobody came to cut the two men down or cared enough to give them a proper burial.

EPILOGUE

There is an old saying "each ending has within it a new beginning." The unknown question becomes will this new beginning be for better or for worse?

From the meeting in the cave Peter took Maria and Marika to live with Mathew and Elizabeth. From there he moved them to a distant village into the safety of Believers he knew and trusted. Here he hoped they could grieve and wait for the birth of Marika and Jesse's baby in peace

Peter disappeared. His grief and guilt drove him away from those who loved and cared for him. There were rumored sightings, but that's all they were.

Within hours of Heinrich's death Rohm and his shadow government, aided by the resistance and Believers took over. Without any opposition they occupied the radio station, newspaper offices, police station and Heinrich's building and office. In the ensuing days mobs destroyed every flag, symbol and picture of Heinrich's was systematically destroyed.

Heinrich's rule had decimated the country. Rohm's greatest challenge was to bring stability to a country torn apart by hate and death. Food was scare, and jobs more scarce. Businesses remained closed, children cried because they were hungry and mothers wept.

People were shattered to learn how many died and how many families were torn apart in the indoctrination camps. Those who survived had little, if anything to return to. Their lives, and those of future generations, were changed forever.

Rohm pleaded with the citizens to leave retribution of the Brown Shirts to his police force but too many had suffered at their hands. His pleas went unheeded; retaliation was brutal and swift. They were hunted by the resistance and citizens alike. Some were brought to trial, others imprisoned at Duvenwald prison. Many more were beaten and killed. Shortly after Rotter's death the inner core escaped to a neighboring country; eventually to regroup and become more dangerous than before.

While Rohm desperately tried to put his country back together, a new foe, Brussia, appeared on the horizon. One by one it moved against its neighbors – first by encircling and then absorbing them.

These countries ceased to exist, their leaders either dead or spirited away. The citizens were forced to live under a harsh new doctrine. The state owned everything and all work was done for the state. Private enterprise ceased to exist. The state controlled all political, social and economic events. All other organizations including religious affiliations were banned unless they were approved by the state. Once again the Believers were under siege.

Then, over one weekend, a fence of barb wire divided the country in two. Families were separated, land holdings claimed and businesses shut down, all in the name of the Brussian Government. People were no longer free to come and go. Rohm was powerless against this new stronger enemy; all attempts at negotiation failed.

The movement started by Jesse's teachings spread across borders and soon the world. New leaders carried on his legacy.

His name became synonymous with hope and forgiveness and, as predicted by the white haired man, became the light of the world, and, as Jesse predicted Heinrich's name became one of the most despised in the annals of history.

ABOUT THE AUTHOR

Judy lives in northern Alberta Canada with her husband Bob, ten year old Shih Tzu, Missy Sue and is the proud grandmother of five boys. When Judy retired from her business career she turned to her first love - writing. A late bloomer, she has self-published ten books and has more waiting in the wings. Judy is an advocate for women and strives to write in such a way that her books offer a message of hope to each woman who reads one.